Watteau in Venice

Also by Philippe Sollers

Women

Une curieuse solitude

Paradis

Le Parc

. . . .

Charles Scribner's Sons / New York

Maxwell Macmillan Canada Toronto
Maxwell Macmillan International
New York Oxford Singapore Sydney

Watteau in Venice

....

a novel

Philippe Sollers

Translated by Alberto Manguel

Charles Scribner's Sons
Macmillan Publishing Company
866 Third Avenue
New York, NY 10022

Maxwell Macmillan Canada, Inc.
200 Eglinton Avenue East
Suite 200
Don Mills, Ontario M3C 3N1

Macmillan Publishing Company is part of the
Maxwell Communication Group of Companies.

Library of Congress Cataloging-in-Publication Data
Sollers, Philippe, 1936–
[Fête à Venise. English]
Watteau in Venice : a novel / Philippe Sollers ; translated by
Alberto Manguel.
p. cm.
ISBN 0-684-19451-1
1. Man-woman relationships—Italy—Venice—Fiction. 2. Art
thefts—Italy—Venice—Fiction. 3. French—Italy—Venice—Fiction.
4. Venice (Italy)—Fiction. I. Title.
PQ2679.O4F4813 1994
843'.914—dc20 94-11797 CIP

Book design by Chris Welch

Macmillan books are available at special discounts for bulk purchases for sales promotions, premiums, fund-raising, or educational use. For details, contact Special Sales Director, Macmillan Publishing Company, 866 Third Avenue, New York, NY 10022

10 9 8 7 6 5 4 3 2 1
Printed in the United States of America

WATTEAU
IN VENICE

1

. . . .

As always, here, towards the tenth of June, there is no drawing back, the sky turns, the horizon displays its unchanging warm mist, one enters the true arena of the evenings. There are storms, but they are restrained, compressed, besieged by force. One walks and sleeps differently, one's eyes are the eyes of another, one's breathing becomes hollow, sounds find their exact pitch. In snatches, this small planet is worthy of attention.

* * *

ON SEPTEMBER 18, 1846 Le Verrier writes his famous letter to Galle, who received it on the 23d. On the following night, using a recent map and after correcting a minor mathematical error, Galle observed through the telescope, for the very first time, the presence of Neptune. Some say that Le Verrier had a foul temper. Perhaps. Among other names, I like his, "The Glassworker." I like the fact that Henri Beyle, better known by his pen name Stendhal, records that he had begun the writing of his memoirs on June 20, 1832, "forced like the Pythian prophetess." He's forty-nine years old, he's in Rome. He stops writing on July 4 of that same year, abandoning his manuscript with these words: "The heat dries up my ideas at 1:30 in the morning." One should leave everything unfinished, it's best that way. Often, Stendhal doesn't spell his real name Beyle, as it should be spelled, but Belle, meaning Beautiful. He thought of himself as ugly, fat, with the face of an Italian butcher. "The eyes that are to read these words are now barely opening to the light." Yes. "My future readers are 10 or 12 years old." Yes, yes.

I CAN HARDLY hear Luz on the second floor. I've drawn the curtains, I set the slide projector in motion, I'm showing the paintings, their details. I stand up, I stretch my arms, I repeat to myself things such as: "To reenter one's own body *mysteriously,* minute after minute, step by step, clouds, the end of an afternoon, a fixed schedule." I'd better explain the hallucination I had a little while ago in the garden: the skull, held in my hand after death, a feeling of intense pleasure. Or rather: the falling corpse, a sudden vertical line in the other direction, a darkening seal, opposing pyramids, light. A sketch might represent a flimsy character drawn upside down, a skeleton arrow downwards, a spiritual arrow, if you like, upwards, big bang of beginning, heaven and earth. "In my youth, when I used to improvise, I was mad." Once again, yes. New lines, new colors.

I'VE CHANGED. The phrase is weak, but what other one can one use? It's not as if I'd write a fantastic story, as for example: No one doubts that I've taken the place of the Other, of the one who preceded me under this skin, he has left and I have entered, the substitution worked as smoothly as a letter dropped in the mail. It certainly wouldn't be a bad subject: imagine an actor confronted with a thousand daily details, confronted with friends and relations, forced to wait, to observe, to apologize—"oh yes, of course, I had forgotten"—seeming more and more lost, soft in the head, a tumor, senility, when in fact it's the contrary (he's getting accustomed to his role, he's feeling better). People glance at one another as soon as his back is turned, a knowing look, shrugging their shoulders. The Self, the Other. The Self hiding the fact that he's inhabited by the Other, but which Other, and since when, from what point onwards, with what purpose? Sickness or cunning plot? His old maniacal delight in secrecy, as question of principle, for no reason at all? Why lend him more credence today than yesterday or the day, before? The truth is that no one—neither father nor mother, brothers nor sisters, officials nor lovers, friends nor children—would notice the replacement, and the discovery would be there, huge and laughable.

* * *

CERTAIN ROMAN OR African sarcophaghi of the first century A.D. bear the following initials: NF.F.NS.NC. This reads, in Latin: NON FUI. FUI. NON SUM. NON CURO. That is to say: "I haven't been; I have been; I am not; I care not." I wonder how this inscription arrived here, behind the spindle trees and the well. And from where. Large block of stone, no name, letters, someone. During his life, I imagine, the formula must have read: "I haven't been, I am, I will not be, who cares." Or perhaps in Hebrew (but God alone, of course, had the right to think this): "I am who I am, I'll be who I'll be, see you then, next year or in several centuries." Or else: "I haven't been, I've been, I am, I will not be, I'll be once again, and so what? Why should the verb "to be" be so very central? What blindness forces us to think that we cannot be and have been? Little piece of paper stitched to the jacket, sudden illumination, drunkenness, fiery night, bliss, bliss, tears of bliss, all that. "The final act is bloody, however pretty the rest of the comedy might be; dirt is thrown on the head at last, and that's forever." Forever? Who can say? And so on, the film continues (children shouting along the quays, ships' sirens in the darkness.)

LUZ HAS GONE down to the swimming pool and now she's floating on her back watching the oleander bush under which, in about ten minutes, she'll lie down. She swims better than I do; we avoid swimming together, I'll go later, when she's asleep in her room, before dinner. What is she reading there, in her white sarong sprawled over the blue cushions? *The Last Tycoon*, the last novel, a flop really, of Scott Fitzgerald, dead of a heart attack in Hollywood on December 21, 1940, while the world watched on with indifference (war in Europe, the Nazis in Paris, Christmas preparations). The day before, he had started on chapter six. Final note, in capital letters: "ACTION IS CHARACTER." Or rather, the question in front of the mirror, at six P.M.: "Do I look like death?" Or this, an ideal rhythm: "It was a gentle, harmless, motionless evening with a lot of Saturday cars." She'll also see a tick on the margin next to: "There are no second acts in American lives" and also "Girl like a record with a blank on the other side." I must have also marked this: "Cleverly stated, the contrary of any idea commonly accepted can bring in a fortune." (I must ask her if, as she read that, she thought of Richard.)

WHO ARE YOU in the new reality? A shadow. Who were you before you were born? Less than a shadow. What will you be once erased? A disappearance. One is no longer a dear departed, one disappears. The dear departed, long ago, had the possibility of reappearing (memory, documents, ghosts, religious ceremonies); the dead who disappear, made of another stuff, don't. Will they suddenly feel, over there, that I'm transforming them into potentialities, into sketches? Oh please, you're not harping on that again! What? You intend to rock the market by seeking out the painters' interior landscapes? The lost nervous system? The little veins of that ancient business? The fingers, the eyeball, the upstroke, the folds, the insolent tuft, the red background coatings, the white ones, the glazes, the thin layer of opaque paint, the *empasto,* the drawing made directly with the brush? Canvas, wood, copper plates? Just like that, off the cuff, with sentences and words?

In front of us? But the space has long been taken, my dear sir, and time as well! You haven't got the pass, the cipher, the access code! An assigned ghost, like everybody else! Go sleepwalk! Get out of here! You're delaying the sale!

Geena, two months ago, in New York:

"It's best not to know too much about some things."

"Such as? Money?"

"Sure. Both extremely complicated and extremely simple. You know nothing of the Temple and its two columns: Sotheby's and Christie's. Plus a forest of cathedrals, basilicas, churches, chapels. Or if you prefer, museums, galleries, visible and invisible collections . . ."

"Tell me."

"It'll take too long."

"Make me part of your network."

"Maybe. After all, we do need people like you. You know how to look, you travel, nobody keeps an eye on your schedule, your quirks are more or less acceptable, you can be discreet, listen without being noticed, we'd try you out, you'd get to snoop around . . . We'll think about it."

Eight in the morning, West 52d Street, thirty-third floor over the Hudson, black tinted windows of the skyscraper full of offices, a cutting sensation, pierced with light, in the back, left and right . . . Radio, all-day classical music, sonatas, breakfast, tea, coffee . . . How Geena has changed these last few years; a quick remodeling in an acid bath . . .

She:

"What are your living arrangements these days? Still with Bella?"

"Still."

"Your daughter? Fleur?"

"She's twelve. Some progress on the piano."

"Your muse for the year?"

"No one" (I lie.).

"I've got someone for you."

ANOTHER BEGINNING:

I arrive, the small palazzo is in order, the sun is shining on the gray telephones. I went out through a secret door at the airport, to the right; I took the boat, quickly; she was waiting for me on the dock, hello with her hand two hundred feet away; we went into the library, I showed her the briefcase, the bags, the photos and the tickets. Then we went up to her room, made love in a hurry, had dinner, slept, got up early, jogged around the customs building, seven o'clock. Stretched out on the terrace, I watch the first ocean liners come in.

Or rather: "Every morning, my face turned against the wall, and even before having seen, over the big curtains drawn across the window, the shade of color of the first sunlight, I know what the weather will be." I sometimes try to imagine how Proust would have gotten on in New York. Fine, I'm sure. He'd have adapted his instruments. One would have seen him at the Pierre, he'd have been buddies with Truman Capote and Andy Warhol, instead of dragging Montesquieu and Jacques-Emile Blanche along with him. He'd have become a formidable connoisseur of Wall Street. Balbec? Long Island. Charlus? Obvious. Bloch? Loads of them. The Verdurins? All over the place. Only Gomorrah would have presented certain difficulties to transpose, not to mention the aristocratic decor: good-bye to that. Would he have ordered kosher meals on the plane? Maybe (they're better, not so heavy). He'd have been a celebrity fascinated by faxes, an instant telegram and resurrection of the art of handwriting with which he'd have inundated his friends.

"OK," says Geena. "I'll call London."

She takes a black felt-tip pen, writes "Hello, what's new?" signs *Mozart,* dials a phone number, slips in the sheet of paper.

"Mozart?"

"Code name, why not have one? We should have Cézanne's answer in a second."

She's right, big scrawly writing on the return message: "Blue sky. Congrats for Jacopo. Kisses. *Cézanne.*"

"Have fun if you like. Give my number."

I write to my Italian publisher. "New York, Monday, 9 A.M. Can we meet in Milan next Monday? I'd like to discuss again with you my Serbo-Croatian rights. Sincerely, *Crebillon fils.*"

The Italian secretary is efficient, and ten minutes later we read: "Mr. Nessuno regrets but he'll be in Rome on Monday, Mr. Crebillon. Would Tuesday 4 P.M. be convenient?"

"Clever girl," I say. "Who's Jacopo?"

"Jacopo da Carucci, Pontormo, over thirty-five million dollars for the presumed portrait of Cosimo, the second Medici duke of Florence, first grand duke of Tuscany. Better than the ten million paid five years ago for Mantegna and his *Adoration of the Magi.* The Getty Museum in Malibu, once again. Would you use Crebillon as your pseudonym?"

"I don't think so."

"Funnily enough, the rise in prices followed the expansion of the fax."

"Fax tibi, evangelista meus . . ."

"What?"

"Nothing, I was thinking of the inscriptions in Venice. Would you have anything for me there?"

The Heart and the Soul Gone Astray was written in 1736. Claude Prosper Jolyot de Crebillon is twenty-nine years old. First line: "I entered this world at the age of seventeen, with every advantage that might lead one to be noticed." Beginning of the fourth paragraph: "The idea of pleasure was the only one that held me."

Geena laughs: "A planet on which everything is for sale."

So: as usual, here, towards June 10, stretched out on the roof terrace, I watch the blue, white and yellow ocean liners pass me by. Luz has just left the house to buy cigarettes and champagne. Where do sentences come from? Instantaneous circles of air, clasped movements, laws.

USUALLY, FUNERARY INSCRIPTIONS are silly, naive, vaguely mystical, edifying or melancholy. Some are cleverer. "*Et in Arcadia ego*," or "He lived, wrote, loved." But there are also terrifying ones, and the uncontested prize goes to the inscription on the base of Masaccio's *Trinity* in Santa Maria Novella, in Florence. The image of a prone skeleton, a neurotic and pseudodemocratic slap in the face of the viewer: "I was that which you are, you shall be that which I am." Yes, you, passerby, man, woman, tourist, lover of art who are alive and well, millionaire, clerk, scholar, secretary, journalist, cop, philosopher. Skeleton? Manikin? A tomb with a view! On the contrary, my coffin among the spindle trees, fallen from the skies or brought to this place by a discreet freethinker, aims at having a far different effect. It could be the last refuge of a painter or musician who had seen or heard quite enough. "I haven't been, I have been; I am not; I care not." How dare one state simultaneously that one *is not* and that one *cares not*? Not to be, would that mean a being in a positive sense? Not to be, would that amount to being diffident? To be, not to be, there is no question? Neither to sleep? Even less, to dream? No nothingness, neither fear nor reproach? Enough with the shifting scene of little bones lashed by the scythe, the buried alive, the stakes through the heart, the rattling of chains, séance tables and cries in the night, the captive moon, the haunted drapes and sheets, the black sun from which the night shines forth, the skulls knocking against each other under the moss, the aligned charnel houses, the slaughtered men and women kindly laid out side by side in the woods, or perhaps vanished into smoke, but always present? What? Nothing? The wind? Either I'm crazy (certainly not) or this piece of information is unique. He must have been persecuted everywhere, like the seven scandalous assertions in the Epicurean credo: 1) The universe is infinite; 2) the number of worlds is infinite; 3) our world will come to an end; 4) the vacuum exists; 5) the gods take no heed of human affairs; 6) our soul is made of material substance; 7) death can be compared to eternal sleep. Let's add an eighth: women, including prostitutes, admitted to Epicurus's garden. As to the others: "They die of the efforts they make not to die." Or Epicharmus: "The elements have assembled, have scattered, have returned there whence they came: clay to clay, soul to on high. What evil is there in this? Surely none." No need for a soul, in fact; unnecessary mist. A stone cube, a carved-out message. Instead, Masaccio's propagandistic skeleton who calls to you, alone with Holbein's horizontally dead coroner's Christ that so impressed Dostoievski, is *painted.* The silence of painting strikes one as hard as the silence of death (mummys' coffins covered with comic strips from beyond, TV boxes that condemn the slave to watch himself and to believe he's watched). A skeleton speaks to you: it is difficult to deny sex more precisely. Death and painting, stock market and triple-combination safes gone crazy. Van Gogh's suicide? Cézanne saying over and over again, and for a very good reason, "to die painting, to die painting"? But, as in the proper departures of nowadays, no one truly dies or lives anymore (to do so would be to upset the wheels of finance), go ask at the Company Headquarters if anyone is irreplaceable. The Company (tunnels, highways, insurance policies, advertising, planes, ships, supermarkets, factories, office buildings, breweries, oil refineries, banks frozen produce, stores, periodicals, movies, electronics, spaceships, museums, politics, inseminations, tapes, pharmaceuticals, records, computer software) owns, directly or indirectly, the TV and radio networks, the publishing companies, the newspapers. Like clockwork. End of story? End of *your* story, rather. Individual and worldwide looting of incredible complexity, each point of the circuit attached to all the others. And you? Are you going to sit and watch the destruction of Venice (ancient universal and jealous hope), a rock concert, inane young crowd all high, sleeping bags, common garbage can, a guy in jeans and leather jacket taking a piss, in the early hours of the morning, against the portal of St. Mark's? And yet, a few hundred feet away, silence, light, a scribbled notebook, flowers. What can one object to when someone has enjoyed something so fully? Not a thing. A sarcophagus lying among the leaves: *sum, non sum, non curo.*

IN A SINGLE CENTURY, from Urbain Le Verrier to Edwin Hubble (who died in 1953), galaxies have taken on a different turn—and it's only the beginning. Explosion, contraction, big bang, big crunch, the choice is yours. However, here on this earth we must carry on our miscroscopic existence, *ain't that so,* dear brother virus, dear sister cell . . . In orbit, twelve hundred feet above our disoriented sphere, the space telescope (completing a circle around us in an hour and a half) will cast a farther-reaching eye back to the beginning of our novel. There where we used to see a star, the telescope will show us sixty thousand. Camera with a wide planetary angle, camera for objects of faint luminosity, spectographs seeking out quasars, ultraspeed photometers for black holes . . . The entire thing cost two billion dollars: sixty Pontormo canvases.

IN OTHER WORDS, from now onwards we should speak of a "disappearing box," as one used to speak of a Time Machine. It's obvious that the latter was conceived at the end of the nineteenth century: a given length of time, a straight line to follow, the Puritan spirit, macabre obsessions, social messianism, the yoke of profit. But nowadays, a ball of bubbles? A conspiratorial web? A multitude of blisters with no direction, no future? Accumulation had its tragic side, overabundance has a side that is both funny and terrible. A swarm of mayflies? All aboard in the box! As usual, the science-fiction movies made for TV lead the way: interstellar spaceship, a chessboard of computers and, from time to time, dematerialization of bodies and recomposition by wave transfer. You stand under the nuclear arch, you evaporate, in a few light-years you are reconstituted inside another cosmic spaceship, and you go home. If in the process you are killed by the laser beams, you are reduced on the spot to a puddle of atoms. Everything's in the control of the reactors. I even suggest a new measuring gadget: a disappearance detector. Here or there, just try it. A buzz, a few numbers, and all the dear departed at your disposal, *en masse.* The shoving and pushing would be unbelievable, it will be necessary to screen them out, thereby giving rise to a host of new inventions. In the meantime, you can concentrate on the classical departed. "I'm calling Watteau, Jean-Antoine." "He's extremely busy right now, sir, very much in demand." "I'm calling Mozart." "You must be joking, impossible to speak to him for another four or five years, even on the infrared number." "Marcel Proust? Stendhal?" "Same thing." So you fall back on lesser-known names, but even Danchet, for instance, the coauthor, with Campra, of the 1710 ballet *Festes véniliennes,* gives a busy signal. Even Pecour, the choreographer. They are mobbed, the recent arrivals surround them, the faintest witness of the ancient world (from the time when a world existed) is worth his weight in gold. The really dead are constantly busy.

"The victory of masks," says Geena. "The spectral society. Not bad, on the contrary."

"It all depends on you. Do you know how much an Ethiopian makes a year, on average?"

"No."

"A hundred and thirty dollars."

It was fun, that session of mutual infiltration between Geena and me, in New York. I haven't been much out of her apartment for a whole week. This time, it was she who had decided to get in touch, after a year of near misses. Physical sequences? Nine times out of ten, selective tests of power. Late afternoon, we'd go to *Palio* for a drink, not far from the MOMA. After that friends, and back to her place. Excellent, just reflexes, nothing more nor less.

"Richard says he fucks more than you do."

"Maybe, but he enjoys it less."

"How do you know?"

"Because he talks about it. Another slogan, like everywhere else, and that's why prices go up like that. Big business, big problems. Lot of images, not much content. Hundreds of paintings, seldom any depth. Gallons of sperm, barely a few ounces of levitation. It's surprising that this disproportion has been the subject of hardly any investigation, as if the representation or even the act itself had any value per se. Fruitful or liberating stereotypes, censored sensations. It's the words that are missing. Listen: 'I'm working on his portrait, the head wearing a white cap, very blond, very bright, a blue suit and a cobalt background, leaning on a red table on which are placed a yellow book and a foxglove plant with purple flowers."

"And?"

" 'The trunk of a pink pine and then the grass with white flowers and dandelions, a small rosebush and more tree trunks in the back, high up on the canvas.' . . . 'In the middle a rose border, to the right a gate, a wall, and over the wall a walnut tree with violet leaves' . . . 'I saw the fields after the rain, fresh and full of flowers' . . ."

"Van Gogh?"

"Not bad. It's from the end of his life, when he talks about Giotto and when he started to reread Shakespeare's historical plays. He compares Shakespeare to Rembrandt, 'that sorry tenderness, that superhuman infinity revealed, and which seems then so natural.' How much do you think these lines are worth?"

"The manuscripts? Not bulky and easily convertible into cash. A stolen Artaud notebook, for instance, has just been priced at eight hundred thousand francs, even though it had been insured at four hundred. Narco-dollars? In his case that would be funny."

"Not the manuscripts, *the meaning*."

"But . . . Nothing, of course, what an idea! I can give you a piece of information, however: they're going to find, just by chance, two van Goghs stolen in the Netherlands, one of them a version of the *Sunflowers*."

"Just like that?"

"Just like that."

GEENA IS RIGHT: sense means nothing in itself, it all depends on the point of view determined by the interests of the proprietors at any given time. It might be said that our time resembles no other in that it has outlawed the expanded verbal conscience. In its place, painting is supposed to stand out as a permanent real estate transaction. Artaud's book, *Van Gogh: The Man Suicided by Society* was published in Paris in

mated, human dome, circles alive above my head" . . . And one can be certain that his goal was not "to bring back a catalogue of outdated images, from which Our Time, faithful to an entire system, would at most draw a few ideas for posters and patterns for its fashion designers." Here he is, leaving Mexico on October 31, 1936 and disembarking at Saint-Nazaire at the end of November. His experience of the asylum, after his stay in Ireland, couldn't have been very different from that of van Gogh—even more terrible, if that were possible, because of the war (forty thousand dead of hunger between 1940 and 1944, a gentle extermination, French style). Diagnosis of Artaud's case, dated April 1, 1938, at Sainte-Anne: "Delirium of persecution syndrome: a conspiracy of policemen trying to poison him, magic spell distorting his language and thought, in an attempt to commandeer them both. Split personality: he knows little, and only through hearsay, the personality bearing his name, Artaud; he is far more familiar, through personal recollections, with a second personality bearing another name. Ease, self-sufficiency, an effort to be clear and concise." A fortnight's certificate: "Literary pretensions."

And here's the testimony of a nurse regarding life at the asylum at the time:

"THE PATIENTS WOULD arrive in a bus. They would be led into a large room comprising a dozen showers; they would then be asked or forced to strip naked and wash, while the nurses would take inventory of their belongings which had been confiscated at arrival or sent on from previous institutions. The new arrivals seemed confused and did not understand what was happening to them; the old hands seemed resigned. Upon arrival at the building, they would all lie down. Nothing was left to them of that which would have linked them to a wife, children, parents, job, their past and their daily life; no identity papers, no wallet, no ring, no belt, no lighter, no glasses, no shoes, no underwear, no shoelaces, no money . . . The toilets had, at most, half a swinging shutter to prevent the patients from hanging themselves behind closed doors. The meals served at set times would be dished out from a trolley steered between the tables. There was one knife for every six men, and its use was strictly supervised; no one was allowed to leave his place before all the knives had been collected."

After the arrival of the Germans, when the Public Health Department eliminated the food budget, one could see the patients eat tree bark, grass, even their own feces.

ARTAUD'S MOTHER WOULD come and visit him twice a week, bringing him parcels and cigarettes. He wrote to her on March 23, 1942:

"YOU MUST FORCE them to deliver walnuts, hazelnuts, pistachios, almonds and chocolates for you to bring to me . . . Tomatoes, olives, bread with cheese and mushrooms . . . Malaga grapes, crackers, bread, a small flask of oil, dates, stuffed figs . . ."

ARTAUD DIED ON the night of 3 March 1948, aged fifty-two. He was found in the morning lying at the foot of his bed. Shortly before his death he had written to a friend: "I must tell you a secret. What makes us die is that, since childhood, we believe in death. We see ourselves between four boards inside a coffin, that is what makes us die, but if you won't allow yourself such an idea, you will never die. I mean my physical body. I'm immortal and I shall always continue to live as I live now. You see, from today onwards you must reject death. That way you too will never die."

A LETTER ADDRESSED to André Breton from 1947 (the year of *Van Gogh: The Man Suicided by Society*) gives us his final feelings about art:

"You've asked me for a text for an art exhibit;
please excuse me

but I can't change my view of this International Surrealist Exhibition which will take place in a capitalist art gallery (with a hefty capital, the fact that it was drawn from a communist bank is immaterial) and where at all times both dyed-in-the-wool surrealists and OTHERS are sold at exorbitant prices;

André Breton, you've known me for almost thirty years now, I don't want to write in a catalogue that will be read by snobs, by rich art collectors, in a gallery where you'll never see either workers or ordinary people because they all work during the day."

A thought after World War II: Fifty years later, one can parade "workers" or "ordinary people" on a guided tour in front of a series of van Goghs, and they'll still not read Artaud. Neither will the bankers, the snobs, the rich art collectors, the postcommunists, the postmodernists, neither will the artists nor the postartists. Forty thousand dead? A minor detail.

Geena: "Narco-dollars? That would be a laugh in his case!"
Luz: "That's beautiful. Moving and beautiful."

I SLEEP, I come down around four in the afternoon, not a sound in the walled garden, it's the moment when the swallows swoop down over the pool to drink, their bellies skim the water and turn blue, they graze my head, they punctuate the silence like bullets. Luz is in her room; we have only just exchanged our sleep, at a distance. Bed, table, pool; and again, bed, table, pool. Yesterday we made love, we'll do it again tomorrow, today is a day in brackets. The large wall, bordered by acacias, shields us from the quay; no one can see inside the white and pink building. Life is reduced to this, finding the place, the time, the appropriate other. As if we were aboard ship, without the bothers of navigation, plus roses and butterflies, the place found, the time open, the skin verifiable.

Stendhal, *The Privileges*, article 14: "If he who is privileged wished to reveal one of the articles of his privilege, his mouth will not be able to utter a single sound and he will be racked by toothache for twenty-four hours." This was written on April 10, 1840 at Mero, that is to say, Rome, which he also calls Omar or Amor. ("But tell me something, Stendhal, is it just for yourself that you transform these privileges abolished by the ancien régime? Don't you in the least long for the revolutionary opinions of your youth? Do you recognize your mistake as regards Napoleon, that archcriminal? No? No self-criticism? Not the tiniest *mea culpa*? You refuse to admit that, to put it mildly, you've been *careless*?"—Noisy approval from the Restoration benches, voices rise, among them, recognizable, that of Baron Norpois: "Self-criticism! Self-criticism!") Nevertheless, nothing forbids me from amending the text, as follows: "He who enjoys a privilege will be permitted to talk about and reveal all the articles of his privilege, certain that no one will either realize what he is doing and that no one will believe him. He will do so with the intention of encouraging others to enjoy such privileges in times to come. Let him go even further: man is perfect, progress exists. Niseve, 1989." *Venise,* Venice, can also be written *Vienes.* July 1, 1836 the first issue of *La Presse* is published. September 6, Mole's first cabinet. The press? "The rascally cowardice, the profound Jesuit sympathies of the editors of *Le Journal des Débats.*" Or this: "Prolonged social intercourse with a hypocrite is starting to make me feel seasick." Or this: "People appreciate me but don't like me. This comes from the fact that mumbling inanities twelve hours a day bores me to death." Change the names, the dimensions and the dates, the comedy remains the same. Rearrange the technique, the conceits, the lies, the criminal acts, the cold-blooded exploitation of both needs and desires, you're still left with the nervous system of the whole setup. Inside it, at times, a dreamer at work: right now, it's me. Noticing, for instance: the only way out, a great notion, a grand vice. If possible, both at the same time. Find a way of making them think you're just like them. Or that you're nothing at all. Alternate these thoughts in their head, *and spend there the night.*

"No way out?"

"We've got to wait till it's over."

"But later on it will be the same."

"I didn't say wait till it changes; I said wait till it's over."

"But we'll all be dead by then!"
"So what?"

WHAT MATTERS, HERE, now, is the body to be dragged from one end to the other of the large liquid rectangle, the blue stuff in the eyes and mouth, the swallows diving right and left, the intermittent thought of Luz naked in her room, the pleasure of being in hiding together, of having escaped surveillance for the time being. "I've got someone for you." Good old Geena, ever young and always so professional, not a moment that hasn't been thought out, the men are restless, the women pretend not to be by not moving a muscle, a canvas of sound waves, information exchanged over the droning of male bumblebees, additions, corrections, decisions. "I've got someone for you." Who does she have in mind? Nicole, in Paris? Probably. All sorts of advantages, the network of museums, she'd be able to keep an eye on her through me, no doubt she finds her lately too cautious or too independent. To know what someone does, where he is, with whom, what is it he is pondering and planning, what his mood is, his health, his financial situation . . . Stendhal, in 1830, finds the *congregation* responsible for this control: "It has made denunciations and spying the norm everywhere. Its leaders wished to find out the name of each newspaper bought by each household in each little village in France, and they've succeeded. They wished to know who came to call on any given day and they've obtained the information—all without expenses, without costs, exclusively through the voluntary spying of ordinary concerned citizens."

What has happened since? The shattering of the illusion

that there might be heretical citizens. The disappearance of the fluctuating anonymity of the large cities in exchange for a generalized provinciality. This hygienic and malevolent thoughtlessness is everywhere, and in compensation makes the devilry of the art market seem so much more logical. To make it yours, to obliterate it. Since when? Barely ten years? For how long to come? Impossible to say. As long as there are reserves (and there are plenty). So the money is there, oozing, swelling, being aroused, crossing and crisscrossing, multiplying itself by two, by three, by four, by ten, five times more for a Gauguin, fifty times more for a Picasso, it seems as if the works of art increase in price all by themselves, but in a negative way, and our business is now to deny their exorbitantly priced nature by fighting back with a few billions deftly wielded. The business of fakes organizes itself, thefts are as common as dirt, deals in the dark never stop, the middlemen are worked off their feet, cathedrals and castles are systematically denuded, panels, books, enamels, chimneypieces, statues, stamps, furniture, vases, medallions, jewelry. In Switzerland they don't know how many more numbers they can add to an account, telexes crackle, faxes become nightly scriveners, sales follow one another in waves, an everexpanding ice floe, spottings, estimates, intoxications, raids, a card game played with different books and different styles. Japan immemorial and electronic kowtows in front of sensual Monet on his barge? Money! A new made-up retrospective, an insidious rewriting of catalogues, an exhibition that changes when other perspectives are needed, all this must assist the rates of exchange. To bury paintings in a safe has become a worldwide pastime, played with passion. Can you hear, at the edge of the forest, the cries of a sick old lady locked away with no food and no care in the left wing of her manor? Her heartrending pleas for help? They are simply *taking away* her Murillo, her Titian, her pastels by La Tour . . . Her voice becomes weaker and weaker . . . Her emaciated body falls at the foot of the bed . . . Already half her armchairs are in Zurich, her Louis XV clock in Bâle . . . Does she have nothing else to sign away in exchange for a bowl of broth or a pain-killing shot? No? Then unplug her! Next! I'm told there's one over there, in Auvergne . . . The backwater country is spewing up unsuspected treasures, lost chapels, monasteries more or less in ruins . . . See these strange tourists, these hurried men, these elegant women, their cameras, their inquisitiveness, their oh-so-refined taste . . . How they love the country! And they come from so far away! How thoughtful they are, how keen, how polite, full of concern, respectful of local customs, educated, lovers of ancient beauty! That charming couple has just returned from Nepal, they are about to leave for Italy, or Spain . . . Or rather the South Pacific . . . Before returning to California after making a detour through Greece . . . Two Apollos sighted here, a Buddha there . . . A minuscule and exquisitely pure Aphrodite here or there . . . Not to mention the *big job* being planned right now, in that villa near Vienna . . .

OK: towel, cigarette. Time to inspect our private little work of art lying on her bed. Am I wearing my invisibility ring? Article 4: "If someone privileged is wearing a ring and clasps it in his hand while looking at a woman, the woman will fall passionately in love with him, as we believe Héloïse fell in love with Abelard." Another turn of the screw and the affair becomes, so to speak, more engaging. Two more turns and deep darkness shrouds the scene from alien eyes.

SHE HAS HER own phone, she can go out when she wants, she can come and go as she pleases. Only one rule: not to speak about me to anyone. Were she not to follow it, I'd find out soon enough. She's in Venice, "staying with friends."

Now I watch her sleep, or pretending to be asleep, just like I sometimes ask her to do. A blond and round ball (blond: her name, even though to hear it you wouldn't think so), rather petite, finely featured but nevertheless well rounded, her deep blue eyes closed, the same eyes of her mother, I imagine, Swedish mother, Italian father, the Spanish name Luz bestowed by the father's mother, while the Nordic genes won out. Twenty-three years old, born in 1966 in Los Angeles, young girl, young woman, of the Ingrid Bergman/Rossellini mythology, ice and lava, grace and earthquake, she is a physics and astronomy student at Berkeley, I've known her for six months. She had flown to Paris for Christmas, chance encounter at the Louvre, yes sir, that's how it is, an anonymous writer said so: "Whatever needs to happen to me happens whenever it needs to happen; there's nothing I can do about it, I hang on." Or, according to Luz's favorite saying: "Singularity is the name given to the central region of a black hole." Which becomes, from time to time: "Don't forget that singularity is . . ." etc. with a blond-blue smile that brightens at once both her cheeks and her short hair. For her, a writer (Stendhal, Proust, Artaud, the others) is a sort of black hole in the human cosmos, a sort of dealer in antimatter, swallowing up everything, even light itself, not allowing anything to escape, not sending anything back in return. Reproaches? Certainly, but lively. No, no, she's not been imprisoned, she's been *misguided*. Scientific mind, but an aesthetic curiosity (in a way, it's because of her that I've gotten into this business with Geena, each new woman forces you to examine the corridors of your life that have led you to her, experiences, sensations, knowledge, I would not have thought myself still capable, fatigue, certainly not, never by chance, luck, since we move about in a world which more and more lacks memory, an enormous black hole, indeed). She's wearing only a white T-shirt, she's very tanned, white-bronze blond, warm legs, I continue to observe her from the armchair, shutters half closed on the acacias and the oleanders, distant traffic on the quay, the bed is perpendicular to the wide shining canal through which the cruise ships pass, it is parallel to the swimming pool, down there, lying open in the garden, night will fall in cool and uneven stages. She is truly asleep, the fleshy mouth half open, sweet lips, not at all scientific at present, or rather yes, but in another sense, I see her scutinizing her computers, tapping away at the keyboards to conjure up the data, the equations, the curves, the numerical images from corners invisible to the naked eye, all this is apparent in her look, an early familiarity with that which lies beyond appearances, a kind of calm and somewhat brutal frankness, an absence of fear. Yesterday she wanted to hear on the radio a pianist she knows, a fourteen-year-old girl, Vanessa Perez, gliding with ease through Haydn's sonatas, a true Californian, like Luz, on her way from Venezuela to give a concert in Padua . . . There's talent everywhere. Instantaneous talent: they are filmed, they are recorded, and it's as if no one knew how to speak about them: never have there been so many phenomenal talents accompanied by such an overwhelming aphasia.

I stick to my tableau: the glass doors, the fading ray of light, the bed, Luz's pink and tanned face, at an angle, on the white pillow, her golden head, her breathing, her left ear, her ethereal left ear with its half-buried dimpled face, her blond sex, her breasts under the crumpled cotton, the right one between the letters B and E, the left one between E and Y, Berkeley, her warm forehead, her apricot-flavored chin, her hips, her wrists, her knees, her ankles. All this must be seen and felt simultaneously, touch by touch. I rise in the same way I entered, without a sound, I cross the long corridor, I go to my room hidden even deeper above the garden, I think, that's a well-built situation or setup, as it used to be called, and I watch the butterflies down below all around the gladioli and the roses. I'm also thinking of taking up again that article on Stendhal, which is already past its deadline: "That refined and singular soul would not even deign to express his disdain, and at the slightest appearance of vulgarity or affectation he'd fall into an invincible silence."

"DO YOU LIKE dance?"

She had turned towards me ever so slightly, still watching. It was early in the morning, there were few people around, I'd come with no definite intention, but I rarely miss an opportunity to see these paintings. For me, they are the most mysterious paintings in the world, I've always thought that something wonderful would happen to me because of them. I still keep, in an exercise book from my childhood, mediocre and yellowed reproductions of these brilliant presentiments of a perfect uchronia: *La Finette, L'Indifferent.* Any other contestants? More deeply pearled, outlined, free? How can one not be condemned by such verdicts? Until next year, in front of *L'Indifferent,* until all next years in front of *La Finette.* Let them be called like that, I don't care, even though these titles rather prevent one from seeing them. But after all, why not have masks? Watteau is the most secret of agents, the real agent W., as they say in the secret service to refer to him or her in charge of penetrating the inner sanctum of the enemy . . . Reserve, change of identity, cover, a laser pen or lighter, specialist in codes . . . Elementary, each apparent letter corresponds to another, A for O, for example, B for S . . . Other funny business . . . As in dreams, as in no matter what discourse, I say this but I think that, aha, the better to deceive you, I've just said exactly what I thought . . . Other black holes, painters . . . Bang in the eye . . . Dislodging the retina, burning the iris . . . The powerful buy that which they can never hope to penetrate, or rather that which locks them up forever in their blindness. "It is the very fact of characterizing something as 'valuable' that strips the object thus valued of its dignity."

"Do you get the message?"

This time I've intrigued her. We walked about for a long time, that day, I and my little Luciferian physicist, a beautiful January Sunday, harshly blue, silvery . . . She lived not far from me, high on the Boulevard Saint-Michel, we walked around the Observatoire, I showed her, in the front courtyard overgrown with weeds, the statue of Le Verrier, the inventor of Neptune, proud, leaning a little backwards, his papers in his hand . . . For the first time, I noticed that Rue Cassini (Balzac's street) has no number 13, and yet I take it every day . . . We were suddenly behind the long white wall, we were walking down another imaginary street, nameless, parallel to the other . . . Just as astonished when coming upon the inscription on the facade of the disaffected church that closes the perspective: Sanctissimae Trinitati et Infantiae Iesu, Sacrum; lost building, a telegram with no addressee in the stone. I kissed her there, under the naked trees. It was she who then noticed the proliferation of cupolas and images of the terrestrial globe in this neighborhood: the zodiac fountain by Carpeaux (a contemporary of Watteau who executed his statue in Valenciennes); a statue of navy lieutenant Garnier (1839–1873)—Indochina, Mekong, Red River—ashes repatriated from the Far East and deposited in the base only in 1987, he's therefore there in person, *ground to dust,* beneath lascivious women and bronze crocodiles, in the middle of the crossroads. Luz asked what the Convent of the Visitation (visitation?) was; who exactly was Marshal Ney (statue by Rude, 1853, Prince of Moskova, Duke of Elchingen, retreat from Russia, sabre unsheathed, three wounds at Interthur on May 21, 1799, executed *here* on December 7, 1815 at 9:00 A.M., he himself commanding the firing squad: "Soldiers, aim straight at the heart!"). Amazing the number of dead who ask to speak to Luz, they're usually neglected, poor things, in the chinks of time-space . . . My young American is a medium . . . She stops suddenly in front of the plaque at 34 Avenue de l'Observatoire: "Jean Cavailles, professor at the Sorbonne, a hero of the Resistance, was arrested here before being shot by German soldiers in early 1944. "Did I know who Cavailles was? I know a little . . . Not really . . . How come? A first-rate thinker! One of those rare Frenchmen who found himself immersed in the problems of mathematical infinity, translator into my language of the Cantor–Dedekind correspondence! Haven't I read his biography, written by his sister: *J. C., Philosopher and Fighting Spirit*? She must lend it to me, she's certain I'd be interested . . . He talks a lot about the Luxembourg Garden in his letters, he had just read Spinoza . . . We observe the vistas: the Sacre Coeur, below; the Senate backed into a wall of black chestnut trees, green with exuberance in summer . . . I say to myself that Paris is full of surprises, that I've been oblivious to it lately . . . A few more kisses . . . When is she coming back? Beginning of June? For three months? Can we make a pact between Physics and the Visual Arts? Fiction and Mathematics? Astronomy and Music? For the end of the century through the centuries? But what about her? Does she really want to see the microfilm, Watteau's top secret cipher?

In my notebook, dated the following day, I find this: "To be continued: The Louvre, sharp little round laughing blue-eyed blond, 23 years old, Italo-Swedish American, quick on her feet. Scientific bent, delectable skin. Only child, mother biologist, father cardiologist, lives in California. Visited Le Verrier, Neptune (explored this very moment by the *Voyager II*). Found her in front of Watteau's canvases. Spanish name (Luz). Coming back in the summer."

In a case like that, the first thing to do is: reinforce as far as possible the security system, the general disinformation. The more you find yourself involved in new and serious business, the more you should appear relaxed, drained, run off your feet, worn down by banality, entrenched in easily observable habits. Add the more or less notorious clandestine activities, those which the self-appointed police routinely continue to attribute to you. This is a private war, the only war that matters, the most delicate of all wars: art. War by day, war by night, locations and time frames, the tiniest details are important in order to disorient the radar, the poisonous magma of socialites. Anyhow, it's important to preserve one's contacts with the self-appointed police, three men, four women at least, listen carefully to the reverse of what they're saying. *The magnetic field is the same everywhere.* One day I'll have to write my secret instructions, my *Monita secreta*, my *Catechism of Agent W. in Action*, my *Protocols of the Elders of Sound* (a word in your ear), the *Rules of My Disorderly Order* . . . Article 1: He who hasn't started from the cradle, he whose eardrum hasn't been, from the very beginning, offended, pierced, persecuted to the point of screaming because of the din, within himself, caused by the religious stupidity of humankind, is lost. Article 2: Deep, immediate, relentless silence to resist the lies, but a silence *that must not be seen* and which implies being able to dance or speak beside the point. Article 3: Spinoza: "The man who is free and lives among ignorant people must try as hard as he can to avoid their kindnesses." Article 4: Keep every day in front of your eyes scenes of delirious crowds (Mecca, Benares, Lourdes, Berlin, etc.), stadiums and military parades, i.e. the congregate shape of community. Article 5: Don't take into account anything except the cold calculations of a banker on his job (listen to him at least once a month). Article 6: Seek behind every apparition, male or female, the mother figure, and behind that, the figure of the mother's mother, and

confine yourself to it (to be left aside, however, during m ments of pleasure). Article 7: Remember that *The Charterho of Parma* will not be read by 99.9% of the inhabitants of th planet at any given time (and badly read by ¾ of the res and that this fact is not of the slightest importance. Articl 8: Stop being astounded by the realization that sex is th object of such misunderstanding and of such automatic clumsiness that it implies either a universal loathing or a universal veneration (which are much the same thing). Article 9: Don't forget that a billion people live on less than a dollar a day. Article 10: It's your body that's in question, only your body, stop imagining that it's you, your body rarely has a reason for being somewhere—check to see when, with whom, how—know that for everyone, with no exception, you're better off dead. Article 11: All the preceding articles are useless, the will itself is enough. We live a rich, full nothingness, and we're off!

It was she who phoned three weeks later, just before my trip to New York. Let's meet there? Sure, a stopover.

And now she sleeps at the end of the corridor. Dinner in a couple of hours.

Geena:

"Not only the impressionists. Picasso, van Gogh, Gauguin also is on the rise. When you see that *Tahitian in a Red Pareo* slipped unnoticed between New York and London, you'll know that the computer's had goose bumps."

"How much?"

"For the time being, one million dollars. But I'm sure she can double that easily. The Marquesas! Atuana! *Sancta simplicitas* of the climate!"

Two months later: "*Tahitian in a Red Pareo,* a watercolor by van Gogh estimated at more than a million dollars, was stolen from a hangar at Heathrow Airport in London, England, last June. It's owner, the American art gallery Beadelstone, did not report the theft until Sunday, July 23. The *Tahitian* was part of a consignment of four canvases that arrived in London on June 21 on a plane from New York."

A curious hangar . . . Mysterious crates . . . Supposing the painting never left New York . . . Which are the three others? Why or how did the negotiations fail? Unless they were indeed successful? Is the information intended to lower or raise the prices?

The Dutchman of France, the Frenchman of the Marquesas, what a couple! . . . Let yourself drift to those islands in 1903, thirteen years after van Gogh's death, when Gauguin writes that he likes his women "fat and lustful," the same man who would give this piece of advice to those who wanted to be left alone: "Nail something indecent prominently to your door." Gauguin: "I remember Manet, there's someone else who was never bothered by anyone" . . . In Paris: "About this fashionable idea of sending pure-hearted girls to study painting with the men, the remarkable thing is that all these virgins sketching a totally nude male model, pay much more attention to the accuracy of the you-know-what than to the face. And after leaving the studio, these young virgins—most of them foreigners, still very respectable, eyes modestly cast slightly down, glimpsing through their lashes—go find relief on Lesbos." I showed Luz this passage, of course, to amuse her, but also these two small sketches: "On the veranda, delightful siesta, everything at rest. My eyes see without under-

standing the space in front of me, I sense the unending of which I am the beginning."

My eyes see without understanding . . . The end of which I am the beginning . . .

And on Mallarmé's *L'après-midi d'un faune*: "I wish to perpetuate those nymphs . . . And he did perpetuate them, that loveable Mallarmé: carefree nymphs, wise in love, flesh and life, near the vines that embrace, in Ville-d'Avray, Corot's majestic oaks with their golden hues pungent with strong animal smells, tropical tastes, in this place and elsewhere, in all ages, from here to eternity" . . .

Mozart? I'll buy him! In the bag! It's a deal, I'll take those Tahitians, those oak trees, those nymphs! And where are the canvases of this Mallarmé? What? A poet? You've got his manuscripts? No? Get going! What's that? "A throw of the dice will never abolish chance"? High up, maybe? Are you sure this nonsense is worth anything? Guaranteed by our Paris agent? The new one? What's-his-name?

Ah yes, my a.k.a. . . . My fax-name . . . All right then, Froissart. Like the medieval chronicler, simply changing the Jean to Pierre. Oh, he too is from Valenciennes, like Watteau and Carpeaux . . . "So, Mozart, what's new?" "Froissart advises us to purchase this manuscript by a certain nineteenth-century poet, sir. A pure masterpiece, a rarity. No, no, nothing to fear, there're very few of them, it's a piece of considerable historical value, closely scrutinized by Jean-Paul Sartre. A discreet and certain rise in value, constant, no unforeseen circumstances, a strong investment." "OK, buy!" "Is it to be sent to Switzerland, sir?" "Of course!" "You wish the Gauguin as well?" "Public or Circuit B?" "Circuit B, sir, unless you should care to wait." "Do we have a Gauguin already?" "Two, sir." "Get it then. Nothing else." "School of Sienna, fifteenth century." "Where was it?" "Medical College, Paris." "That's funny. You'd better be there. And you're certain about that Froissart?" "A hundred percent, sir. Cultured, discreet, competent." "On a level with W?" "I think so." "You're not forgetting the two da Vinci and the Guardi? Worth how much?" "A wad. The Guardi is unique" "More Venice?" "Who's to complain, sir?" "Salesroom?" "Sotheby's, Monaco." "The lot will travel first?" "Usual circuit: London, Tokyo, Los Angeles, New York, Paris." "Paris?" "Just for appearance's sake, sir." "Your advice?" "The whole lot, sir." "Even the Guardi? There are so many fakes!" "More reason to own a real one, sir. Don't forget that Venice is sinking." "Tourists, tides, seaweed?" "Young bums, chemical pollution, renovation projects." "I saw a guy with a beard, on television, piss against the portal of St. Mark's, right after a Pink Floyd concert: isn't that a laugh?" "Sidesplitting, sir, but perhaps a bit *too* much." "Aren't we in charge of good and evil, destruction and construction, perversions and their cures? And speaking of that, what's happening to our psychoanalysts?" "They're still asking for funds for their world congresses, sir." "Give them the funds, give them the funds! And the writers we're subsidizing with grants? They're writing proper stuff, I hope?"

Banal conversation, airy stuff . . .

"Be careful with how you prepare the catalogues for the public circuits. Serious scientific curatorial jargon plus a touch of poetry."

"What would you like for the Gauguin?"

"Ecology, exoticism, dreamy atmosphere, greenery. Savages to protect, rain forest, endangered fish and birds, ozone layer. Get a writer who can embroider on that. Preferably phototelegenic. And above all, no sex. 'Fat and lustful women.' Certainly not."

"I've got the man you need. He's just written a particularly moving best-seller on India. Hefty, healthy, athletic, shy."

"Pure of spirit? Nostalgic? Mournful? Golden age? A religious twenty-first century or bust?"

"Exactly."

"Fine, ask him to contribute. But a rock solid critical apparatus, OK?"

"Rock solid, sir."

ROCK SOLID ACADEMIC, that's Nicole. She encompasses scholarly research, contacts with museums, universities, specialized magazines, publishers, embassies, government departments. Just as Geena—big, copper-colored hair, always relaxed—might appear in one of the innumerable soap operas of American success stories, Nicole—dark haired, middle sized, smiling and tight-assed—represents the European tradition of never having to spell things out, "Business, me? It's just *one more* aspect of my job; that's not the problem." The truth is that she's even more financially minded than her dollar-obsessed friend, but in a muffled, neutral way. Paris is another showcase, modern art, or postmodern if you like, but we Parisians were already there . . . I understand why Geena chooses rather to control her from inside: Nicole, in spite of her cynicism, now common to the whole profession, would *certainly never* confuse a Monet with a Jasper Jones—in spite of their having almost equivalent market value. Geena would, yes, and with a certain aloofness, showing both tolerance and pity. Nicole can dream of Alan Bond, Australian gold-mine owner, who bought himself (without being able to pay for it) van Gogh's *Irises*, but not of Samuel Newhouse, Condé Nast (*Vogue*), who put 17 million dollars down on the *False Start* by the most expensive living American painter (after de Kooning who died peacefully, at a very advanced age, of Alzheimer's: painters must now be dead or well behaved, Jasper Jones is perfect, absent, almost invisible). Geena would choose Newhouse or someone else with no hesitation, and thinks of that gilded James Bond as somewhat mentally retarded. War of the continents . . . Nineteenth and first half of the twentieth century, against second half of the twentieth and twentieth-and-a-half . . . To be continued . . . Nicole tires of her latest husband? The anticommunist political editorialist is in decline, next to his old reconverted adversaries? Too openly rightwing-leftwing for the leftwing-rightwing business (never drive on the wrong lane)? She was the girlfriend of Meilhan who also died five or six years ago . . . Swallowed up by married life, Meilhan was. The kids, the noise, the holding back, the daily dissuasion, the conjugal debt . . . Why bother writing another ten lines wrested from the enormous and microscopic usury of the passing days? I know his wife: she has unflinchingly made use of the unstoppable strategy of expenses and irritability, tantrums and bills. This will finish off any man as quickly as anything, just pin down his bank account and his ear, force him to press his eardrum against his

bank statements, in between two bouts of sickness, against a background of cries and melancholy. I saw Meilhan again recently, a man afraid of everything now, suffering from sleeping disorders, drunk, haunted, disgusted, spiritless, this man, the author of *Mascarade*, a success, for once, based on the work's quality . . . Yes, but the taxes. . . The ever-increasing disappearance from the best-seller lists, the twenty most popular novels, stories, nonfiction, essays, reportage, travel guides, comic books, detective novels, how-to's . . . Ah yes, the latest Meilhan didn't sell, too complicated, not reader-friendly enough . . . What can anyone do against Marion Zimmer Bradley? "Who is she? *The Fall of Atlantis, The Mists of Avalon.*—First I've heard of her.—What ignorance! The epic of the *Illiad* resurrected!" . . . Nice man, Meilhan, trying to be mean just to survive in this jungle . . . Thoughtful, forcing himself to joke about it, already resigned . . . Marion Zimmer Bradley . . . I've just seen her name in an ad. On the other side of the page, in large letters: "We love our clients and we still have loads of love to give. Media-System, the first communications agency for human resources." But of course, human resources are limitless, like love, like communication itself. Meilhan refused to communicate, like so many others. He reread Heidegger: "Eksistenz is the ecstatic position in the truth of Being." Or: "Only Being grants the unscathed individual his ascent in serenity, and the wrathful his feverish course towards ruin." Heaven, hell . . . His wife's voice: "Dinner's ready!"

(Maybe he's just read the same ad, Meilhan has, and also the one next to it:

SEX: HOW WELL ARE YOU DOING?

Have a psychoanalyst answer all your questions by phone—daily!

Thursday: Man and polygamy.

Friday: The discovery of femininity.

Saturday: Men who love both men and women.

Monday: Men and their fear of commitment.

Tuesday: The need for a father figure.

Wednesday: The role of the uterus in reaching an orgasm.

Thursday: Erotic seduction.

Friday: Premature ejaculation.

Saturday: Dreams and homosexuality.

Monday: Female erection.

Tuesday: Loss of desire in a relationship.

Wednesday: Sexual inhibitions.

Thursday: Men and foreplay.

Friday: Sexuality in boys.

Saturday: Pleasure and the unconscious.

Monday: From adolescent to adulthood.

Tuesday: The role of sexuality in creativity.)

Like Laugier, "whose name hardly anyone knows nowadays," Richard used to say with the contempt of that which exists for that which doesn't, that which doesn't being that which hasn't been spoken of in the past three weeks. I hear him and see him too, Laugier, rather high-pitched voice, clear; rather pale; he was never filmed or recorded, that's his masterpiece, a real black hole . . . Three short books, one or two photographs, slumped, drinking beer, stays cloistered at home, plays chess. He's chosen a fully clandestine life, ineffable illegality, "several illegalities at once," those are his words. A new kind of mystic, hyperrational, a mass of nega-

tivity, he's pushed to suicide the society within him, not a martyr, only a presence, demonstrating simply through his refusal, the wished for, the orchestrated unreality, the permanent falsification. "Ah, Laugier!" . . . For some, the name sounds sometimes like a sort of dreaded final judgment, shame, a reminder of the dates and files of generalized corruption. One of his best friends was murdered; he wasn't, how strange. Not did he kill himself, which is even stranger. Nor did he go mad, in spite of the explicit and constant wish of his contemporaries. "Laugier? Paranoid" . . . The cliche was used a hundred times, by senseless dummies stuffed to bursting . . . If at least he'd been a terrorist or a sentimental anarchist: but no, his was the classic style, cold reason, irony, a bit like Meilhan, both deluxe furniture on sale. They didn't sell. Nicole broke off with Meilhan (one mustn't speak to her about it; her eyes immediately cloud over) when she understood what his decision was: rather vegetate than give up his language, rather remain silent than reel off the requisite vacuous thoughts. "They're assholes," Richard would say, "you only live once." He lives his life at full speed, he does, his one and only life of an image among images, nerves laid bare on the screen, drugs through ads . . . He *exists*. Does he suspect me of not believing in his existence? Nor in mine, the way he conceives it? Yes indeed, distrust. I'm of two minds. He grimaced when I told him, in passing, that we should reinvent Gide's *acte gratuit*, the deed done for no reason whatsoever. *Acte gratuit?* What for? I insisted: "After all, the books haven't dated, *The Immoralist, The Vatican Cellars* . . . My sense is that it will make a comeback, the *acte gratuit*." "Hmm." "Crime without passion nor reason, disinterested, by chance, reclaimed as

such, no justification whatsoever. Apathy. Signed, *Gide.* "Gide's dated." "We could update him." "You think so?" I enjoy embarrassing Richard, his face grows long, thirty seconds' calculation, who knows if this *acte gratuit* thing isn't something marketable, after all this idiot has good ideas sometimes. No . . . In the end . . . To whom could one offer this dubious gadget? "It sounds reactionary, even fascistic." "So what?" "No, you need a motivation, nothing can be done for no reason whatsoever . . . Satanism, if you like. The thirst for evil, with a thousand psychiatric explanations, American TV is full of them." "Of course not, pure rationalism: I find those two words thrown together quite explosive: *acte, gratuit.*" "OK, maybe." Richard's thoughts are already somewhere else . . . I can't simply recite for him Article 13 of the *Privileges:* "He who is privileged may not steal; if he tries, his organs would refuse to act. He is entitled to kill ten human beings a year, but none to whom he has spoken on more than two separate occasions." The gratuitous murder, yes (it's one of the Fine Arts), theft, no. The exception for the first year is a delightful touch. The prohibition of having spoken with the victim is of great moral elegance. Ten murders a year, in 1840: would we go up to a hundred by the end of our century, taking into consideration the population increase and the grandiose massacres we've witnessed since? Is it too much to ask? Am I being sufficiently restrained?

Richard's name, in the network, is Andy, like his hero: Warhol.

I'VE RETURNED THREE or four times to Luz's room to watch her sleep . . . I watch her breathing, I put my mouth close to

hers to feel her breath. At this very moment, the entire city, the little streets, the interlaced canals, the walled gardens, the balconies, the bridges, the worn marble of its floors seem to concentrate and evaporate against her eyelids. Softly, I open the shutters to let the evening into the room, the perfume of the oleander bushes and the quiet water through the leaves. She opens her eyes, fails to recognize me for about three seconds, then smiles. While she gets ready, I go sit outside, behind the spindle trees, on my tomb. I haven't been, I've been, I am, I am not, I'll be, I won't be, I am.

GEENA:

"Have you noticed that Warhol has the same initials as Watteau?"

"A.W.? A shortcut of three centuries. Difficult to make a loop."

"Rosenblum says he's the Manet of our time. You think that's an exaggeration?"

"Not at all. The idea of portraits in a series is very powerful. One has to see them in perspective, the skulls beneath the skin. Marilyn Monroe, Elvis Presley, Marlon Brando, Liz Taylor, Mao, wanted murderers, just anyone, himself. Accidents, electric chairs, skulls carried off from the shallow common grave of consumer goods. Look at the *Camouflages*. The theology of the dollar."

"Theology?"

"Spectacle and grace. Mass at St. Patrick's after his bizarre death . . ."

"A badly set up instrument at the hospital. Negligent nurse."

"Yes but, twenty years earlier, a woman's revolver aimed right at his chest."

"A loony."

"Not so loony. She was a fan. Imagine a Madame Bovary who, in order to save the feminine ideal, became militant and stabbed Manet because of his *Olympia*."

(To save Woman or God, same battle . . . I think of the fanatic who stabbed Spinoza, the Spinoza thanks to whom we have the *Ethics* . . . All his life he kept the torn cloak in his room. One more "black hole" composition: *Spinoza's Cloak*. "We pronounce the excommunication, the expulsion, the anathema and the curse of God against Baruch de Espinosa. May God never forgive him!" Good Lord! . . . And Voltaire: "We could suppose that without the stabbing and without the black candles snuffed out in blood, Spinoza would never have written against Moses and against God. Persecution irritates; it emboldens anyone with a sense of genius" . . .)

"But wasn't he a homosexual?"

"Warhol? What's that supposed to mean? What's that supposed to mean in his particular case? One of his most abrasive lines seems to have been: "Sex is so nothing." A specialist in nothing (sex, money, appearances). But that "nothing" must be known and challenged, one must register to the bitter end its contortions, and the maniacal belief people have in it. I spent an evening with him. He didn't say a single word—tuxedo, watching the extras, I'm a machine, nothing but a machine, and you are, for the machine, nothing but transitory images and preconceived images, poor ruminations on your pseudointerior images as they flit by on their way to becoming nothing. A modest man, carrying his tape recorder with him (everyone is warned: the inanity of each word, but everyone is *forced* to speak, right?). What it comes down to, is that he had transformed himself according to the example of those huge ears now flapping away almost everywhere on this planet on account of secret services: radars, active and passive sonars, hydrophones, submarines, satellites. That's how I'd paint him. For all that, a perfect gentleman."

"Would you bet on his going up in price?"

"Certainly. Even if the puritans wage their requisite campaign against him."

He's in Venice in September 1977, Warhol, after an earthquake (I remember, the day after there were swarms of wasps everywhere). He writes in his journal, on the 17th: "I took a fast boat to get to the airport, we flew over the waves." This good Catholic of Czech origin, an expert in all vices, went to mass every Sunday. After a trip: "I went to give thanks for having returned alive." Sunday, February 13, 1983: "It was snowing outside, it was wonderful, not too cold, went to church." But also: "I must be too weird for TV because it's always the same, they don't know what to do with me."

Last canvases: Madonnas and child, after Raphael, Last Supper, after da Vinci. "You like them?" "Very much." "Richard says it's totally uninteresting." "He's wrong." "According to you, what's his best work, off the top of your head?" "His later canvases, the self-portraits, the skulls, the dollar signs." "So it seems that America has only had one dandy worthy of mighty Europe?" "In a nutshell."

Another entry: "I told him that after they tried to murder me, I was no longer as creative as before because I stopped seeing weird people." And also: "Ah, I forgot: at the table,

Bianca took her panties off, passed them to me, and I pretended to sniff them before stuffing them in the pocket of my suit. I still have them."

Luz, sipping her champagne on the terrace:

"You were saying: Save Woman, and you save God?"

"I could have used another example:

"Of the eons of geological periods recorded in the stratifications of the earth: of the myriad minute entomological organic existences concealed in cavities of the earth, beneath removable stones, in hives and mounds, of microbes, germs, bacteria, bacilli, spermatozoa; of the incalculable trillions of billions of millions of imperceptible molecules contained by cohesion of molecular affinity in a single pinhead: of the universe of human serum constellated with red and white bodies, each, in continuity, its universe of divisible component bodies of which each was again divisible in divisions of redivisible component bodies, dividends and divisors ever diminishing without actual division till, if the progress were carried far enough, nought nowhere was never reached."

"Christ! Who's that satanic author?"

"Joyce. Too bad he's not around anymore so that we can condemn him to death. It's true that today his book would not be published, or else would fall majestically flat on its face."

"You mean that science is still bearable, but not the words and perceptions of everyday language that would translate what science knows?"

"Exactly."

* * *

IT WAS LUZ'S father who wanted her to learn French and travel to France. Her mother wanted her to become a musician, that is how she was made to listen to the entire classical repertory during her childhood. Music, math . . . She underlined this passage in Cavailles's correspondence (June 9, 1931): "Mozart's quintet in A major: those glissandos as well as those linear dualities, rounding the edges of sound and making it more complex and, in the larghetto, those patient depths where we are given a kind of foreshortening of cosmic duration, or rather the coming of another world with dark links between points in time, and superior as something atemporal and immobile." Not bad? Not bad. I would never have read that without her. Nor this (March 13, 1934): "Last week I spent a delightful morning at the Luxembourg Gardens preparing a class, trying to hear the birds and the tree buds—such a time is auspicious, and I took up Spinoza once again with real joy, in spite of all the restricting obstacles." Cavailles's sister remarks with charming naiveté: "I've always been struck by how his mood and even his intellectual activity were influenced by sunshine." And one of his friends at school reminisces: "Of my conversations with him during that year (1931) what I remember most is the ever-growing attraction that the Catholic liturgy seemed to have for him." Cavailles was a Protestant, so was Luz's mother, she didn't underline this passage. But she did draw a line under this one (written by Cavailles's sister): "I know not how he met the Norwegian woman who had then (1936) such an importance in his life. But her portrait which I often observed on his desk was proof of his attachment to her. The woman in the portrait directed her insistent gaze towards Jean, unwittingly revealing the ties that existed between them. She was very beautiful." Somewhat further on: "The young Englishwoman, the Norwegian woman, but also all those who were not able to resist his charm . . ." This sister of his is of exemplary honesty, but we will learn nothing more about this all-important subject which sheds equal light on his love of the sun, his delight in Mozart and Spinoza, his inventiveness in the field of mathematical logic, his attraction to Catholic liturgy, his abilities to organize clandestine armies, the strength with which he kept his secrets to the end, becoming John Doe #1 at the mass cemetery of Arras, finally identified thanks to his small green wallet turned black in the earth. "Condemned to death by the military tribunal of Arras at the beginning of 1944 and immediately executed." In the Resistance, Cavailles successively called himself Marty, Herve, Chennevieres, Carriere, Charpentier, Daniel . . . In London, in 1943, the secret service had christened him Crillon. "Next to his tomb," writes his sister, who had come to identify his mortal remains, "in an abandoned corner of the cemetery of Arras, there was a white rosebush planted there by chance, a white, vigorous rosebush."

I study his photograph: an oval face, large forehead, rather round cheeks, big meaty mouth, pale eyes, hair brushed backwards, thick eyebrows, with a happy, translucent air about him. His eyes have a direct, insistent look. You'd say he's about to throw himself on the camera. The book his sister wrote on him (republished under a different title, *J.C., A Philosopher in the War,* instead of *A Warring Philosopher,* an important correction) lies on my table next to *Memoirs of Egotism,* on the cover Dedruex-Doroy's portrait from the Stendhal Museum in Grenoble. No resemblance, but striking family ties. Literature and group theory have much to say to each other. "A lonely theory," wrote Cavailles, "still incomplete, uncertain in the eyes of many, an arm reaching out towards the sky . . ."

"It's so much fun to blow up a viaduct," he says one day, "to be the one to set fire to the Bickford line." . . . "His sister comments: "In a certain sense, he wasn't 'well behaved,' he loved life, good wine, travel, at times even luxury and elegance, he used to accompany me to help me choose a dress." I take pleasure in placing next to one another that recollection and the following sentence: "By a revolutionary reversal, the number is expelled from perfect rationality, and infinity is invited in." Powers of continuity, watch over us. Do you mean to say that there are as many points in the side of a square as in its entire surface? Yes. Elementary. However, the day Cantor reaches this conclusion, he writes to Dedekind: "I see it, but I don't believe it." Blessed are those who have seen and have not believed! Praised be Galileo, Newton, Cantor, Einstein, Cézanne, Picasso, Joyce! Silence, you, the powerful and profane, sunk in the shadows: buy, buy back your sins: "It is only through the prejudice of realists that we busy ourselves with objects, when all that matters, in our sequence of assertions, is that which commands the sequence, i.e., the actual intellectual labor."

Cavailles, a.k.a. Crillon or Daniel, lived then on the top floor on 34 Avenue de l'Observatoire, in an apartment that looked over the whole of Paris. He was 41 at the time of his execution, and his work had hardly begun. We forget that Spinoza (1632–1677) died at the age of 45.

Prison of numbers . . .

"WHAT'S THAT GOT to do with Warhol?"

"Idea for a party: you invite whoever you wish. There's no reason for the party. What's very well-known is little-known, what's not known should be made known. Tell me again about group theory, infinity, black holes."

"First of all, in physics, zero and infinity don't correspond to any measureable object. Then you have two horizons that mark their inaccessibility: the cosmological horizon of relativity due to the impossibility of transmitting signals faster than light . . ."

"Turn the light off."

". . . and the quantum horizon due to the principle of uncertainty which does not allow zero to be the result of any physical measurement. OK. Now, the black hole: a condensed body whose gravitational field is so intense that it does not allow any substance, any rays to escape it."

I listen to her, I quickly think of something else, waves of memory wash over me, I get her to talk so as to better watch her in the dark. It's hot. She was sitting opposite me in the library; she has just stood up to switch off the chandelier, it's eleven o'clock, we've just come back from our nightly walk, the moon enters at an angle through one of the French doors, one for the road, one last little chat. Tableau: "Writer of Dubious Proclivities Listening to Young Woman Physicist, in the Moonlight, One Summer, in Venice." Or this one: "The Cosmology Lesson." Definition of a *singularity*? A point in time-space where the time-space curve becomes infinite. Of course. Time-space? A four-dimensional space in which the points are events. Crystal clear. Are we, point by point, a singular event? Nothing contradicts the notion of my sensing things in this manner *at this very moment,* right? Stroking her hair, her shoulder, her cool arms? Closing from time to time her lips (small mouth), sucking her mobile tongue that has just spoken? By the way, is a black hole a condensed body or a time-space region? Both? Necessarily. Have there been any great women physicists recently? Of course, Jocelyn Bell, for example, of Cambridge, the pulsar business, in 1967. And Chien-Shiung Wu, in 1956, another American, who demonstrated that a weak interaction does not follow the P. symmetry (whereby all physical laws are the same for each situation and its mirror image). *Oh, this interests me.* And many others, more and more. Does this surprise me? Not in the least. Don't I share the current prejudice which consists of believing that women are incapable of innovations in math, chess, music—in a word, the abstract dimensions? Far be it from me to conceive of such an idea. Are women under a biological yoke? Unfortunately yes, most of the time, but advancing in the other direction, that would be ludicrous, q.e.d. I'm fully convinced, I love her. I'll make up a song about my little scientist, light of my days and my nights, eyes born again beneath the sky, blond curve, to the tune of my love is like a red, red rose, June, tune, sun, run, there, very close, barely two darkness-year seconds away. Had she never heard this story about Warhol's murder? No, she was three years old at the time. Ah yes, of course . . . But it's all so long ago . . . And the *Scum Manifesto,* the plan to castrate men? Right in line with the great Protestant lunatics of the nineteenth century? Mary Baker Eddy? Man, dumb ox, big ape, and finally *pig*? Yes, well, all that was probably exaggerated by our great-grandmothers, but you've got to see it from their point of view . . . Prose by Warhol's assailant: "The only men who will not be sent to extermination camps will be the fags who, through their magnificent example, encourage the other men to become nonmale and thereby relatively inoffensive." But *was* Warhol the symbol of maleness? Someone so pleasant, so reserved, so sickly sweet, behind his Polaroid, his Instamatic? Someone who was an expert in phone-sex? Someone who said: "I think we're too caught up in love relationships, and it's not worth it . . . We do it just like we watch a movie on TV"? Curious. Or is it that very distance which was felt as murderous by the will to murder, endemic, alive? Was it because he was more dead than the rest that he had to be murdered? Look, I'll paint a portrait of Andy Warhol as Watteau: he moves forward, unemotional, in the midst of a landscape that becomes one with him, a dancer motionless and pale. We're at a New York party, he pinpoints the frenzied, comic irreality. All aboard for Hell . . . Lots of money floating around, ruining him just like the human scabs who attached themselves to him, ruined him: "people transfer," "people are so amazing that you can't take a bad photograph."

There are nothing but bad photographs.

There are nothing but good photographs.

In photography, it's never a question of good or bad.

And in painting? Ah, painting . . . The work of a friend of Warhol's, Basquiat, is priced one day at two hundred thousand dollars. This, Basquiat finds depressing. He wants to try something out: he goes to some people's house, rings, and offers one of his paintings for two dollars. They don't even glance at it, they refuse. Next day, they learn that they've just lost two hundred thousand. Then Basquiat dies young, and he becomes even more expensive. Two dollars! The cost of a photograph!

Record voices. Take pictures. Show the voice and the image together without preconceived connections. Cut. Start again. "No story, no plot, only *incidents*." At Warhol's *Factory*, in the golden years, every newcomer was automatically filmed. You who come in, know that you're but a reflection. "I never wanted to be a painter, I wanted to be a tap dancer." Challenging Hollywood, challenging that whole reality which had become a worldwide soap opera, challenging the novel as demanded by the ever-present Medium. from point A to point B, with death lurking in some corner., "Write me a real novel, the public demands it" (and we are the public, keeping watch over TV channels and forthcoming books).

I have already five hundred photos of Luz, in the swimming pool, lying in the garden or on the terrace, on board ship, eating an ice cream on the quays, on her bed, sitting at her desk, in front of the windows (profile to the right, neck, profile to the left), she looks a little like Edie Sedgwick (overdosed in 1971), Warhol's female star of the sixties, concentration, grace, shapely slenderness. The technique consisted of: take as many purposeless shots as possible, purposeless movies, endless still shots, a tiny change after one or two hours, close-up of a kiss, a man asleep, the Empire State Building during eight full hours, a blow job shot live fixed on the face of the guy about to come, a haircut, transvestites, of course—

that's it, transvestites are at the root of that gunshot. Film wasted deliberately, messed up, burnt, unwatchable, just to show the flip side of the immense packaging operation, images of images of images, brave new world, ruthless and void, chosen to replace the body, decondition yourself, every instant of your life is of interest, or none is, no more hierarchies, no more pathos, frenzy of Feeling, of Property, of Goal. This is S/M kitsch, the very heart of showbiz, its constant pulse (a black hole is a cosmic S/M machine), leather, dance to a whip, coke, heroin, amphetamines, noise for the sake of noise, integrated sleepwalking. A witness to the time may well describe Warhol at the core of this self-defeating excitement as the frigid eye of the storm or as a meditating Buddhist, but he wouldn't be able to avoid mentioning, without drawing more than a conventional conclusion ("repressive education," "a taste for decadence"), that all, or almost all the protagonists were Catholics: Warhol, Linich, Ondine, Malanga, Brigid Polk, Viva, Paul Morrissey, many others. However, there's a simple reason for this: there is in all of them, apparent, a perverted drive; they are pros of perversion, they take action. Unveiling, antidote, cold shower, explicit disintegration. A blasphemy on the lips of the new darling behind the scenes, a struggle to be once again in control. Who'll win? Standardization, as it always does after the plague. But we'll have had time to catch a glimpse of something through the keyhole What? Nothing. There was nothing. Nothing was happening except that which was happening at the moment when it was happening. People are so amazing, in the future everyone will be famous for five seconds (fifteen minutes is far too long), send on the TV game shows, the permanent stupefying effect, the measured manipulation in the studios, it's only the beginning, it's impossible to miss a show, the perfect dream.

And painting? *Painting?* But what painting? Real painting? Fake painting? Real-fake painting? Fake-real-fake painting? Real-fake-real-fake painting? Guaranteed by whom? How? For whom?

Richard's plan has its method:

"But don't you see, it's one *duty* to put works of art back into circulation, *in a state of feverish intensity*. It's in their nature, after all. The financial excitement surrounding pictures? Why not? Psychoanalysis of *Der Kapital*. Would you rather have the old-fashioned museum, obligatory visit, shoving crowds, opening, closing, antiseptic denial, vague glimpse, mind-wandering students? Do they get put away in safes, these pictures, so as not be shown? Yes, they're radioactive. They *emit* money at every instant. More and more. They sleep and yet they work, sometimes they don't even move away from the place in which their sale took place, they don't have time because they're bought again in the following days or months. Money starts turning around immobile irises, the minted sun moves in relation to fixed sunflowers. We give art back its dignity and its memory, time, space, the walk-on actors are defined in relation to it, nudes, portraits, flowers, trees, contortions, colors, gestures. For the first time, people kill one another in cold blood over a canvas. Andy said it very well: "Art as business comes after art." This means that life itself is nothing but business, from beginning to end, emotions, dreams, beliefs, sperm, thought. Body factory, stuffing of brains. The hypocritical humanist-romantic-pathetic protesting will change nothing, on the contrary, it's been scheduled as part of the show. 'Froissart'? Where did you get that?"

"A chronicle writer from the mid-fourteenth century."

"Art has always been an outlaw, only outlaws guarantee it the respect it deserves. Is it bearable to know that a Titian lies rotting among a bunch of morons who don't even look at it, that there are still Holbeins, Van Dycks in private estates? All property holders must surely feel threatened, pay fabulous insurance fees, ultrasophisticated security systems, armed guards. They must earn tons of money, and even more, or sell. Skirmishes, ambushes at the stock exchange . . . The X store chain against Z Import-Export Co., the stakes Picasso's *Acrobat* and *Young Harlequin*. The German Baron T. attacking some British admen. Internal strife, staff replacements, deadly jealousies and, in the center of the conflict, a simple rectangle doodled one fine day by a guy who's more subtle or crazier than the rest . . . For his personal use . . . To commemorate god-knows-what sexual fantasy satisfied or not . . . Afterwards, the unworthy and neurotic owners tremble. Is my Monet still in its place? My Turner? Is my Pontormo a masterful fake? My Greek Kouros a failed real-fake? We, we are the artists' avengers, the army of genius humiliated throughout the centuries, the commando of convicts or exiled writers, the hosts of Judgment Day, here, now. You want a van Gogh? To keep you alive? Fine, you'll pay for it with perpetual disquiet, it will buzz in your ears during the night, it will grimace at you in an Artaudlike fashion, ulcer, impotence, cardiac arrest. We turn out the drawers, topple the banners, the intimacies, the religions. God? Christ? the Virgin? the angels? Well, it's high time you learned that only Michelangelo's God *is*. Ditto,

Rembrandt or Tintoretto's Christ. Ditto, El Greco's Virgin. Ditto, Giotto's angels, or whoever's. We are the ones who have done it all, and even with the sound track: Monteverdi, Bach, Mozart. What's that you say? A God without images? You're joking! The imageless God, once having reached a satisfactory position, puts all His efforts into buying images: *He sets himself up*. The sunflowers are angels, the impressions at sunrise an assumption, the acrobat a crucifixion. And let it rip! The clergies and the banks brought to heel by the easel, that's our justice. Yes, that is our *noble* mission, Froissart, and I would ask you to be more aware of it in the future. It doesn't matter if our clients are not capable of understanding our revolution: it's here, it marches forward, nothing will stop it. The people of India will reclaim the impressionists when all their temples are finally plundered and they've made their fortune. They'll bicker over Renoir, gone with the Ganges. Same thing for the people of Iran, Russia (who are even now, as we speak, renegotiating their Matisses), Algeria, Libya, China, Africa (if there are any Africans left) . . . *Mao wanted a Warhol*, that's what Andy realized. One of his most beautiful series, just after the first steps on the moon. The woman who shot him saw clearly through her delirium: she emptied her gun not at the rotten decadence, but at a brave new world, a world in which the artist finally becomes that which he's been ever since the caves of Lascaux and always: the measure of all things. Aha, you'll say, that's exactly the moment when there's no more artists? Just zombies? Indeed. *Except us*. It's a splendid joke, Froissart, but remember: 'No one can give me as much pleasure as myself.' Having said that, let's calm down and look at things carefully. What's the fax whispering now?

Nothing from London? Silence in Rome? A hush in New York? All's quiet in Hong Kong? You've found an interesting manuscript? A haunted castle? A manor full of mysteries? An ecclesiastical network? Religious objects? You know my plan: during the night, replace with perfect copies the statues and paintings in a church. Easy to do, no one will notice. The Vatican is deeply in debt these days, correct? We could start in a place that's not much visited, you'll know which one . . . Anyway, I've got the right Japanese for the operation: he'd give anything for an original Tiepolo ceiling, and the lives of both his kids and his wife for Raphael's *Stanze*. So?"

LUZ TOOK MY proposed experiment very well. At last a clear, free, determined, rigorous spirit; at last a nervous system both stable and flexible. Life as a permanent and desired work of art, when art itself has become impossible? But isn't life impossible these days? Certainly. However. And yet . . .

We started with the recordings: video camera, playback in the evening, no commentary. Memory must become the memory of recorded moments, and of other moments. *Where's the difference?* In a week, time reenters space and vice versa, they take turns. You set the stage, you live on it, you forget it, you exit, you remember, you return. On the TV screen which later shows our tapes, our life proceeds as if it were a newscast, fiction, reportage, documentary, and these two unknown people having a bath, talking, sleeping, caressing (her), reading, are our doubles who have become more real than we are through the upside-down all-powerful intoxication of great all-pervading film.

The camera is a Japanese JVC, burgundy and black, with

built-in microphone. The results are as convincing as that of any TV channel. If you want to know what someone's really thinking, ask him to take your picture or film you: the result is blatant, unquestionable. Focus, atmosphere, projected nimbus, murderous intent, sometimes tempered, of him or her who pressed on the button without—especially without—thinking, everything is immediately there, love, indifference, hatred, reticence, rancor, the whole rainbow of attractions and repulsions. So that's how it is, she loves me about 70%, that's a lot. Usually, I barely reach 40 or 50, smiles sometimes, positive declarations, but disastrous cliches, bleak reproaches. Where were we? What, twelve hours of reels already? In dry weather, in muggy weather? *Mug,* a good eighteenth-century word for face, nothing happens by chance in language, pan, mush, kisser, bring on the animals, let them relax, escape their own selves, show their true colors, their fake colors. Me, I love Luz 90%, it's obvious, look at close-ups of the neck, of the nose, of an ear. And the hands. At length. At great length. At an unusually great length. No hand ever had so many fingers, Picasso was coy. And the ankles, the breasts, the buttocks, the back, images of massage, shoulder blades, shoulders. The elbows. The passion fruit ice cream: tongue and lips, corner of the lips, zoom (she films me under the oleander writing this very sentence). Luz floating belly-up in the swimming pool, black cap hiding her blond hair. Swallows dipping in to drink, gulls higher up, tight movement, deeper still. *Voyager II* circling Neptune, the whole group dedicated to Le Verrier, to the Observatoire, to Stendhal, to the unknown in the sarcophagus, to van Gogh, Manet, Spinoza, Cavailles, Mozart (the real one). And the eyes, the eyes, the eyes, all those eyes, again and again the eyes, turn on the light, turn on the light, again and *more of that blue capable of sight.* It's my fantasy, of course, the page watching you, from the other side of the looking glass or the grave. Yes, don't ever stop making those eyes shine bright, those eyes, and tell me once again that to see, to touch, to hear, to listen, to speak are but a single impalpable knot, there, out in the sun. No, let's start again. No, no, begin at the beginning. The weather is gray and rainy, we'll work on mother-of-pearl. Put on this blouse, no, the black sweater, no, the mauve silk dress, a slight thin rain on the silk. You climb on board the boat, you go to the back, you stay there, you allow yourself to get wet, yes, quickly and then: a hot bath. Do I bother you? Sure? One should classify all the different varieties of laughter, pout, giggles, fake laughter, bouquet of flowers, remember to mark the day down, take the felt-tip pen, time flies, we forget three-quarters of everything. But to forget in this manner changes oblivion into another kind of forgetting. In French there's no difference between *time* and *weather,* you don't say: "weather is money," a mistake. What's Richard's usual phrase, in that singsong voice of his? "Five minutes OK." And yours, your phrase?" "One might think so." Go back. Explain to me once more what's this radiance from the depth of the sky or how is it that, the farther away a galaxy is, the faster it pulls away, it's not at all obvious, this notion of drifting towards red. Let's drift towards red ourselves. Or this: how time and space are finite, but without limits, *without borders.* What's the speed at which a spaceship must move to escape the gravitational pull of the Earth? Twelve km per second? Well, when I see you, you're no longer there where I see you, an infinitesimal distance, a second of a second of a second. What a lovely word, second: You second me, I second you, we second one another.

"Go ahead, carry on with Watteau."

"Another time."

"No, now" (Pause). "Please."

". . ." (A full shot of the swimming pool.)

"Newsflash: Watteau's secret, *La Toilette intime.*"

(Phone rings).

"Shit."

It's Geena. Luz records the conversation.

2

. . . .

In these days of networks and satellites, there's nothing left but networks and satellites. Parasites reign supreme, the racket increases the sounds within a thousandfold. Nothing is actually said or listened to, but everything is repeated, heard. No thought, merely a swarming of signals, froth on the froth, a maniacal and tense reduction of everything. As always, there are the overseers and the overseen, but the overseen have become overseers; why? how? they have their own excellent reasons. Spying on principle, they no longer remember why or for whom they're spying, both sides, against one and all. Anguished question in a magazine regarding the possible existence of extraterrestrials (the press must have something to sell during the summer months): "If a signal is received, what should our Earth do? Should we answer? Who is to decide?"

Hello? We're an intergalactic intelligence far superior to yours. We command that you deliver to us in one week's time each and every one of your works of art, otherwise we will destroy everything. You must deliver immediately the complete works of Titian, Vermeer and Rembrandt.

Mr. President, what have you decided?

Watch out, Céline would have said, "esoteric precaution." "Hell wasn't cooked up in a day." "One moment of bliss, not a second more." "I'm at my best in the realm of music, small animals, the harmony of dreams, of cats and their purring." And he adds (in a letter to Henry Miller): "Be discreet! Always more and more discretion! Know how to be mistaken. The world is full of people who are always right. It's enough to make one sick!"

Geena is now, as they say in novels, my officer in charge. Geena MacBride, a.k.a. Mozart, after having consulted Richard Milstein, a.k.a. Andy, and Nicole Vuillard, a.k.a. Dürer, rings up Pierre Froissart to find out where he's at, or rather what he's hiding. It's unnecessary to have me followed, to have my phone tapped night and day, to waylay my faxes or to open my mail, a few words on the phone are enough, a direct sounding of my voice. Hi, how's it going? It's my tone that interests her, not my answer (which she doesn't listen to), the high or low pitch, nervous or calm, my *audio-spectrum.* Then she'll know, with unerring instinct, if I'm tired, alert, confident, bitter, wallowing in belief or disappointment, more or less dangerous, vulnerable. A physical presence provides less information, except of the kind that interests only one's partners nowadays: looking good, not looking too good, put on weight, lost weight, looking sick, looking beat, looking fit, maybe get rid of him, or proceed with care. Why tell me you're going to Rome so that I think you're really going to London when in fact you *are* going to Rome? That's not a quip but the trigger of every conversation. You've got to have your chessboard or your deck of cards handy. Guess what mistake the other expects you to make, aim at the other's constant desire to blame you. "What does a woman want?" a good writer once said. "A man to blame." Given this point of view, a woman frequently becomes the one to blame, and all men can certainly become blamers. Hysterics, is the push button. It seems that there's a mystical sect, something like the Sufis, called "the blamed people." They take upon themselves all basic reproach and reprobation, the fault of every given moment. Imagine a calling card: "*X., Someone To Blame.*" It makes them so happy, why deny them the pleasure? You might even go as far as committing *the most blatant of faults,* the one they never dared hope for, there it is, they've got you now, you've had your moment of weakness, you've been caught unaware, you've been had because of your greatest shortcoming, you've lowered your defenses: you've put the blame on someone. While this takes place, you might simply be doing something else, moving to another address, changing your phone number, following up on your wicked deeds, i.e., those deeds which in fact are the most innocent, the most natural ones, those which, obviously, *no one ever suspects you of*. Learn to allow others to second-guess your intentions, but to misunderstand those intentions; prepare delayed perceptions of yourself; a good agent is like a star whose light doesn't reach its observers until it's dead or has left one area and established itself in another. You're on the lookout for extraterrestrial messages? Really? Come ask me questions. Why tell me you're going to Rome so that I think you're going to London, guessing nevertheless that you're going to Rome, when you really *are* going to London? Spirals . . . There's not a single human relationship that's not based on destabilizing, and the best little devils are those who know this, puppets of a bored soul intent on constant denial. Another trick: make a number of random statements. They'll contradict you at once: fine. That will keep them busy. Throw them a bone, another bone, hurrah for this, hurrah for that. Never travel without a bag of bones. Hold on to the priggish pedantry of spinning plates on a stick, it won't let you down. The game of spinning a plate, plus a certain undefinable smell of formaldehyde, can be unmistakably recognized in this: there are certain subjects that are serious and others that are not, *there are subjects you don't joke about* (tight-lipped variations according to the times).

Voltaire: "The world is a chaos of absurdity and horror, and I can prove it."

The magazine never supposes—how strange—the existence of *dishonest* extraterrestrials. Who would answer only in order to deceive and destroy. But a rival magazine goes one step further: revelations from beyond the grave, visions of death, getting in touch with the disappeared. Be part of it. Is there extraterrestrial life after death? Are we extraterrestrials in spite of death? It's not impossible. It's being discussed. Sponsored research is underway.

From my great-great-grand-aunt to my great-grand-niece, the subjects you don't joke about have been listed as follows: priests, nuns, army, family, fatherland, children, motherhood, racism, human rights, the people, suffering, work, democracy, concentration camps, famine, women, money, death, animals, nature and finally, as always, god.

Voltaire, in a letter to D'Alembert (1773): "There is no conformity any longer, no confidence, no consolation; everything is lost; we are in the hands of barbarians."

A contented barbarian, reading these words, would be bound to think: "Nonsense, please don't be upset . . ."

SO GEENA WANTS to know what I'm doing in Venice? My purpose is simple: I'm a writer-cum-tourist, taking notes for a coffee-table book, an amateur photographer, the insatiably curious visitor of palaces and churches, the mole who can be prodded again into action whenever so desired. I know there'll be ships, which is why I've been lodged not far from the Church of the Salute. The *Player II* registered in Gibraltar will meet the *Sea Sky* from London here. I'll be warned, I'll oversee the operations.

Yes, but Luz wasn't part of the plan, and even though I've suggested that she'd be an ideal cover, Geena can't help feeling out my surroundings at a distance. Jealous? No, she's too much of a professional, and yet . . . The "I've got someone for you" reflex.

I press on the button marked "typical disenchantment,"

detached banalities. Morose cold-bloodedness. What would she do about Watteau's hidden intentions? Two months with an American student? So what? Everyone needs a break. Student of what? Physics? Astronomy? Berkeley? Met where? Looking for what? Nothing in particular? No file? Nothing in the archives? Parents, boyfriends, embassy? Professors, lovers, girlfriends? CIA? FBI? NSA? Drugs? Nothing? Midsummer night's smile? These Frenchmen . . .

"In Paris, late June?"

Don't I have the right to some fun? Provided, of course, that from time to time, I pay my dues.

Luz isn't an expert in profitable secretions, like Geena or Nicole. To reach that state, one must usually marry, have several children, alimony, keep an eye on the law, bank, administration, real estate, doctor's bills, the eternal competition. Careers come first. Luz does her first stint, she's gifted, she doesn't yet carry the bitter wrinkles and the locked jaws that signal the final electrified frontier, nor will she be hardened, at least I don't think so now, but you never know. I take advantage of that, which you could say isn't very nice. There are those who start off as homophobic, and then there're the projective homophiles who become homophobic little by little, the phobic growth is the rule. The later the better. Take courage, your slightly grimacing head, your skull is not yet among the stones nor up for sale, let it roll freely from day to day.

Steal a glance at the oleanders.

"I PICK UP at random that which chance places in my way."

Stendhal underlined this himself in his *Memoirs,* and then added: "This sentence has been my pride for ten years."

We know his schedule (very proper for a real-fake consul):

"When I arrive in a city, I always ask:

1. Who are the twelve most beautiful women.
2. Who are the twelve richest men.
3. Who is the man capable of having me hanged."

He might have added: Who is the woman advising the man capable of having me hanged.

I think of the terrace and of the winter mornings on West 52d, and of the icy wind in front of Central Park. I love the crushing loneliness that makes you want to scream, of certain days in New York City. More than once, I've said to myself that this is where I should depart to, sorry, I mean disappear. Bang, now you don't. Non sum.

Luz knocks gently on the door: "I'm going out."

IN MY THOUGHTS I follow her through piazzas and narrow streets, over bridges and along the quays, the clichéd image is accurate, the ideal city was conceived and built at least once. Is it possible to overcome the shame of human flesh, to establish a dictatorship of the spirit in the republic of the body? An aesthetic and mathematical solution. Partition, drain, fill-ins, angles, invisible features, profiles, dams, docks, openings upon openings, covered passages, incisions, corners, suspensions in midair, reflections. There one can imagine a bright population busy with its sums, a society of discreet Chinamen. No noise, except the ship's foghorns, the bells, and at times, increasing the number of hollow spaces, the hammering of the hulls being repaired before setting off to sea, each percussion a promise, a good omen, commerce, gliding, silence, the evaporation of atoms, slow time, fast, airy. Amsterdam might have had this charm for philosophers, but now, if we really want it, nothing can trouble us. Let your hand glide along, find yourself, oh mirror of mirrors. I enter Luz's room, everything is tidy, framed by her window I see the dome of La Salute, I flip through her books full of equations I don't understand. I'm under her protection, I'm in love with a fairy child, through her, fate keeps watch on me and keeps me in line . . . But how can we possibly believe what you're saying, none of it is real . . . Too bad . . . Neither was it real when I was ten, at the bottom of the garden, far away ("Are you listening to what we're saying? Have you seen a ghost?" . . .) You have no doubt thirty or fifty sad stories to tell us, handicaps, nasty bits, frustrations, humiliations, tantrums, terrors? Yes, no, I forget . . . Man must not create unhappiness in his books . . . I wait for night, stealthily, I'm familiar with the passage, on the left . . . We reach the white hole (from the year 1550), the swallows utter a few last cries in the blue-black sky, we can see less and less, we thumb our noses at each other, why would I make these things up, too bad, too bad . . . Blue Moon, Blue Haze, Billie Holiday, Miles Davis . . . Black man of the golden age of blues . . . Against the whiteness blue not really blue unless it's steeped in black by the hand of time. White cornea, black iris, blue apple of my eye. And Blue Monk, Black and Blue, all titles with the word "blue." Sh! Not a sound! Only seagulls, swallows, the rubbing of wood and ropes . . . Relax, the constant scraping seems to say, take a rest tied to the dock, all the canals are on your side, canals, sunsets . . . Your hand, your arm, a change of hand and arm—quick. See-smell-hear-touch anywhere and everywhere. Slightly black-and-blue on the right shoulder.

WHEN COULD WE have met in earlier days? She came to Italy for the first time with her parents, eight years old, 1974, Rome, Florence, Venice. She doesn't remember much, churches, paintings, churches, paintings, but the light yes, the water, it was in May, I was there, I was on my way back from China, maybe we crossed paths near the Academy or the Rialto. Then she's in New York aged twelve, 1978. Uptown. I'm living in Lower Manhattan for three months, I remember the large white loft, the mattress on the floor, Geena carefully preparing the lines of coke on the table (the mauve plastic straw for her, the red one for me), Indian summer, weekends in Long Island, swimming and naked afternoons on the grass. Again in New York the next year and the year after, I too, millions of moving bodies, and her eyes see the same rain as my eyes see, the same clouds reflected on the same green skyscrapers, her skin whipped by the same bracing ocean breeze, she visited the Met several times, I could have isolated her in the crowd, noticed her in front of Manet's *Woman with a Parrot.* In spring 1983 she's in Paris, aged seventeen, April in Paris, where she saw *L'Indifferent, La Finette,* but just like that, no particular impression, her strongest memory is that of Versailles, the Seine. And once again in Paris, after London, three years ago, she was twenty. I must try and remember the first time I read Hemingway's "A Very Short Story," which begins: "One hot evening in Padua they carried him up onto the roof and he could look, out over the top of the town. There were chimney swifts in the sky. After a while it got dark and the searchlights came out. The others went down and took the bottles with them. He and Luz could hear them below on the balcony. Luz sat on the bed. She was cool and fresh in the hot night."

I have no idea how, but now of course it's one of my favorite texts of the whole of literature. It's only two and a half pages long. It's World War One, Hemingway is wounded, she's a nurse, they have "a joke about friend or enema." They want to get married, he returns to Chicago, she writes to him (no phone in those days, nor fax), ends up preferring someone else, someone who eventually won't end up marrying her, she writes him a letter to break the news, and the story comes to a sudden close: "A short time after he contracted gonorrhea from a salesgirl in a loop department store while riding in a taxicab through Lincoln Park." It's good vintage Hemingway, brutal and fine, right in the eye. Unforgettable: "There were chimney swifts in the sky." In Padua.

Chimney swift: bird similar to the swallow, but with narrower wings and shorter tail (length: 16 cm). Nests in France from May to beginning of August and hunts for insects during its quick flights. (Order: Micropodiform.)

IT WAS LUZ who showed me the article in the *New York Times*, "The Skull of Amadeus." "Mozart's skull has been identified. The composer suffered from a very rare deformity of the frontal sutures." Big photograph in strong black and strong white, alive, burning the page, cutting through the World News, Stock Exchange, Obituaries. A frontal bump, precocious sutures . . . The conclusion is reassuring: "This deformity did not prevent Mozart from possessing a cerebral capacity slightly above normal, some 1,585 cubic cm." What relief! Bang in the middle of the paper, the skull. To its left, a controversy over petrol and pipelines. To its right, the prickly question, which is becoming increasingly hot tempered, concerning supernumerary embryos. They freeze them, then the parents fight over them. Title: SEE-THROUGH TEST-TUBES. (In Russian: *glasnost.*) Good, good, everything's in order. Mozart, as everyone knows, dies of acute rheumatic fever on December 5, 1791, at 12:55 P.M. (and not 56, as a current error has it), at 970 Rauhensteingasse, in Vienna. He's thirty-six. A third-class burial, Cathedral of Saint-Étienne, Saint Marx (*sic*) Cemetery, in the suburbs. You must have seen it all in the film. In 1842, the year Constance died, his wife (not as unfaithful as you'd like to make her out to be), the Austrian anatomist Jacob Hirtl discovered the skull. (This is how they tell the story: I draw your attention to the very peculiar logic that requires an anatomist to discover a musician's skull *after the death of his wife*: why, how, who knows?) The transfer of the skull takes place at the Salzburg Mozarteum in 1901 (what happened during all that time?). As there are still doubts concerning the authenticity of this piece of bone, from which no melody drifts even during nights of full moon. It is locked up in a library cupboard from where no one tries to steal it (thanks, it won't be long: "Mozart? But that's crazy! Quickly, do something about it!"). It's just been scrutinized with scanner and electronic microscope. The craniostenosis, the premature closure of the metopic frontal suture, is now a subject of study, thanks especially to the thirty thousand skulls at the Musée de l'Homme (no, no, I won't give away any secrets about this). Mozart's portrait, painted by Lange, his brother-in-law, corroborates the diagnosis. For more information, see *The American Journal of Physical Anthropology* (or push 33.33, the code: *Eine kleine Nachtmusik*).

Conclusion: as this is the first description of this malformation in an adult male, Mozart, without knowing it (but he would have found it amusing, is that what you're saying?) assisted in the advancement of science. This brings him even closer to us. Exhibitions are being planned throughout the world to explain how is it possible that his more than famous mortal remain was, for two hundred years, buried, exhumed, shelved, taken off the shelf and finally recognized for what it is.

Give me an aspirin.

I fax it all to Geena: Froissart to Mozart re: Mozart's skull. Small intimate concert, one day, in Japan? In California? Nice day among the trees, orchestral tunes, opening of the safe before and after, ten armed guards, glass box carried by the prettiest girl in town, golden cushion? Like Mathilde, in *The Red and the Black*: "she had placed on a small marble table, in front of her, Julien's head and was kissing it on the forehead . . ."?

"Mozart's skull, sir—Excuse me?—The authentic skull of Wolfgang Amadeus Mozart.—Authentic? Scientifically guaranteed?—Here are the documents, sir.—How much?—You understand, it's an extraordinary piece.—You're certain it's not *already* one of the ten copies being sold under the table?—Not at all: Mozart himself.—No one will suspect the substitution?—No one, sir.—You know I'm very fond of that young singer . . .—That's exactly whom I had in mind, sir."

I can see it now: the last guests have left, night falls. The lucky one, new cosmic Mathilde, dazzling in her long black sleek dress, neck circled by a stream of diamonds, is lighting the torches in the great halls. She places the skull on one of the mantelpieces. Oh yes, she imagines how she'll faint as her lips approach the immortal brow! How her breast swells! How her bosom heaves, her ankles burn! She brings her mouth close to it, her mouth which has just sung *vibrato*, once again, the celebrated high-pitched solo of *The Magic Flute*. At last her lips brush the skull, with her lace handkerchief she wipes off the slight trace of lipstick on the bones, it will always remain the strongest emotional experience of her life. Dead secret, of course. What palpitations when, lying by the pool, under the palm trees, a yellow silk scarf around her neck, she raises from time to time her eyes towards the terrace guarded day and night, the terrace of the president himself, and she recalls that He, beloved of the gods, genius among geniuses, Love Itself, *is there*. Saved from the paupers' pit and, even worse, from the display cases. At last, His Head, but it's all in the head, isn't it? Let's hope He won't be sold immediately, she doesn't possess Him yet, and she might have as her rival that ambitious and hot brunette next Salzburg Festival . . .

Thefts! Sales! Thefts at the sales! Learn how to distinguish the skulls in armored boxes, like the skull-signature in Holbein's *The Ambassadors*.

(Give a thought to the thirty thousand skulls at the Musée de l'Homme.)

Did Warhol have Holbein in mind? Certainly. His *Skulls* are from 1976. The one I can see now on my screen, silk screen ink on synthetic polymer paint on canvas (335.3 ×

381 cm) is part of the Menil Collection, Houston, Texas. White on black, the grinning bucktooth skull on a green and blue background, set on a disk of shadow rimmed in red. He made another one, same dimensions, in pink, yellow and apple-green. And nine small ones, which he kept for himself, multicolored. And the self-portrait carrying a skull on his left shoulder (1978), hanging from the self-portrait with hands strangling him from behind. And finally four versions of *Philip's Skull* (1985) (private collection).

(*Almost*) A DREAM: SKULLS

Have you got Shakespeare's skull?"

"Don't pull my leg, sir. You know perfectly well."

"Galileo's? Einstein's?"

"We're working on it."

"Marx? Freud? I'd very much like to make an ashtray out of Marx's skull. And present Freud's in a humorous fashion, maybe on a phallic base . . ."

"Maybe we can arrange something for Marx through London. But as for Freud, don't even think about it, sir. He was cremated and placed in a Greek urn by the Princess Bonaparte."

"Fine, buy the urn."

"We'll try. But we can get pretty quick results with Lenin, Mao, Ho Chi Minh, Che Guevara."

"Oh yes, ashtrays, ashtrays. They still haven't found Sade's skull?"

"The quest continues. But the roll on which *The One Hun-*

dred and Twenty Days of Sodom was written is available. We could make an offer."

"The Russians must have kept Stalin's skull after the splitting-up?"

"Of course. But they're asking an exorbitant price."

"Let's hear it. Have we got the artist to give the whole thing some class?"

"No problem."

"And Bach? Beethoven? A few popes? Columbus? Philip II of Spain? Michaelanglo? Napoleon? Queen Victoria? Luther? Goethe? Kant? Hegel? Nietzsche? Get a move on, will you!"

"Yes sir. But France is growing restless. For a good price we can get Pascal, Stendhal, Proust."

"Not bad."

"Joyce, via Zürich."

"Not bad, not bad at all."

"Van Gogh, Cézanne, Picasso."

"But of course! Sold!"

"Warhol."

"Alas, poor Yorick! Perfect. What a pantheon right in the middle of the Pacific! Houston's syncretic temple set well in! What a sublime behind-the-scenes view of the universe! Mozart in the center! You understand, my dear, this is really the end of History. We now understand everything since the beginning and for all time. Imagine: *we can no longer be wrong! No more damnation! Time will sit in judgment no longer! Art was nothing but a childhood disease!* My ideal is this: Skulls and seagulls! The Ocean! No more waves! Oh, skulls! Oh, gulls!

*   *   *

A VOLUPTUOUS BODY now haunts the world and the world's funds: the flesh of blazing landscapes in lost paintings, obsessing the ghosts of living dead. A sensitive surface has nothing to lose except its chains.

Luz:

"My horoscope says I'm living out a great passion."

"You read your horoscope?"

Let's go back to where we left off. Wasn't Mozart buried in a pauper's grave, one snowy day, his hearse followed only by a dog? Indeed? So how could his head have resurfaced from the muck? Did it climb up all by itself? You're not going to say that it was cut off *before* the burial by his wife, following a hunch about what the future held in store, like Johanna, Theo van Gogh's wife, rewriting Vincent's letters to his brother, having them buried side by side, after having forced the painter to commit suicide over a question of *paying the rent*? My God, all is so muddled up, so chaotic . . . Constance Mozart, in the Saint Marx Cemetery, holding a lantern . . . Having the sack pulled up, leaving with the head . . . Who's the hunchbacked little man by her side? And Goya's skull? Why wasn't it in the coffin opened up in Bordeaux? And where is the skull of duchess of Alba, the maja sometimes dressed, sometimes naked? My headache is getting worse. Give me back Artaud's skull! The priest of Ivry stole it to have it rebaptized! Vehement denial by the archbishopric. They say Warhol's thighbone cures AIDS in India. Three fake van Gogh jawbones have been confiscated at the Swiss border. And still that old woman dying in her own feces, crying into the night: "Murillo! Murillo!" "Master, explain this Dance of Death to us." "We can't do anything about it, the sacred is in crisis." "The Middle Ages?" "Sort of." "Tomorrow they're selling Monet's right hand." "Not surprising." "And the day after tomorrow, Picasso's shinbone preserved by his wife, who committed suicide." "Of course." "The Japanese lead a wild search in the barns of Auvers-sur-Oise to find hidden canvases, only yesterday they tortured an illegitimate descendant of Dr. Gachet, van Gogh's friend. Real hyenas. Where will it all end?" "Nowhere." "Three children have cut their own ears off after their art class." "Indemnify the families." "But it makes no sense!" "What makes sense these days?" "Excuse me, you don't happen to have a few fat and lustful Tahitian women?"

"Excuse me?" "No, nothing, I was just thinking of Gauguin . . ."

IN NEW YORK, I thought of Venice; now in Venice, I think of New York; the lines cross one another, vertical and horizontal, cold and hot, stone and steel, avenues and passages, giant bridges and tiny bridges made of wood or brick, churches and towers, air conditioning and curtains fluttering in the afternoon breeze, in front of me. Between English and Italian, French functions as a sort of acoustic filter, a pliable and logical keyboard. You meet whoever necessary, whenever necessary, however necessary. Luz, yes, but also Geena, just when it became necessary for me to go underground for a while (what bliss, also, to walk about oblivious in such beautiful weather with one's embodied skeleton, the rest is silence and in the future). Life? New actors, partners sometimes met again, other plays, other parts, reinterpretation of the past, turning point of the present, the future even more doubtful . . . Not the same death at all, a *totally different* corpse waves at itself. I was, I am, I'm not any longer, I am.

I enjoy reading, in Stendhal's *Journal*, dated January 1, 1834 (he's in Florence): "Lovely weather. I'm full of ideas about astronomy after having read Herschel." Herschel, a murky story between brother and sister—Frederic-Guillaume and Caroline-Lucrece—bagging between the two of them Uranus, Saturn, several nebulae, several double or triple stars, but there still another discoverer, Herschel Junior (Jean), 525 nebulae, three or four thousand stars.

June 25, end of the twentieth century, Venice: lovely weather, she talks to me about Neptune, I stare at her head turned golden in the sun.

Voyager II, four and a half billion kilometers from us, carries on with its business. Espionage helps the progress of science: those who augment their science augment their information network. Simultaneously (you mean to say you really see a link between the two?) the art market retracts, ignites, takes off, changes its course. Right now, what I'm interested in is in that contracted heart of ice right in the center of Neptune and Jupiter. Since its departure in 1977, *Voyager* is headed towards its goal (Neptune, Nereid, Triton) at a speed of 27 km per second. It passed Jupiter in 1979, skimmed by Saturn in 1981 and approached Uranus in 1986. After Neptune, it will leave the solar system, towards darkness. Voyage to the beginning of the night.

Luz was eleven years old at the moment of departure; this story is part of her biography as future planetologist. From time to time she thinks: "Imagine, my eyes advance at this very moment at 27 km per second, my eyes or rather the counting through my eyes, my eyes as envoys present there where my body could not follow for even a second." Reader, everything is hidden from you. Too many dollars, kilometers, technical systems, you can't take it anymore, you collapse. You asked for a god, he's descending, here he is. You race to the TV to make sure that reality is already capturing itself on the screen. Neptune: from the word *nare,* to swim . . . "At every given moment, *Voyager* forces us to eliminate the previous data and to rewrite that which we know; at every given moment, something happens: instant science."

Minus 200 degrees blue-gray. Methane cirrus and azote geysers. Bombings, continuous gas cyclones. And the extraterrestrials? Not to worry, they're farther off, always farther off. Have you thought of the message to be sent out? Just in case? In case they want to contact us for a chat? The recording of the fundamental bits of Dante? The whole score of *The Magic Flute?*

The *instant novel* is another world (a pile of tapes in the living room closet).

PIERRE FROISSSART, 52 West Broadway, Calle di Mezzo, Venice. The distance between Paris and Venice is 836 km. You fly over Troyes, the Alps, Zurich, Milan. On arrival, heat, police dogs sniffing the luggage. I exit through a small door on the right, then take a water taxi, it's faster. In the boat I immediately put on yellowside black trekking team sandals, cloth and thin rubber soles, like shadows. Kiss me, kiss me again. They'll come and take pictures of the site, you'll see. How come all this happened without us knowing anything about it? That's inadmissible! Didn't we suspect anything at the time? Didn't we do anything? An American physics student? Ships in broad daylight, neither seen nor heard? And the others set up their old network? They met again after all these years? 1968? Twenty years? Each one of them, during that time, following his own thing, in the States, Germany, Italy, England, Holland, Spain? And this one, in France, accompanying them from a distance? And yet we thought we knew him. Checking his income, his ambition, his wife, his children, his friends, his mistresses. Personally, I've always considered him a clown. Double life? Triple? Quadruple? And on top of all that, a member of the "inner sanctum"? No, if that's the case, he'll never talk about *the other three.*

I've always practiced. As a child, I pretended to be with them, to go into their homes, I knew they too wore masks to disguise and conceal, always with one single scene in mind: the cemetery. That was their only concern. Tell me something, was this a spontaneously "scientific" attitude? Tell me something, was a little white-yellow-blue light transferred from South to North and smuggled back here? In the end, the characters are nothing but colors. Geena, red and black; Nicole, gray and green; Bella, and Fleur too, white and blue; Richard, carried away by the sound of his voice, discourse/racecourse, same word, light gray. And I? Green and blue, wouldn't you say? The colors know one another, we are variations according to one another. You know yourself better thanks to me, and I myself thanks to you. You don't have much to say to me but many things to declare in my presence. Fine. Bashful skin, in the future, amused indifference, mimed aggression, we'll shake up this scumbag, this deathbag, we're not made to come to this *end,* are we, my sweet? *Afterdose,* a novel: the story of a guy who's experienced everything, not a sad story, really, on the contrary, and who has become incapable of arousal, except as part of a game.

So we're here, in one of the twists of the game:

La Fête à Venise is a painting by Watteau which reappeared on the clandestine market more or less at the same time as the sudden discovery (communicating vessels) of *La Surprise,* disappeared since 1801 (incredible adventure story, secondhand furniture dealer in the Vendée, petty crooks in a garage, back room of a *brasserie,* easy police raid). This brings to mind the famous canvas at the Prado, in Madrid, *Fête galante devant la fontaine de Neptune.* It belongs to the same period as the *Fêtes vénitiennes,* in Edinburgh (between 1718 and 1719) and is its double. I prefer it: the dimensions are the same, and yet it appears to be more spacious, more at ease, more far-reaching, of a deeper red. Watteau accentuated several of the pentimentos of the other canvas, for instance, shortening the dresses (he must have painted *La Fête à Venise* immediately afterwards). He added two new female figures: a second woman-fountain, bursting with sensuality, still following the model of the nude in *Nymphe et Satyre* (now in the Louvre) and a second circumspect dancer, thereby playing as he often does (a sign of his time) with the contradictory notion of an inanimate object—stone or marble—more animate and carnal than the living body.

It's a magnificent painting. It has never been shown in public, its existence has only been suspected; therefore the transparencies I have in front of me are in themselves remarkable. And yet no one will know anything about it, barring some improbable accident: this is nothing like the amateurish muddle in the *Surprise* episode. Yes, yes, some day no doubt . . . In the year 2036 . . .

No, it isn't a fake.

It arrived on board the *Player II*, will travel on the *Sea Sky*, I'll oversee the transfer, the rest is none of my business.

That's all.

Of course, I didn't tell you. Sleep well, read well, swim well, we still have time. We're in the town in which Montesquieu wrote in 1728 (seven years after Watteau's death) that here one can "go out in full daylight to see the trollops, wed them, not receive Easter communion, be wholly unknown and independent in one's actions." "In Venice, you are not asked to display carriages nor servants nor fine clothing: white linen makes one equal to everyone else." And also: "A mask is not a disguise but a secret identity." Tell me, do you enjoy your casino? Your room? The garden? Your lover? A little? A lot? Not yet not at all? White linen . . . In a taxi, the other day, along the Seine, do you know what I was thinking as the gray-blue morning began to awaken the facades of houses, the shutters, the trees? I was thinking of a fresh bouquet of paintbrushes done up tightly. A white shirt, brushes, open air, time and shadows, brief breath of certainty in the hollow of the damn skull, you know, there where a sensible glimmer persists. Brushes, water spaces: scales of tactile memory.

"PAINTING HAS NEVER been so powerful: let yourself be carried away!"

Time-Life has done it again.

"Dear reader,

"Have you ever felt, when wandering through a museum, an intense emotion at the sight of tens or hundreds of works of art, each more beautiful than the next, all witnesses of our past, of our heritage?

"Open your eyes and allow yourself to be astounded. You will come back to these magnificent reproductions again and again. Because the more you observe a masterpiece, the deeper it touches you.

"And this isn't all. A brief text introduces the works, the artist, and also the techniques used to obtain the desired effect, as well as the circumstances in which the painting was created.

"Great art historians will help you discover, in turn, French painting, modern painting, Dutch painting, Renoir, the painters' Venice, the impressionists, etc.

"Send in promptly your request for this first volume which you can keep without payment for ten full days. As a gift, you will receive a folder with five reproductions of van Gogh's most celebrated paintings, plus, if we receive your answer in the next eight days, a traveling clock, elegant, refined and useful."

Or this:

"Nice, May 13.

"Sir/Madam,

"After having worked as Auctioneer in Paris for many years, for the past eight years I have made my home in Nice while still keeping an office in the capital.

"My assistants and myself work for important collectors,

including Japanese, seeking out modern and impressionist paintings, eighteenth-century masters, and objects of exceptional value such as: sculptures, jewelry and furniture.

"A simple call to my office either in Paris or in Nice and we will travel at our own expense for all purchases at current international market prices."

THE EXECUTIVE, THE image of today's voluntary slave, is thus at the threshold of the vault of treasures. In French, the word for "executive" is *cadre,* which also means "frame." He is a *cadre,* he must be filled. To begin with, he can be defined as someone who, having started off from a lowly station in life, demands nothing except the right to confuse the original with its reproduction. *This is his very identity.* He trembles, our executive, when he reads that Gerome, "mediocre painter now forgotten by posterity," bars President Loubet from entering the hall in which the impressionists are exhibited: "Do not go in, Mr. President, sir! This is where France is being dishonored!" Our progressive executive's rival is also called Gerome. Our executive is a potential Loubet. Our executive will go in to admire the impressionists in spite of Gerome, if necessary over Gerome's dead body. With great enthusiasm he will realize that a huge revolution is taking place, in spite of this anguishing question: "1850: photography appears, what will become of painting?" Yes, what will become of it? And with the advent of film? Television? He begins to sense that art is advancing towards him by tortuous and unforeseen ways. Because it is for him, no doubt whatsoever, for him, *the real Loubet,* as well as for Madame Loubet—and also for his son and daughters, Christian, Francoise and Isabelle Loubet—that van Gogh displayed his uttermost daring, his *via crucis* under Pontius Gerome. And also for him, infallible Loubet, that the jewels of Western art were experienced, shouted sometimes in the deserts of the ancient conservative bourgeois. Look at Delacroix: the theme of the struggle is essential in his work, wild beasts against wild beasts, men against men, assistant managers against managers, top executives against top executives. "So many battles of which the canvases express the physical tension, while he experienced them daily as a moral struggle." It's about Delacroix, but also partly about Loubet that Baudelaire writes this: "A volcanic crater entirely hidden by bouquets of flowers." Also, Loubet rhymes with Courbet who must be considered the apostle of brutal realism, at the cutting edge of the academic art of his time. Courbet didn't beat around the bush. "Beauty is in nature," he'd grumble. And then add: "Nature's sense consists above all of artistic conventions." Loubet agrees wholeheartedly, even though he doesn't approve of the fact that Courbet, a Maoist in his youth, had strayed towards quaintness—young ladies along the banks of the Seine—and anarchism—the Paris Commune. Madame Loubet is more reticent. Manet and that stark-naked woman, among those fully dressed executives . . . Secretly, she asks herself whether her husband would be as accepting if it were herself among his colleagues from the office. She doubts it. In fact, she's certain that he wouldn't. Those painters were pretty neurotic. What's that? Napoleon III spat on *Les Baigneuses*? How absurd. All you need to do is change the conversation, turn the page, even go as far as preventing the publication, the reproduction, the distribution. We're not shocked, we don't horsewhip anyone, we don't make a fuss, we're not in Islam, we don't censure: we simply dismiss it.

Classification of ads in sales brochures: 1. Felix Vallotton, *Le Ballon* (child in straw hat, greenery, remember that it is usually the women who open the mail at home). 2. Millet's *Les Glaneuses* (sense of economy, quiet strength, the angelus in the distance, rural stability, a reminder of the progress women have made in society since that time). 3. Van Gogh's *La Sieste,* after Millet (here he is at last, that terrifying van Gogh, but without his madness, not yet sick). 4. Courbet's *L'Enterrement à Ornans* (he was not all that much of a Maoist, he showed respect where respect was due, priest in full view, childhood memory). 5. Manet's *Le Déjeuner sur l'herbe* (there's nothing wrong with a pinch of well-balanced eroticism; also there's no lack of humor in the painting, and placed next to Courbet's burial scene it looks quite all right).

Scientific guarantee: "You will appreciate the exact tones of these unperishable works of art. Each volume has been rigorously vetted by a specialist who carefully examines the colors."

Exact, unperishable, rigorously, carefully.

Bang, into the mailbox.

Madame Loubet, devoted user of the *Trois Suisses* sales catalogue, sends in her answer within the eight days to receive a traveling-clock just as artistically fashioned.

Good work, Nicole. There are no profits too small to consider. You can only sell properly that which you might consider buying yourself.

I'M GOING TO see the docking of the *Player II* and the *Sea Sky*. Not with the port authorities, of course. There's a port within the port, like there's an airport within the airport, a taxi station within the taxi station, a bank within the bank. The society within the society honorably defends society's society. "Froissart? *Sicuro* . . ." Concerning the difficulty or the simplicity of entering Italy. I like *Assimil*'s typical example which allows me to remember the password while climbing the stairs: *"lasciando scivolare la mano sulla ringhiera."* There have been operations *farfalla,* butterfly; *impalcatura,* scaffolding; *temporale,* storm; *fulmine,* lightning; *nubifragio,* hurricane. We are now in operation *ringhiera,* banister. "Amsterdam? Larnaca? Three days? One next to the other? *Aspetta un momento* . . . *Sicuro* . . ." I have something belonging to the society to transmit to the society via the society. Watteau on the banister. No, there were never thirteen of us, only four. One day I'll tell you a portion of the story. "Allowing the hand to slide along the banister."

Luz, on the bed:

"I'm happy to be here. Are you listening?"

I pretend to be sleeping.

Quick beauty of the word *listen,* often at the beginning of her sentences. Often also, to say *oui* in French, she says *si.*

LISTEN, IT'S NOT by chance that Watteau has titles such as: *L'Amour au théâtre français* and *L'Amour au théâtre italien*—"Love on the French Stage" and "Love on the Italian Stage." These canvases are in Berlin. French love is in the daytime, a dance, the prima donna offering herself. Italian love is at night, masks, torches, lute, stage front. It's one or the other, or rather one and the other, we jump from one scene to the other changing character and set. A spot in the forest, a spot on the stage. Curiously, *La Fête à Venise,* like *Fêtes vénitiennes,* is closer to *L'Amour au théâtre français*: the same central dance at the end of an evening, the same display of arms and legs, the same gathering both attentive and distracted. Of course, one couldn't care less about being in Italy or in France, on the Moon, Mars, Jupiter, Uranus, Saturn or Neptune. Watteau simply wants to signal the place in which Watteau can be comfortably played out, Cythera, Venice, Paris. Straight chronological line: Greece, Italy, France. Love and war, war in love. Lack of importance of dying, and on the surface an explosion of women and flowers.

"The speed with which they undertake that upon which they have decided, makes these people a unique case: every time they set out a plan, hope and possession become for them a single issue."

Thucydides also says this: "When the Athenians are good, they are good to the highest degree. Only amongst them does excellence spring from the source, unfettered, by divine grace. Amongst them excellence is a profound truth rather than a laborious veneer."

Make love well and make war well. Don't take one for the other. Don't prefer one to the other. Scale, music lesson. *Madrigali guerrieri e amorosi.*

Let us go in.

The instant novel must be as feisty as a married woman getting ready to meet her lover. The pleasure of getting ready to lie, to conceal, to deceive. Why are novels so boring? Because they lack this technical cunning. Look: she's in the bathroom, she washes herself, she perfumes herself, she makes herself up, she dresses herself. *Red nail polish.* Her husband or her mother (same thing) barely question her, he's in a hurry to leave (perhaps he is the lover on another stage). She looks at herself, she seems concerned, she smiles at herself. She straightens once more her stockings, has put on the panties he likes. She slips away without a sound, she has her plan. Geena is doing all this now, and Nicole tomorrow, they are so beautiful, suddenly, how well the space approves of them. The day isn't murkier than the depth of their heart. They are like dark arrows poised for the attack, the entire theater groans with uneasiness, with jealousy, with fury. A young bride's buttocks on their way to the brothel through sheer perversity and with the satisfaction of accomplishing a profound deceit, *without actually having any real desire to do so,* are the most beautiful things under the sun. Instead of suffering from it, she will enjoy her own frigidity, she will make fun of everyone else's stubborn credulity.

She must be seen in the street, in a taxi or on a bus, her slightly tightened buttocks must be imagined, her smile, her measured force, her thoughts of revenge, her innumerable sordid machinations, conceived in her own interest, an intelligence both innocent and criminal. She opens her purse, she offers several bills, coins, she's on her way to be paid back for an endless boredom, she stops in front of a few store windows, she passes by the Cafe Neptune on the square with its fountains (there will always and everywhere be squares with their fountains), she goes into one of the stores, she's decided to buy some perfume and some *underwear* for her lover so that he thinks of her from time to time, when he is all alone, very simply, unconsciously during the day or even if he's with another woman (a thought which irritates her deliciously). In a word, an entire halo of sharp and confusing sensations in the luminous air or in the rain (the rain implying that the gesture, upon entering, will be to go place the umbrella in the bathtub). Love on the French stage? Here's the ultramodern apartment building where her playboy lives: twelfth floor, elevator, hall, door. She's on time, her heart is beating. He's there, behind the door. Immediate action, mouth, fingers, sighs, what a relief, *let yourself be carried away, painting has never been so powerful.* At last she'll be able to talk for the sake of talking, babble on, run on, a hundred meters, two hundred meters, a straight line, fences, five thousand or ten thousand meters, last lap, the bell, it's time to go back, finishing line, champagne, cigarettes. Still fifteen minutes left. "Everything OK?—Sure, how about you?" A well-deserved holiday, something unforgivable has just taken place. What? A painting.

ON THE OTHER hand, let us suppose that we're dealing with an expert in self-consciousness, but someone alert, imaginative, music, colors, shapes, words. Philosophical contemplation is not enough, action is what's needed. Even if he doesn't particularly feel like it, he too, it must be done. He concentrates on the waiting. He tells himself that walls have ears and that he must become those ears. Does she who is about to arrive guess what very impressive cries the one who has preceded her uttered the day before yesterday, exactly in this same spot, on the experimental bed or on the ritual carpet, prone on the east-west axis while she finds herself in the north-south position at the moment of suffocation? Let us not compare their inflexions and tremors. Every canvas is unique. Jealousy is a belief in reproductions. Our painter in reality is a sort of saint of the modern megalopolis, and if he reaches an orgasm in the end it is rather because he's sorry for himself, the times are tough, asceticism severe. A workshop tradition preserved among the skyscrapers. As secret and improbable as the presence of the chopped-up body of a bum lodged in the cement of a parking lot. Or of an artist of times gone by, master of the motif, sunflowers, water lilies, haystacks, barges, mountains.

Secret reports from inspector Marais, towards 1750, so dear to the heart of Louis XV: "Monsieur de Blagny assures me that Mademoiselle Raye of the Opera ballets is an excellent enjoyment, and I believe that this must be held to be true, because the above-mentioned Monsieur de Blagny has had enough practice in this matter to be able to emit a sound judgment." Or this: "Mademoiselle de Charme has asked for an increase in her diamonds. Young, pretty, very good musician, she plays the harpsichord marvelously." Mademoiselle de Charme . . .

What were the terms used at the time to designate the female sex? *Periwinkle, orange, oracle.* And the verbs to denote the action? *Tiffing, doing the naughty, emptying the trash, bulling, tomming, tupping, covering, hauling the ashes, putting the lid on the saucepan, mounting, quiffing, niggling, foining, nubbing, nugging, rump-splitting, sarding, mending the kettle, grinding, dipping the pen, dunking the wick, having congress, groping for trout, snizzling.*

I confess to a weakness for *snizzling*.

And today? Humping, sleeping, free-flying, belly-bumping, bobbing for apples, having it off, doing it, playing the national sport, playing the old ball game, fiddling about, fitting, fixing, pumping, going for it, plumbing, diving, one-step dancing, saucing it up, warming it up, feeding Susy, giving

Johnny a ride, making Henry happy, plugging, riding, *attacking*.

And so on.

A question of palette.

This mustn't make us forget the little-known provisions of colonial law (the executioner's fees in Martinque in 1740, *Black code*):

Hanging	30 pounds
Breaking on the wheel	60 pounds
Burning at the stake	60 pounds
Hanging and burning	35 pounds
Cutting off at the wrist	2 pounds
Dragging and hanging a corpse	35 pounds
Putting the question extraordinary	15 pounds
Putting the question ordinary only	7 pounds & 10s
Honorable fine	10 pounds
Slashing and withering the hamstrings	15 pounds
Flogging	5 pounds
Collaring	3 pounds
Cutting out the tongue	6 pounds
Piercing the tongue	5 pounds
Cutting off the ears	5 pounds

This said, the narrator takes note of his position and observes his magic rectangle in front of him:

1 2 3
4 5 6
7 8 9
* 0 #

If he wishes to do so, he can call New York, London, Paris, Tokyo, San Francisco, Rome, Amsterdam, Madrid, Frankfurt, Larnaca, Barcelona, Berlin, Gibraltar, Geneva, Naples. These must be sold soon: Corot's *Liseuese interrompant sa lecture,* a St. Lucy altarpiece; Watteau's *La Promenade* (floor at more than a million dollars, expected to go for more than twice that amount); Picasso's *Portrait d'homme* (same estimate, probably higher); Monet's *Le Train è Jeufosse* (more than two million to start with); and finally *Details of Renaissance Painters* by Warhol (based on Botticelli's *Venus,* under one hundred thousand dollars). The Watteau sale is organized by Sotheby's Monaco, Warhol's takes place in Paris, organized by the Gersaint group. However, the narrator is waiting for a rendezvous that draws nearer step after tiny hurried step along the avenue. He has begun his countdown: half an hour, fifteen minutes, ten minutes, five minutes. The last three minutes are priceless. He can sense her crossing the courtyard, long or tight skirt, split or not, this will change the position of the hands in thirty seconds. From far away, time sinks into space. He hears the drilling sound, messenger of a deep sleep. He abandons the sentence he is writing in order to pick up exactly where he left, later on. Because he's highly cultured, he recalls that the poet Mallarmé, a friend of Manet's, said somewhere something about "wedding the notion." He says to himself with an irritating giggle, that here he is, he the narrator, ready to bugger the concept. It isn't just an airy formulation, or rather yes, it is: a breath of air, a biblical breeze.

Want to play, my lovely? Learn to lie to tell the truth, forced refraction in these matters? Want to be expected in this manner tonight? When the pink walls rise while the blue fades away? Fine, cross the garden, the trees have been trimmed this morning, branches and leaves shipped away on barges, boring through the alleyways, the flowers stripped bare against the red background. Black skirt, light blue blouse with white polka dots, very good. We meet in the corridor while behind us the ships sound their foghorns (the *Vistafjord*, for instance). Your mouth, while they glide slowly behind their tugboats, towards the port. French and Italian stage. You have no need to learn to dance. Waiting for you, I'll have seen in the distance our neighbor getting ready in her bathroom full of green plants. God knows towards what and towards whom she's headed, this one as well, godspeed. Afterwards, ice creams on the dock, next to the freshwater barges that feed the ships. The barges are flat, green and gray, and there are three of them: *Risorta, Gigi* and *Liana*. They are laden to the brim for next day, sunken in the regular rippling of the water, they draw a demarcation line between two kinds of black: the liquid, shiny, vast black of the Giudecca, and the dry, velvety black of the overcast sky. The air (once again the air) is like a cat's ear, or like a thin closed eyelid. We walk beneath the laurels and the honeysuckle, immersed in their scent, past the *sottoportego* to our left. The dockside once again: this is where the *Player* will dock, and over there the *Sea Sky*. Tomorrow morning the gulls will float in their proximity, waiting. You want to go all the way up to La Salute? Isn't it too late? Don't you get bored with those great polished steps? Sixteen steps on each of the five sides? Covered in rice on wedding days under the gaze of the angels? No, let's go back. I still have two or three more calls to make.

* * *

ON JUNE 30, 1939, the German museums, yielding to Hitler's personal pressure, put up for sale in Lucerne one hundred and twenty-five contemporary paintings and sculptures considered "degenerate." Among them, several Picassos, van Goghs, Gauguins, Matisses. A van Gogh portrait (notorious degenerate before becoming—but perhaps following the same logic—the Christ of the dollar) goes up, in Swiss francs, from 145 to 175,000 and is adjudicated to Dr. Frankfurter of the *Art Review*. Picasso's *Deux arlequins* go from 52,000 to 80,000, but no one wants the *Buveuse d'absinthe* nor a *Tête de femme*. Matisse arrives with difficulty at 8,000 francs. Multiply all this in today's prices by at least two hundred: Germany is now trying to recuperate certain of these paintings, but the German museums are overwhelmed by the Japanese overbidding.

And by the way, was there really in the twentieth century a Second World War in which the big losers were the Germans and the Japanese? Oh yes? Really? How curious.

Still following this logic, the celebrated German collector Ludwig orders then a bust from Arno Breker, Hitler's favorite sculptor, and exhibits it at the entrance of his museum in Cologne where most of the stars of American pop art are also exhibited. A riddle: exactly what logic are we talking about? If you don't know the answer, or if you think that it's just a coincidence, don't worry, it's nothing serious.

HITLER, AS WE know, was in the beginning a sensitive and delicate painter of academic watercolors. On July 18, 1937, in Munich, he says he can recognize in the depraved and degenerate art "cripples and malformed cretins, repulsive women, men closer to beasts than to men." These "stutterers of prehistoric art" see "blue grass, green skies, sulpher-colored clouds." Conclusion: "There are only two possibilities. Either these so-called artists actually see things this way and believe in what they depict, and in that case their eyes should be examined to know whether their ailments are due to mechanical causes, which would be unfortunate for them, or are due to heredity, in which case the Reich's Ministry of Interior should be in charge of them at least in order to prevent a further genetic transmission of these cruel afflictions. Or they don't believe in the reality of such impressions but they strive for other reasons to disturb the nation with these absurdities, and in that case their conduct falls in the realm of criminal law."

It seems that, when one of the more moderate councillors proposed the idea that the impressionists should perhaps be "perceived at a deeper level," Hitler roared back: "You can't forbid me from seeing them at any level I want!" The councillor was arrested a few weeks later and sent, without regard for any depth of level and even though he wasn't Jewish, to Auschwitz.

One can never be demanding enough as far as *levels* are concerned.

Gerome (re: the impressionists, always the impressionists): "We're in an age of decadence and imbecility. For the State to have accepted such garbage, a colossal moral decadence is required."

I'll spare the reader the tons of communist literature stigmatizing this Western art as degenerate, depraved, decadent, schizoid, antisocial, perverted, parasitic, and pornographic.

Today Allah, tomorrow something else, the day after tomorrow something else again. And now, after such *recommendations* and so many deaths, how not to invest frantically (since repression obviously achieves nothing) in order to better stifle it all in *this?*

"SAY, MOZART. WHO in particular is *blacklisted* these days?"

"No one, sir."

"You sure? Not a single artist dragged through the mud? Treated as dirt? Scandalously underestimated?"

"Things no longer happen that way, sir."

"Well, keep an eye open all the same. I want to be personally informed of any *very bad reputations*. I insist. Not those decided in advance by our Margins department; I mean the *really* bad reputations. Find them."

"I'll do my best, sir."

THIS?

Luz: "Fine. And now *La Toilette intime.*"

I'm coming to it, I'm coming to it . . . First I had to see to the *fourth*. Ah that's it, I mean the last of the squares about to become a triangle. A "death in Venice" interlude . . . Guillermo arrived exhausted from Barcelona, half dead, to end up here. I'm back from the hospital, I held his hand for an hour, he barely recognized me, I managed to avoid an inquest. Things were more or less known and, as usual, nothing was really known. True, in New York, this winter, he had seemed to me on the edge of exhaustion. We walked in the snow through Greenwich Village, in the wrecked village, an old story, end of the downtown area, deserted docks. Fine, I'll have his body sent back to his Basque village. One Italian and two Frenchmen left, including yours truly.

"It's difficult to find the right words when even the reality of facts is admitted only under duress. The well-informed and forewarned listener is likely to be deceived by what he hears, taking into consideration what he expects and what he knows. And someone uninformed might well, through jealousy, suspect an exaggeration, when being told about acts beyond his possibilities. The praise of someone else's acts is bearable only if one believes oneself capable of doing that which is being praised. If an act surpasses our capabilities, our envy will make us skeptics."

We had recalled the Warhol of days gone by, the one whose technique consisted of being there in order not to be there, effortless work to unglue the retina trapped within itself, constant self-awareness and meaningless presence. Gratuitous and useless act, doing nothing: something that seems blasphemous today. We spoke Spanish for laughs, he had serious trouble breathing. "The power of adherence to images always tries to stifle the iconographic experience of the non-image." "At a time of massive and organized narcissism, everything consists of disconnection and interruption." Of course, Guillermo was convinced that W. had been murdered at the hospital, leaving no traces. "It happens every day." "But who would have killed him?" *"Nobody."*

Death is so nothing.

So there. He too dies and we haven't had time for even a drink in Venice. I think of an author he liked and who, in fact, was here some twenty years ago to attend a subversive and clandestine assembly. "To seize from moment to moment the time to feel alive, is to find oneself free from both the right and the obligation to obey and to command." "The peremptory demands of making a profit have the power of privileging everything—except gratuity." "A fulfilled desire breeds ten other ones that promise the same fulfillment. Which is why a happy man doesn't find in his heart the slightest reason for desiring the death or the punishment of anybody."

Balzac forced things a little in his *Story of Thirteen,* but then he pursued "the endless pleasure of having a secret hatred against one's fellow men, of being always armed against them, and of being able to withdraw within oneself with one idea more than however many ideas even the most remarkable people have." What did those to whom the book is dedicated—Liszt, Delacroix, Berlioz (the *Requiem* performed at Les Invalides on December 5, 1837)—think of the following lines: "Their feet in every salon, their hands in every treasury box, their elbows in the street, their heads on every pillow, and, with no scruples at all, allowing everything to feed their fantasies. No leader commanded them, no one was able to assume such power. Only the most violent passions, the most demanding circumstances became essential . . ."

An object of which Guillermo was very proud, to the point of never parting with it (it lay in his travel bag, at the hospital), was the first edition of *Les Fleurs du Mal,* Paris, Poulet-Matassis et de Broise, 4 rue de Buci, 1857. *Concordiae Fructus.* On the gray cover, Theodore Agrippa d'Aubigne's epigraph, *Les Tragiques,* Book II:

"Science hath not begat the Vices wilde,
Nor is clear Virtue Ignorance's Childe."

Here you are, Luzita, an unexpected Venetian gift. Open it from time to time, later on, wherever you might be, coming home from your planetary computers. Don't ever give it to anyone else, and if you yourself don't sell it, then burn it.

BY CHANCE, Courbet's female torso, reputed to be obscene, known as *L'Origine du monde,* was being exhibited at that same time in Brooklyn. Both Guillermo and I knew where it was coming from and where it was going. It's part of those "suspended operations" which have been, several times, on the point of succeeding. Travel to somewhere in the Gulf has for some time now been possible: Allah is great and merciful, but above all terribly curious and libidinous. After all, that divine piece of flesh, so strangely *squared off;* those breasts, that belly, that red-haired pubis, so delectable—the pearl of certain specialized collectors, the intimate jewel (long kept secret) of a celebrated psychiatrist—this scandalous painting usually shown to the public hidden behind another, behind an insignificant sliding panel, this masterpiece was, at its origin, a private commission from Islam, placed with the leading artist of the Commune, the destroyer of the Vendôme Column then exiled in Switzerland—because what the painting depicts is the anatomy of a favorite of the Bey. Portrait of a paradisaical whore. No, don't reproduce this image, you're crazy. One of the great pornographic works of all time. Surrounding it, what a commotion of adult children who refuse to see since God Himself, as is well-known, having glanced in that direction, became blind. I myself would give two thousand highly priced abstractions for this cunt, one of the first true soundings of Venus. I'd be curious to see the results of a televised public auction, whether it would go for more than the *Irises,* so much more allusive but just as explicit. "You're really obsessed." "Look who's talking." Don't get impatient, Luz, I'm simply preparing a worthy backdrop for *La Toilette intime* and *La Fête à Venise.* Courbet in Brooklyn! No kidding! Humankind behaves oddly with its paintings; one might say that they conjure up, automatically, that which takes place in the bed of what's left unspoken. No, no, we'll sleep no more, we'll dream no more, and if necessary, we'll live no more. Aren't we dead in the end because we can buy anything we want? Get this into your thick skull: everyone remains steadfast, *no one dies anymore.*

Chance then, or lack of chance, decreed that I carry with me *The Book of Seasons* by Niffani, an Arab mystic of the golden age. The author's name means "fleeting," "fugitive," "he who eclipses or disperses himself." I suggest reading this book in New York, in winter, on a thirty-third floor, after a long taxi ride and several difficult transactions. "To that which is silent within you, bid silence, and that which is eloquent within you will by needs speak out." Or this: "He who knows the veil is above the unveiling." Or this: "My vision neither commands nor forbids. My absence orders and prescribes." Unless one goes as far as this: "I reveal myself when I reveal unto others," which wouldn't be a bad definition of literature. Niffani in front of the Courbet? "Your body after death occupies the same space as your heart before death." Always *levels.*

Oh, if that torso were able to write its memoirs! To tell

everything it has heard about itself or about other subjects—as if other subjects were possible! To tell the life of its several owners and of their friends, their occupations, their manias, their favorite fantasies, the exclamations and the scent of cigars, in the evening, after dinner, when it was finally *revealed* as the core of all things! Some believe it was in Germany in 1936 . . . That Hitler asked Goering to organize a thorough search for it . . . For ages there seems to have been a price on its head (if I may be so bold) somewhere between Jerusalem and Mecca . . . That our psychoanalyst who, according to certain sources, also examined Artaud at Sainte-Anne ("literary pretensions"), owed to this concealed treasure some of his shamanlike powers . . . What won't they invent to come up with these legends? What won't they come up with in the sanctuaries, read into the unclear din of oracles and prophecies?

WHERE AM I to find you, yourself, in Watteau? Most everywhere. White and graceful your back towards me, on the vast meadow by the lake with the statues, in *Les Deux cousines*, in Paris. On the left, leaning back slightly in yellow and white in *La Proposition embarrassante*, in Leningrad. Also to the left, green and blond, with a guitar, in *Les Charmes de la vie*, in London. Crouched, blue-low-cut top, pink dress, in the mother-of-pearl dappled clearing of *La Déclaration attendue* in Angers. Neither is it difficult to espy you in *La Récréation italienne* in Berlin or in *Les Plaisirs du bal* also in London. And, in all your glory, in the egg of *L'Automne*, in the Louvre, pruning knife in your hand, dripping peaches and grapes, left arm ending on the terrestrial pumpkin, naked legs and offered knees. You might also be found, if you like, in L'Été in Washington. You rise soundlessly at night, you leave the canvases, you fly here to meet another of your apparitions in *La Fête à Venise* floating on the water, red dress, whispered movement against the monumental backdrop of a staircase. If you prefer to watch yourself asleep, left arm hanging outside the bed, right leg folded, hideous nightmare that doesn't seem to bother you, on the contrary (that bronzed, bearded and decided male who surprises you and embraces you from behind), then you have *Nymphe et Satyre* (still called, with customary prudery, *Jupiter et Antiope*), a perfect ellipsis. At a given moment, you will dismount from your horse in *Le Rendezvous de chasse*. What are we doing *there*? Well, instead of lamenting, as most of us do, that life is a dream or that we're made on the same stuff dreams are made of, a few intrepid explorers took it upon themselves to enter dreams in order to direct them. "It's impossible," they're told day after day. But the dogs bark, the pilgrimage to Cythera passes on. Impossible is not Watteau. Look through the window: laurels and useless gardens. Turn, you estimations! crackle, you telexes! carry on with your intrigues, phones and faxes! We are switched on, we are switched off, we are separated, we are brought together, we are sold and we are resold, we are frozen for a century or two, we are stolen and we are stolen again, we are copied and we are faked, we are locked up, we are damaged, we are restored and we are forgotten, we are brought out into the light again, we are valued at a hundred or a thousand times *that which they think of us*, but they think nothing of us since they were never there when all was well and when, precisely, it was all worth nothing. Always excluded from the paintings, poor things, of course they suffer. That explains the painful legend, fatal mistake. Life, a long agony . . . Moaning and groaning . . . Sound and fury . . . Alas, it is better never to be born . . . Everything that rises must converge . . . Leaves in the wind . . . Youth in shackles . . . Infamous old age . . . Everyone says so, everyone will say it again, just to see . . . To see if he, standing in front of his easel, will finally let himself be convinced by this ocean of common sense . . . Tremble, Watteau! Scram! Give up! You'll die! (Indeed). Stop torturing us with your paradisaical snares! Can't you hear the loud clamor of humanity? Are you then so insensitive and superficial? Already the sense of history condemned your frivolity; now the end of history brings on its execution. You believe, against all the store of experience, that a man might be called happy before reaching the end of his days? Well, in that case we'll say you were anguished, shy, unstable, glum, irritable, melancholy. You will die! (bis). Anyway, your enchanted landscapes are traps: there are at least two sickly snails in your forests, three consumptive sparrows in your trees. Your characters are dancing on a volcano, the void gnaws at their feet, they suffer from generalized cancer or general paralysis. They know that they are already being dismissed as if they were nothing but soundless and empty decorations. You yourself are out of fashion, the new generations have superseded you for many years now, the new young models pay no attention to you, the young girls ignore you, you are old, you will die (I know, I know). Won't you commit suicide? Cut off your ear? Just a bit? No? Fine, our conspiracy of silence in the media will sweep you away.

Nocturnal landscape: the pyramid of the Louvre. Everything is asleep. Watteau, on tiptoe, heads towards the apartments full of elegant furniture belonging to Madame Nicole Vuillaud (a.k.a. Dürer). He opens the door with his key, throws himself in an armchair, stretches his legs on a Regency desk, orders a whiskey from the delightful curator in a light blue *déshabillé,* and allows himself to be possessively loved like the original of one of his paintings.

I'LL READ YOU the current assessment: "Watteau, chronicler of his time, sees life only through the eyes of art. He is a film director who, after making a few observations in his sketchbook, orchestrates a group of settings, lights, emblematic objects and characters, all of which borrow more or less from one of the arts, Architecture and Sculpture, Theater and Opera, Music and Dance. It isn't real life that Watteau reproduces, it's a transposition of the arts of his time that he proposes for our contemplation."

Watteau, "chronicler of his time," an all-rounded novelist? Isn't "real life" the same as that of "art"? Is it more real? He "proposes"? He proposes nothing, he disposes. What? The figure in the carpet, the purloined letter, the gray-plated and pale pink web draped in silver, the mercury whose secret has apparently been lost, the key to the departure hidden in folds and more folds, the finger on the lips. Life isn't an art except among the arts? Without which life isn't really life? Elementary, and that's the endless mystery of the thing. The financial needle will become increasingly magnetized by the single and unique enigma. The slightest act of authentically free life, if still possible, will be the fortune of fortunes, and because of this we mustn't be surprised if insensitivity reigns, anticipates, watches. When Carpeaux builds his fountain at Valenciennes, he lends Watteau the Sanguine features as they are depicted in *L'Iconologie par figures* by Gravelot and Cochin, Paris, 1791. The Sanguine figure is a young man with a laughing face and a vermillion hue. The musical instruments and other signs of gaiety noticeable in his presence show his taste for pleasurable activities, as well as the Sanguine inclination towards Bacchus and the Pleasures of Love, signaled by a basketful of grapes and Venus's doves. This essential book was not reprinted until 1972, in Geneva. Hope springs eternal.

The city has drifted from deep pink to black, the white cloud I was watching a while ago through the glass door of the hall has been spirited away by the night seeping in. Luz has just changed for dinner, the neighborhood is silent, barely a few voices, the gulls, the water slapping the stones. Once again I project the right-hand details of *La Fête,* details on which Geena was particularly insistent in New York. "Pay attention *here* and *here.*" The air grows cooler, words begin to fail me, I turn the light off, I stop.

LADIES AND GENTLEMEN: the honorable court. Here's a decision that's bound to stir things up.

A painting both explicit and hermetical. An art tribunal.

Paris, concerned with the subject of subjects. The Judgment of Paris. Who's the fairest of the Three? Why? Is this jury capable of judging? How?

One would almost think one was standing next to a gypsy caravan, fortune read by the side of the road. There's a quarrel between the three female stars of the troupe, Eden's apple is played the wrong way round, halfway through time. All the media are present in the person of Hermes-Mercury, leaning over to interview the one-person jury. You must imagine the scene for yourself alone or for you and the person of your choice (or who has chosen you, which amounts to the same). Look at the staff, on the left, in a diagonal line; the wand and its wings, more wings on Hermes' head. Athena-Minerva withdraws, furious, to the right, with her spear and her Medusa-crowned helmet. Hera-Juno becomes who-knows-how a nymph and an accomplice, flies away, not as grumpy (she expected the outcome or prefers that this one rather than the other one be chosen). And last but not least, Love is lifting the robes of Aphrodite-Venus, descended from her shell which remains fixed in midair, offering as is proper nothing but her back to the audience. The infant Love inspects her other side, the one we cannot see, the object of the dispute. Paris has indeed seen it. He's disturbed but firm, red-faced, withdrawn within himself, the whites of his eyes showing and reflecting on the apple-planet which he holds in his right hand, somewhat frightened but self-assured, as if saying: "Everything's fine, we're off and running." I must point out that the painter personally insults Athena, Goddess of Thought, the Arts, the Sciences and Industry, while rewarding Voluptuousness (Aphrodite), under the protection of the Messenger of the gods, patron of merchants and thieves (Hermes). The dog, lying on the ground, unconcerned, allows this human and divine story to take place. "Paris, can you give us your thoughts on this matter?" "Later, later." "Are you aware that in doing this you're unleashing the war of wars?" "No comment at present."

"Now follow the red cloth that drapes Paris and uncovers his mortal navel. At the end, what do you see?"

"Where?"

"There. *There.*"

"He's got a hard-on?"

"Pardon me, my child?"

"I mean, he's aroused?"

"Certainly, but keep quiet. The whole shebang has been set up around this almost imperceptible allusion and we are the first ever, ha, ha, to point it out. White cloth lifted for Venus, red cloth barely held in place by the protuberant suggestion for the young mortal, he raises his arm, he's aroused, he chooses, he is chosen, inverse ascensions, infolded peacock, a slap in the face of Terrible Medusa, the crossing of the looking-glass-shield, the shell explained, nothing to see, opening, cause, effect. It is because of this that many will die, nothing else. Either I'm dreaming, or this is the only painting that never ceases *to turn*. It's impossible not to experience it in three dimensions, molded, kneaded into shape, bulging, turned on its head. Aphrodite-Venus's sex isn't there, of course, on the other side of the buttocks; it's nothing less than *the entire canvas itself*. With its conclusion, its trail of eyes, its quick reasoning of colors, its gestures, its concentration, its intense excitement consummated, dispelled. Its sense, in a word, is this: whatever the time or the circumstances, the results of this carefully mounted operation will be the same. You won't spark off a war, but you'll know why one must take place, profoundly, and why this war is of no interest whatsoever except in its telling. Utter certitude. A game of skittles. Bull's-eye. Beauty contest? And the winner is . . . !

Imagine the sale: 2 P.M. in Paris, 8 A.M. in New York, 10 P.M. in Tokyo. Direct video broadcast, Venus auctioned off across the time zones. General mobilization: banks, store chains, electronics, oil, real estate, insurance companies, nations, everyone gathered for the final attack. Banzai! In midair, the golden apple-shaped hammer of Paris, the auctioneer. The Olympus of the secret service on guard. Ach, Paris! *The person, not the place.* And you say that the planet is bored to death, with no new stars, no ideologies, no intellectuals of a universal dimension? So be it. Each new candidate to the promulgation or incarnation of Value—philosopher, scholar, politician, journalist, military man, bishop, pastor, rabbi, imam, lama, economist, gangster—is to be examined *in situ* in front of Antoine Watteau's *Le Jugement de Paris.* What can you make out? What do you imagine? What are your thoughts about it? Uninterrupted broadcast, world satellite transmission, twenty-four hours a day. What fun.

"But isn't it only a painting?"

"*Painting,* you miserable creature? *Painting?* All earthly financial powers are shouting at you that there's something completely different that's defying it, and you call it *painting? Painting* that red detail bang in the middle of Paris? More important than the entire city, than its inhabitants, its traffic, its smog, its noise? This Chinese self-portrait, this attack at the very core, this bulletin of a cosmic victory: a *painting?*"

"What would Freud have thought of it?"

"Well, he would have written *A Childhood Memory of Antoine*

Watteau, I suppose. Or rather, he'd have given up. Michelangelo or da Vinci maybe, but not the French eighteenth century. Having said this, however, you could add several psychoanalysts from the different sects to the lists of interviewees on the program *Paris Calling*. Molière's doctors, a little German Latin would loosen things up. *Lustprinzip,* for instance. They'd repeat this rhythmically: *Lustprinzip! Lustprinzip!* Pleasure principle! Deny reality! Fetishism! Or this: Archetype! Yin-yang bisexuality! Alchemical transmutation! One reproduction would be enough. *Watteau's Sexuality: Episode 1000.* According to you, Doctor, was Watteau's mother an exhibitionist? An early seducer of her little boy? Did she kiss his Adam's apple too tenderly? Did she leave the bathroom door too easily open? Could a mother have been as perverted as all that? Did she have two jealous sisters less beautiful than herself? Who tried to seduce little Watteau at the bottom of the garden? Was Mr. Watteau Sr. usually absent in the mornings? Were customs that lax in this country which has always been the shame of Europe and of the world? Was Watteau a precocious ejaculator? Enuretic? Feeble? Impotent? Homosexual? Compensating depressive? Notorious transvestite? Immature? Phobic? Lesbian? A computerized poll. Question: Did Watteau, in this painting, try to overcome a serious, traumatic childhood experience, for instance, the absence of penis in his little sister? Answers: Yes, 72%, No, 10%; Undecided, 18%. Do you think that today's price tag on his work is ridiculous and scandalous? Yes, 81%; No, 5%; Undecided, 14%. Do his paintings conjure up for you a personal experience? Yes, 60%; No, 20%; Undecided, 20%. Are the Japanese out of their minds? Yes, 10%; No, 65%; Undecided, 25%.

Would you say that Watteau was a major or minor painter? Major, 10%; Minor, 80%; Undecided, 10%. Was he a genteel or a lustful painter? Genteel, 90%; Lustful, 1%; Undecided, 9%. What detail in the *Jugement de Paris* struck you most strongly: the terrible face of Medusa on Athena's shield, or Paris's attitude vis-à-vis Aphrodite? Terrible face, 85%; Paris's attitude, 10%; Undecided, 5%. Does this painting have, in your opinion, a religious or metaphysical significance? Yes, 0.2%; No, 99%; Undecided, 0.8%.

ISN'T *LA TOILETTE INTIME* an affront to the dignity of women? Doesn't it sing the praises of her bondage? It's worth asking the question, as in the case of many ancient works of art and, fortunately in fewer cases, of modern ones. Once again, our Commission has assembled, conscious of the immense task before it: the preparation of an index of the thousand and one literary, visual and musical works deemed suspect. It will soon be handed over to the press and to Parliament. Contrary to what some have insinuated, this index does not carry on from where the Vatican Index left off, the latter having fallen into disuse together with the prejudices from another age, which were its source. Ours is a scientific and democratic point of view, and our goal is to strengthen the collective and individual liberties, and above all the now inalienable right of women to control representations of themselves in both the present and the future, and therefore also in the past. Evil must be torn out at the root and, if that's the case, there is an overwhelming number of roots. Privileges, prejudices, all sorts of exploitations, arrogant luxuries, misleading calm, odious voluptuousness, unhealthy desires, idleness the father of vice, gratuitous exhibitions of intimacies, navel-gazing afflicting artists more concerned with flattering their deviant instincts than with offering humanity examples of complex rationality and justified generosity. Raising the question of Watteau, the Commission and its informant, Valerie Norpois, know that they are facing strong resistance which will show, better than sterile debates, the depth of an evil which is still far too widespread. It's been established that Watteau has always been defended by reactionaries. Defended by Théophile Gautier and his execrable Variations on the Venice Carnival, by the brothers Goncourt, those rabid anti-Semites, those sadly famous misogynists who dared write this: "Nothing resembles love as much as visual arts criticism: it makes use of as much imagination concerning a canvas, as love concerning a woman." Woman compared to a canvas! Nice gentlemen. Yes, Maxime Du Camp was right when he spoke, in 1855, of the "depraved instincts of this rotten society," and Delecluze, as early as 1847, when he accused the artists of his time of bringing back to life "the pornography of the preceding century." In the twentieth century, in the twenty-first century as in the nineteenth century, and all the centuries of centuries, the purulent example of the eighteenth century must constantly be analyzed, decomposed, disinfected, stifled, punished, precastrated. These dainties are the most dangerous of poisons, aimed at paralyzing a real democratization. The taste for happiness at any cost—a deceit, since we know that it is nothing but the mask of an interior failing, a genetic flaw, the just punishment of a cold egotism incapable of any authentic communication—opens the gates to all social excesses, to the rapacious greed of the largest estate holders, to the cynical calculations of money made on the woman-object. At this point, Valerie Norpois-Solanas points out very apropos, that we are not to be swayed by the apparent similarities between certain of our demands and those of certain fascist groups or parties still in business, or with those of the old dying communism or with those of the currently expanding religious ecumenicity. It doesn't matter if ill-wishing spirits believe that we too are playing the game of the iconographical market; according to them, it's inevitable whenever a moral position is taken. Our goal, of course, is different, even if we cannot define it except in negative terms. That is why we demand, among other things, the pure and simple interdiction of all reproductions of *La Toilette intime* by Antoine Watteau, more noxious—as we shall have occasion to show—than a crude and obscene representation.

Morning's end, softness, a touch of gray, I come back from dealing with the formalities concerning the repatriation of Guillermo's remains, I have a cognac in his memory on the dock of the cafe we used to enjoy, the *Linea d'ombra,* across from San Giorgio.I suppose he'd have done as much for me.

First of all, this amazing bed, foamy and interminable, green and black background adorned with shells, quivers and arrows, a bathtub full of milk or cream. The sheets and the large nightshirt blend, a blown-up oyster, a giant ear, a fat clam whose naked flesh darts in and out, a tall and taut bourgeoise sitting on the edge of her ship of dreams. She places her right foot on the floor, her left leg folded underneath her right one. The left hand pulls out the left breast, the right hand accentuates the navel. Her lowered gaze, her contemplative air point straight at her sex. Facing her, somewhat lower, the novice maid, serious, joyful, satisfied, dressed up in black and white, red skirt, offers her, on her knees, a porcelain dish and a slightly damp sponge of the size of a small loaf of bread. Both women's attention is powerfully concentrated on the former one's inner thighs, as if this area belonged to a third woman. A delicate volute of transparent cloth, placed on the right spot, allows one to distinguish . . .

"No?"

"Yes. Her presence is underlined by the empty slippers on the floor, one of which is perpendicular to the naked foot. What's going to happen? The women are placed as if on both sides of an altar, the rite being that of ablution. What pious women, getting an eyeful, with a pricking of conscience in the process! What's the previous sequence? And the one before that? And the one after? And the one after that? Watteau is always forcing you to ask this sort of question, he gathers all the elements just at the point where they might implode in silence. The painting could also be called *The Triumph of the Holy Sacrament* (Raphael's entire composition converging on the porthole of the monstrance in the Eucharist). The real presence is the acting absence. A deluge of silk and cloth, adoration of the shepherdesses, long chorus-girl legs spread wide apart, the *Folies-Bergères* or the *Crazy Horse.* For 270 years now they've been in meditation—and it's bound to continue. "I see, and have always seen my books," Stendhal said, "as lottery tickets." I'll buy all the lottery tickets of *La Toilette intime.*

"Where's the painting?"

"In a private collection."

"On sale?"

"I don't think so."

"Would it constitute an event?"

"Huge. Heading: 'Financial Cripples At Height Of Their Powers Fight To Death Over What Watteau Might Have Seen.' Who'd be capable of telling them? I believe that he simply lived out thousands of tiny private dazzling novels. He painted them, that's all. That's why he'll always be presented as someone who held himself at a distance, embarrassed, a spiritual libertine perhaps, but not one in his behavior. The contrary, that is to say the evidence, would be too serious to consider."

"But aren't these the testimonies of people who knew him?"

"Those who really knew you never say anything. As to the others, the entourage of breathless voices, God preserve us from their portraits if one has led a rather colorful, unusual life. One of those close to Watteau, someone rather well-intentioned, regrets his lack of plot or action, his repetitions, his roads leading nowhere. We still don't know who is that mysterious and innocent a-Christlike Pierrot (which belonged to the very strange Vivant Denon). When he's living in Nogent-sur-Marne, in 1718, with his mistress, we are told that they were not on good terms, but the fact is impossible to verify. White holes, lapses of memory, small vague anecdotes, his contemporaries are like family, busy with defending themselves from the anxiety provoked by the breaking away of one of their lot. It is enough to read the critics of a certain age, their inflexibility, their condescension (when it's not their lunacy), but also those of any age, perhaps especially of our age, so certain of not being mistaken that they can't avoid being mistaken radically and generally. I knew him well, dear boy (Barres at Proust's funeral, the funeral of *"le petit Marcel"*), you don't mean to make a big deal of him? Trite. Be happy that they don't just burn everything to ashes, interest holds them back, money might blow where it will one of these days. Money is a versatile god, but equitable in the end: it always concludes by bringing to light the strong points of desire. It works on its own. Oh, Future Bank, protect us from those who have known us!"

"I would say that . . ."

"You won't say anything. You'll have moments of ineffable memory like everyone else, clearer than everyone else. Intimate hemorrhage or constricted throat, just like when you are told, today, that some guys, during the night, for the fun of it, went and broke the legs off the horses of the Fountain of Neptune in Florence. Stendhal or Nietzsche are taking a late walk, come upon the scene, they go crazy, they're dragged back to their hotel, they lose the power of speech. During that time, *Voyager II* continues on its path towards the Oort nebula, the garbage dump of our galaxy. It doesn't matter. It's not likely that *La Toilette intime* will one day be burned, but who knows. Nothing like the present. Look, there you are, they're writing a script: *A Day in the Life of Antoine Watteau*. He's shown watching his mistress's toilette, drawing her from life, making love to her. Then he visits his dealer, quickly gives a few finishing strokes to *La Fête à Venise* which will soon disappear who-knows-where, has lunch with a collector, goes for a walk, sketching all the while, either to the Tuileries or to the Luxembourg Gardens, calls upon another of his mistresses, lies down next to her on her bed, falls asleep. Or else he leaves for Saint-Cloud with friends, actors, actresses, dancers male and female, musicians of both sexes, who dress up, dine, light candles, and places them wherever he likes, near or far, asks them to forget he's there, mingles with them, stands aside, enters and exits from the game, sketches, tears up the sketches, sketches once more, finds himself with a pliable blond on the grass, behind a clump of trees, quickly seen, quickly felt, quickly done, lovely weather, returns to Paris, to his morning mistress, lies down by her side, makes her come half asleep, waits for her to return, warm, relaxed, fucked, to lose himself inside her splendidly, near and far, right in the midst of the painting, falls asleep, dreams that he redesigns the coat of arms of his friend Gersaint, that he proceeds with more skill on the right-hand side, paintings within paintings, that he's better at depicting the passion of the buyers, their collector and connoisseur frenzy, wakes up early, quietly leaves the bed, jots down certain darker hues perceived in his dream, leaves the house, walks quickly towards his new studio (he's always moving) where a model is already waiting for him, opens the window, takes up his brushes . . . How will he depict himself on the canvas? Lying on his stomach, whispering sweet nothings in the ear of that young woman crouched in the shadows? Passing by, jacket flung over his shoulder, an ironic glance cast on the garland of bodies? With indifference, leaning over a balustrade? A nervous player fine-tuning his lute?

Script turned down: too elitist, too sophisticated, too much culture, not enough history, unsalable for the stupefying sessions of TV in the evenings. We asked for a life of Watteau that was tragic, an account of his last days, and not this succession of encyclopedic clips and digressions. "But Your

Majesty, *the feelings within?*" "What feelings? Whose within? Know that painting, at that price, is sufficient unto itself, be beautiful and shut up. Watteau had nothing left to say, all accounts agree: he had become practically mute. So, art on the one hand, tragic life on the other." "No connections between life and art?" "None. Or rather: a contradiction. He suffers, but he paints, he'll die, that's all."

Stendhal: "The well-mannered type, ceremonious, scrupulously conventional, even now turns me to ice and reduces me to silence. Just add a touch of religion and declamations on the great moral principles, and I'm dead."

"DIDN'T HE EVER COME TO VENICE?"

"No. However, a Venetian lady took a great interest in him. Also, an excellent painter (strange that the gynocratic nebula hasn't thought of advertising her, I offer them the idea, after Camille Claudel surpassing Rodin, why not this one?). Rosalba. Rosalba Carriera. She painted two portraits of Watteau, one still young (Frankfurt), the other at the end of his life (Treviso). Her portrait of Louis XV (Berlin) is superb. She can be seen, painted by herself, at the Uffizi in Florence. She's given herself the appearance of a very proper bourgeoise. But one must hasten to the *Bacchante* in Munich to have an inkling of her real personality. She writes about Watteau in 1728: "I've always been among those who admire this skillful man." She came to France in 1720–21, therefore she met him. Rosalba, rose of the dawn, silken touch. She should go up in the stock market. I'll see to it and pay a couple of visits to find out whether there isn't something of hers left over in some closet."

"Watteau: that merry carnival where many famous souls . . ."

"Why 'carnival'? Why 'famous souls'? I've been to Venice a hundred times and I've never seen a single carnival here, nor have I ever seen one in one of Watteau's paintings. Why 'famous souls' when they're all people like you or me simply having fun? Baudelaire, and Napoleon the Emperor, once again, Hugo's '*melancholy field* of Waterloo . . ."

"*Seek out like errant moths the all-consuming flame . . .*"

"Why moths? Why are they errant? Why do they seek out the flame? Because they are ephemeral? Because they burn? Because they'll die? (Here we go again.)"

"*In dainty halls made light by chandeliers of gold . . .*"

"There's not a single chandelier."

"*That turn the swirling dance into a maddening game . . .*"

"What nonsense. No one swirls even if the canvases swirl, and never was reason more tightly knit, more free from constraints, more crystal clear. No carnival, no moths, no error or errancy, no chandeliers, no turning, no maddening anything, no swirling. The poem is beautiful but false. It would have been better had it been beautiful and true. Afterwards, the dancing flocks of vampire sheep repeat: 'Were they ever bored! Were they ever uneasy and sad! Did he ever foresee the fall of their cruel and frigid world!' The litany has begun, it will never stop. I myself was forced to copy out again and again in school: 'Watteau was a painter who was shy, consumptive and disheartened, unconscious of the rights of man, just like the rest of his contemporaries.' And yet, in spite of the exorcism, a doubt remains, oozing out, climbing, ascending. 'Cythera was an unhealthy place where hanged corpses were found, giving off a pestilential odor . . . Slavery was the norm: women and children in fetters would stand and watch with accusing eyes the errant butterflies come to insult their misery . . .' 'Watteau's dancers would organize filthy orgies, worthy of the Marquis de Sade . . . Those parks were in fact concentration camps where the subjugated people, especially the women, would die in atrocious pain . . .' "

Tell me, in your opinion, precisely what instrument is Finette playing? This fact wasn't established until 1961. It jumps out at you, literally. A guitar, a lute, a mandolin? No: a theorbo. If specialists require that much time to identify a musical instrument, how many centuries would be required to imagine the sensations felt by the body playing that instrument? Who would dare question the luminous gray-white-green moth perched on a stormy evening bench, appearing in profile in a flash of lightning, holding the melodious kalachnikov? Is she a famous madwoman swirling along on her errant way after having escaped from an asylum or from a carnival? It doesn't seem so. Her brocade stillness is frightening. Her weary look, her small candid fruit mouth, her crumpled reptilian body like that of an automatic machine gun, her head like the stalk of a flower flung back, her beret against the sky, her buttocks and endless legs while the backdrop opens as if worn-out, ripped or clawed at—what aggression, what unease. Does she love you? Not at all. Is she looking at you? No, not either. Nothing can come out of the leprous rock star's electric theorbo, that unfortunate coffin, nothing except a shrill romantic complaint, wounding, teutonic, reminiscent of marshes, miasmas, infants drowned in the woods. One can only see her left arm clutching that big indecent organ which she should not have the knowledge to manipulate, while her right arm is plunged in that other world from where she'll hurl at us a sulphurous malediction. She's come from her intimate toilette, the slut, the terrible sorceress, from her venomous quicksilver bath in her private pool. She crawls out of it at the close of the day, in her apocalyptic diver's helmet. A heartrending note is about to be heard. Flee, you good people, cover your ears, bring in the cats, the dogs, the babies, close the shutters. No one survives who crosses the path of La Finette! Impotent men, barren women, polluted nature, plagues, stiflings, convulsions, fevers, vermin, TV and radio sets scrambled, planes exploding in midair, earthquakes cylcones, tidal waves, no more newspapers, no more news, unreality, the abyss. No, no, anything but La Finette! We repent! Help! We even promise to read one page of a book a day!

3

. . . .

The ships arrive in ten days, the weather's fine, a burst of oleander trees against the sky, still shadows. I'm writing as I sit on the sarcophagus at the bottom of the garden. My own boat is obviously called NF.F.NS.NC., and I'd be surprised if these initials can be deciphered by the port or customs authorities. I've lost weight, I take myself for walks, I tire myself out, I put myself to sleep. Luz swims in the pool, we're delightfully alone. From time to time, I come upon a

French newspaper, I read without much attention the news or the interviews with the summer authors, a few lines of their travelogues, their philosophical or political positions (always on the side of goodness, never on the side of evil), their opinions about theater festivals or art exhibits, and sometimes even an extract from a novel, impossible to follow after the first three lines. Here someone's death is celebrated, there, a certain personage passes away. Quoted from muddled poems are copied out devoutly. What's this? The president of the Book Association has something to say about the international Singapore trade fair. Isn't there anything happening in France? Unfortunately, no, nothing much, no, really nothing at all, we're no doubt going through a transition period, I can't think offhand of a single obvious name, but careful here, let's not be rash, look at the nineteenth century when no one recognized the existence of Stendhal, and yet Stendhal was there, wasn't he? You said it, Norpois, the gulls approve. No doubt in 2089 there'll be the same routine, the same laborious charlatans, accepted, moderate, colorless. In 1880, Stendhal writes. His comments on his contemporaries are made for the printed page: "Gloomy fanatic, Jack-of-all-trades." Or this: "A coward to the point of scandal." Or this one: "A sad beast, kindhearted, refined, cautious." He leaves the cafe or the theater repeating like his hero Julien: "Scum, scum, scum." One becomes emotional reading, for instance, in his journal, on November 23, 1839, in Civitavecchia: "Blue slates and green olive tree well varnished. The colors of the sky and the sea, a day of sirocco; the beginnings of the tramontane wind. Slate-colored sky. The sea on the horizon green as a varnished olive tree; this color begins 200 feet from the edge of the sea." The slate no doubt made him think of the math exams of his youth, the teacher's platform, the more or less damp cloth, the unease, the equations, the chalk. We should imagine him returning to the consulate, perplexed by a computer screen. And on November 28 of that same year: "I begin to pick up my old work habits and the low evening spirits. To be expected in absentminded speeches. On the 27th, sister and both brothers to dinner." Sometimes, we're almost there. As in the case of Mme. Le Roy, Jeanne, the wife of his art teacher, "a thirty-five-year-old she-devil, very saucy, with charming eyes." . . . "I lusted after two volumes of La Fontaine's Contes with engravings very delicately executed but nevertheless very clear. They're awful, said Mme. Le Roy, with her beautiful eyes like those of a rather hypocritical chambermaid. But they are masterpieces."

All the spice in the quote is of course in the word *rather*. And also in the repetition, three times, of the word *very* (which a bad writer would not have tolerated).

First he wrote "very delicate" and then corrected it to "very delicately executed." And "with her beautiful eyes like those of a rather hypocritical chambermaid" is an addition between lines.

Not enough mention is made of the sketches of places and situations that Stendhal accumulates in his posthumous manuscripts, a quick and touching topography. Nothing's lost in them, everything can be discovered. I was there, I went from here to here, his memory stands upright in front of him, blackboard, military map, musical score, memories geometrically outlined in a living halo of constraint or happiness. So, when it is announced that Seraphie, his mother's sister, his tormentor, is dead: "I fell on my knees at point H to thank God for his great deliverance." The drawing depicts the kitchen where he found himself (at the age of fourteen) when the news ("She has passed away") was spoken; the small courtyard next to the kitchen; a long table; point O, "a tinderbox that exploded," and his presence at point H (his name is Henri, the name of his late beloved mother, Henriette). On the other occasions, he finds himself in H.H.H. It's much more than an account, it's a cut to the quick, a series of scars, a gravestone. A little like the Greek, who after a successful raid would raise a trophy. To go and live again at point H: that is the goal for someone who has held back, and with reason, in time and in space. The exploding tinderbox, an adolescent thanking God (whom he never addresses, except by the English word *God* in order to obtain, at the end of his life, royal privileges), celebrating the death of his hated aunt, now surrounded by priests—what a scene! Awful, as Mme Le Roy would say, with her beautiful eyes like those of a rather hypocritical chambermaid. But a masterpiece.

Stendhal's mother (whom he never stopped kissing on the neck and who, "light as a doe," one evening stepped over the mattress where he slept next to her bed) died when he was seven years old. His mother's sister, the demoniacal and narrow-minded Seraphie, did obviously not succeed, in the following seven years, in marrying Cherubim Beyle, the father. Odd to have a Cherubim and a Seraphim as your mortal enemies.

Another sketch, parallel lines in the shape of a star: "The path to madness, the path leading to the art of being read, the path to public esteem, the path of all good prefects and state councillors, the path of money. Point A: the moment of birth. Point B: the path taken at the age of seven, often without being aware."

What was I doing at the age of seven? Have I forgotten? No.

Ordinary dictionary, article on Stendhal (1783–1842): "His vigorous style brings to life in fast-paced action, lyrical heroes who hide a profound sensibility under an apparent cynicism.

A MORALIST FROM the end of the twentieth century (a century all in all abominable, perhaps you remember) who was, no doubt whatsoever, one of the few authentic revolutionaries of his time, not without haughtiness begins a book with these words:

"All my life I've seen nothing but troubled times, profound chasms in society and huge destruction; I took part in these disturbances. Such circumstances would no doubt suffice to prevent the most transparent of my acts or of my reasonings from ever being universally approved. And also, I believe that a number of them may have been misunderstood."

This tempts me to begin my *Memoirs* more modestly like this:

"All my life I've seen good times rescued as if by magic from the void, incredible alliances and understandings, intense efforts of reconstruction: I took part in these happy events. Such rarities imply that the darkest of my acts or my reasonings will always be universally understood. And also, I'm certain that a number of them have been very well understood, especially by those who opposed them with all their might and main."

I get up, I close the shutters, I go for a short walk since it's midday. Venice is the invisible capital of the planet in broad daylight, inhabited by provincial folk ecstatic and peaceful. It wouldn't occur to them to reflect on their extraordinary situation. It's what we needed, no two ways about it.

Stendhal, once again: "The pleasure I have in writing, a pleasure to the point of madness in 1817 (in Milan, Corsin del Giardino) . . ."

And also: "One morning, entering Milan on a charming spring morning—and what a spring! and in what country in the entire world! . . ."

I VISIT IN the evenings, Luz comes with me one time out of three, she waits for me at an outdoor cafe, from time to time she allows herself to be cruised, tells me about it. Often, to go home, we take the Number 5, the *Circolare* line. There are lots of people in the popular districts of Giudecca, we are separated, the young men stare at Luz, every so often a pretty girl gets off at Zitelle or Redentore. On other occasions, if we're sitting in the back, our faces are almost in the water, our cheeks are level with the undulating liquid carpet. Dimensions are inverted, the Palazzo Ducale, immense five minutes ago, becomes a litup children's toy sitting on the black horizon. The *vaporetto* hugs the sunless bank, and then starts again along the Zattere, straight towards the great door of varnished wood of Gesuati, a neighborhood of hurried and discreet shadows. We eat in a trattoria somewhere along the quays, but sometimes also on the terrace of *Giglio* or the *Deux Lions*, on the Schiavoni. Or she has a meeting at the American Center, and I eat alone, I read. There was a congress of astrophysics at the Cini Foundation, on the results of the Magellan soundings of the uninhabitable Venus, what has been learned about the Ishtar Region, as vast as Australia; there is to be another one on the biosphere. During the official dinners—bay windows on the Grand Canal, across from the Dogana, red sunset in the middle of the sky—I wait for the moment when I can catch a glimpse of her neck, her chin, her mouth. There are at least ten dozen benches outside that I could mark with chalk: *point Luz*. "After so many years and so many events, there is nothing I recall except the smile of the woman I once loved." One charted memory is worth a thousand. And yet, everything passes so quickly, days collapse one into the other, a telescope turned towards the inside, lenses increasingly refined, powerful, sand made of air. After swimming, walking onto the quay, in the mauve afternoon, Venus shines fixed on the left, a nail, a note at the top of the page, dew. Remember the Trevisan Bridge near the French Consulate, with the house at the corner, a terrace with wisteria, a nestled Virgin with Child and from the Trevisan alley so narrow that one can only walk one behind the other, at the far end the shaft of dazzling light reflected on the water and the white oleander trees. Remember everything and nothing, we catch onto nothing, passing on. To think that it was possible, in the nineteenth century, to prefer Milan to Venice; finally things were set straight. Before us, *le déluge*. *Après nous*, whatever. Anyhow, there never is a *déluge*: the flood never takes place. Listen to the morning bells, in full peal, look at La Salute once again. Go back home and do several backstroke laps in the swimming pool, sun, salad, coffee. "To live in Italy and listen to its music became the aim of all my thoughts." Or this: "I think that a man should be passionately in love and at the same time the conveyor of joy in every society he might find himself." Written with Shakespeare's comedies in mind, *As You Like It*. "I possessed two or three maxims I wrote everywhere and which I'm now extremely sorry I've forgotten. They brought tears of tenderness to my eyes; here's one come back to me now: *Live free or die*, which I much preferred, for its eloquence, to *Freedom or Death* with which they were trying to replace it."

There we are, in 1793. Henri Beyle from Grenoble, alias Stendhal, alias Brulard, alias Dominique, alias Darlincourt (and many others), aged ten. He affirms having met the model for Mme. de Merteuil in *Les Liasons dangereuses* ("You are a thoroughly bad character. Yes, you're an utterly charming woman"), the elderly Mme. de Montmaur, limping, offering a candied nut, *whole*. Later he meets old general Laclos in a box at the Scala in Milan, who, he says, is *moved* when he learns that H. is from Grenoble. In *Freedom or Death* you don't need a subtle ear to immediately and above all hear *Death*. *Live free or die* is, certainly, something else entirely. One could find such formulas almost everywhere in Thucydides, and not only among the Athenian democrats. The Corinthians, for example, express themselves with utter clarity (and this would be enough to justify, if necessary, my *nocturnal visits*): "He who, grown attached to his comforts, refuses to do battle, would quickly be deprived, without lifting a finger, of the pleasures of an easy life; that is to say, of the very reasons that prompt him to hesitate."

*   *   *

GEENA:

"But whatever do you *say* to that girl?"

I could pretend to confess that I tell her almost everything and that from now on, it entails no danger. But why bother to demonstrate to Geena that the whole thing (precautions, faint anguishes, ruses) is over? That the detective novel, appearing all over the place, is to be found nowhere at all? That in the end nothing happens (or something happens all the time, which amounts to the same)? That one can write or act openly without being seen by anyone (unless one is fired by one's own network, or unless one insists and demands to be suppressed by firing randomly on the crowd)? Luz lecturing Geena on black holes? Hopeless. Watteau walking on water amidst the general indifference? Christ being interviewed, one evening, at Foundation X or Z? Why not, on the subject of "*people*? After all, what matters is keeping the man in the shadows satisfied, as well as the man behind him. This latter one is in fact rather conciliatory if one is punctual, practical and detached. Everything sorts itself out, nothing is a bother, and at the slightest problem the film for outdoor shots is ready. To be able to read, simply to read, will place you soon in the rank of the gods.

Understand, Geena? No? It doesn't matter.

I'm in Paris, and she's insisted that my arrival seem necessary, it's a way of asserting her powers, but the truth is that for a woman, it isn't that obvious for her to enjoy a guaranteed, well-balanced leisure, without complications. It's difficult to send a fax: "I feel like making love, I'll be in Paris on the weekend." So the old sentiments are still pertinent to serve as screens: curiosity, jealousy, the semblance of intrigue, allusions, even modesty. One can easily understand why Laclos, after having written his novel, quickly went on to something different; why Sade continued on his outrageous path of destruction; why Stendhal, between two fiascos (that absurd physical appearance), should have chosen to crystallize things at a distance. ("Times are sad and sullen. Under Louis XIV I would have been gallant and amiable; in this 19th century, I'm stolidly sentimental.")

The basic equation was revealed by Laclos (and developed by Proust): one makes love to do someone a bad turn, which is something that, after careful consideration, apart from fantasies meant to overcome boredom, is certainly the only reason to get mixed up in these things. At best, an exchange of information. At worst, mutual blindness. There are pleasures—considerable and just as quickly forgotten—to be found in the interludes. We're lucky if there still remains of these a calmer, truthful version: *Les Champs Elysées*, *Cythère* or *Plaisirs d'amour*. Geena is bored? Probably. She feels like doing someone a bad turn ("that girl")? No doubt. She has invented for herself a little classical soap opera about a love affair in Venice? She wants to interfere and intercept it? Most likely. She's gone back to her idea of spying on Nicole through me? All that and maybe other things as well, without mentioning my satisfaction of traveling thinking that I'd like to know more. And in this she's mistaken, I'm the reserved historian par excellence, I imagine quite clearly what they're hiding from me, I don't need to be told what it is. For whom is our "bad turn" intended, for Luz or for me? For the entire cosmos?

"One might think." A crime as exciting as rare: time theft. For a long time, I allowed myself to be intimidated, thrown off track, to the point of devoting myself to dark and useless tasks. I scared away my true nature, it returned at a gallop. Let's see: do I have the right to talk like this? Have I spent my seasons in hell? Have I suffered from basic shrewishness? Yes. Should I nevertheless blush when I think of this or that action of mine? No. Am I certain I always had *my reasons*? Yes again. Is mine a desperate case? I hope so.

Geena watches me, registers my scarce physiological agitation, my silences, my very sensible abstention. She wants us to go visit Nicole, we have dinner at her place, Boulevard Saint-Germain, but sidestepping the rules, as if there were nothing to it. Geena manages to leave early, I'm obliged to stay on, the conversation drags. ("Venice? Near La Salute? Calle di Mezzo? I was there once"), not a word about the current operation nor about the others (who's going to be in charge of the marvels vanished from the Palazzo Mazzarino, the one of *The Leopard*, in Palermo? What's the forecast regarding the next three Picassos?) Gossip concerning promotions or regressions, the slanted occupying of posts. Then:

"Would you like to stay on in Venice?"

"Why not?"

Here's danger. A test decided with Geena, or a personal proposal? It's one in the morning. She stands up, too soon to let me know more, a simple message, should I kiss her and push a little, she's the one coming towards me, she's the one kissing me, without pushing, good-bye. No trace of Watteau. Next morning, a few technical details with Geena, rather distant, then the plane and back home. I bought Luz a little apple carved out of Chinese jade. I offer it to her next morning in the bathroom.

IN THE *FÊTES vénitiennes* in Edinburgh there are eighteen characters, nineteen if one takes into account the living blond statue of a naked woman at the edge of the waterfall, deliberately lifting her right arm so that one notices no one except her. In *La Fête*: twenty-one. Generalized conversation, in discreet bouts, and a dance against a background of bagpipe music played on the musette. Hotteterre, in his *Treatise on the Musette* (1738), says that the instrument "is always dressed in a sort of skirt called *couverture* . . . Velvet is best for this purpose, since it is less slippery than other cloths. This *couverture* can be decorated as sumptuously as one wishes, either with braids done in Spanish stitches, or with embroideries, since ornaments and finery suit this instrument admirably." Daquin, in *The Century of Louis XV* (Paris, 1745), remarks that "the musette is the instrument of the lovers of rural fetes and festivities, because it brings to mind the fortunate days when the shepherds, to please their beloved or to charm them, would join their voices to its sweet and flattering sounds. The musette seems made for the solitude of the woods and to give vent to a lover's sighs."

Sighs or no sighs, I want to rhyme musette with *finette*. Finette, a cotton nightshirt. Finette: "Cotton cloth with a feltlike reverse achieved by using a scraper." To which we'll add percale, a perfect word, from the Persian *pargalah*, "very thin cloth, tightly woven out of closely cropped cotton."

No Muses, lots of musettes. They draw together, in the

painted air, the grass, the water, the stone, the leaves, the murmuring voices, the faces already concerned with arriving as best they can to the end of this business. "You think so? Can we proceed? So fast? Isn't it a bit too quick? Are you quite certain about the opening?" The female dancers and the single male dancer are busy trying to fill the stage, while the others are huddled together like the feverish scale of a harpsichord. In *La Fête à Venise* the circle is more tightly closed, as if seen from a distant vantage point. Pinks and greens dominate, except at the landing of the stairs with the small blond dressed in red, and, as always, the diagonal blade of mother-of-pearl. On the left (an innovation after the Edinburgh painting), the ground descends one level, as in the *Récréation italienne,* giving the impression that one of the musicians, a guitarist, is sitting at the bottom of a shallow ornamental lake, a small fishpond or a dry fountain, a skating rink in summer, frozen in shadows. Here's point H. Attention, recital, spreading smiles, concentric powers of the absent metropolis. The general impression is that *they're starting again*. Somewhat weary, wiser, intent, on drawing forth a more deliberate, more violent quiver. Since I started running from Berlin to Dresden; from London to New York, Washington or Boston; from Leningrad to Madrid; from Stockholm to Rotterdam passing again through Paris without forgetting Chantilly; from San Francisco (for the sake of *La Partie quarrée*, in itself deserving three months' worth of studies) to Richmond for the sake of the incredible Lorgneur, without mentioning Lugano, Helsinki, Frankfurt, Angers, Troyes (because of *L'Aventurière* and *L'Enchanteur*), and if we add to all that the private (very private) collections, the planet turns around this brush, he's everywhere, he's an octopus, a posthumous parachuted invasion, the cities have no existence any longer except through these improvisations placed in their core, these dimensions, these subjects that are always the same and never the same, a terrifying nightmare. If people knew, yes, as in the case of *La Finette* or *L'Indifferent*, they'd be *truly* terrified. I should steal *La Fête* at gunpoint, keep it with me for a few hours, die by its side. I rent a boat, I leave with the *parcel*, a quick battle at sea, we sink together, I return it to Neptune in the deep . . . Come on, come on, let's escort it.

AT SEVEN IN the morning, the bathroom is dappled in light. At seven-thirty and at six in the evening, a frenzy of bells. All the churches make themselves known at the same time for a full five minutes. The churches: a network of times past, whose practical sequence we have followed. God dead, not dead? Death become God? We don't argue, we work. Anyway, he's very busy, God is, what with armaments, oil and paintings.

I like turning the corner of the alleyway, to the right as one comes out. It's point H., or W., or F., after all, for Froissart, an expert in techniques of departure. There is almost always a cat there, lying in the sun against a door of varnished wood. He pretends to mount guard, to sleep, to be there: a colleague. Between plane trees, I walk across the piazza with its whitewashed well covered by a rusty iron lid; I constantly feel the stones under my feet; I see, in front of the Accademia, the queue of people waiting to see the holy images, the canvases that explain, one hopes, the awkward and clumsy rolls of film wreathing the bodies. The spectator, who knows, perhaps imagines that they're *grateful to him,* in high places, for having gone to meditate in front of these icons, and furthermore, why wouldn't he be recorded for five seconds on a worldwide screen by a hidden camera? As to the rest, that's to say, as to real life, learn for the sake of your computer, the code names:

Catdog? "Cats and dogs united on the same screen, that's the trick of this service. You'll find here all the necessary information regarding the correct nourishment and good health of your favorite pets. For example: your Labrador's nose is hot? Checking for our advice will only take you 4 minutes."

Artline? "Both professionals and amateurs will appreciate this superb treasure trove of data concerning painters and their oeuvre. Other than a detailed biography of each painter, you'll receive all the results of the public sales worldwide for the past three years. 4 minutes to reach a work of art, consult its sale tag and the artist's biography."

Atlasecho? "The economy of 200 countries in the world and their mineral production: our tour de force. Gross national product, inflation rates, population figures carefully scrutinized by the best economists. It will take you 2 minutes, for instance, to become unbeatable regarding the economy of Pakistan."

Psych? "A sudden depression? An existential angst? A child who's slow in class? Don't hesitate: consult our psychologists, they'll answer all your questions. For example: restore your balance, find meaning in your daily life, thanks to *Be One of Life's Winners* and *Self-Confidence*."

Read? "Over 40,000 titles in this catalogue accessible by author or by title, and the possibility of receiving any book in

48 hours: new titles, reviews, advice. An actual bookstore at your doorstep. For example: 3 minutes to find and order the book you want."

ST? "Yes, you got it: ST deals with the stock exchange: rates, gold, monthly payments, secondary markets, investment portfolios. You can find out a rate through the name of the company. For example: we give you the previous rates, top and bottom. Isn't this exciting?"

You've had enough? So have I. And I spare you *Ulysses* to find a job, Pastel to choose a retirement home, *Novalis* for music. Without forgetting the flood of novelties, *Birth*—"whatever happened the day you were born?"—or *Fuss*—"what does your surname mean?" What? Nothing about the probable events of the day of your artificial insemination, nothing about the day of your death? It will come. Enjoy those *carefully scrutinized* populations, those biographies that can be consulted in 2 minutes. Isn't it wonderful? Irresistible? All answers to all questions? All the questions you haven't yet imagined, answered?

"WHAT'S NEW?"

"A Vermeer, sir."

"The one from Boston?"

"Exactly."

"I'm afraid it might be too much. Nothing else?"

"An autographed manuscript of *Rome, Naples et Florence*."

"What?"

"Stendhal, sir."

"Froissart again? No jewelry, no gold?"

"I see your mind is on the crisis, sir."

"You think we have too many hands on deck?"

"Possibly, sir."

BOSTON? THE MOST important business since Monet-Marmottan. Minimum two hundred million dollars. One of the most beautiful Vermeers, *The Concert*; a Rembrandt self-portrait and his *Storm on the Sea of Galilee*; Manet's *Chez Tortoni*; an incalculable Chinese bronze cup . . . The Gardner Museum: a Venetian folly built in 1899 on the model of one of the palazzos here. On the pediment, in French: *Ç'est mon plaisir*. Isabelle Stewart Gardner, a curious character: frequenting boxers and getting drunk on beer, more or less converted to Buddhism after the deaths of her son and husband . . . You get the picture. She had bought the Vermeer in Paris in 1892 for six thousand dollars. In 1925 it was already worth two hundred thousand. These days? Priceless, therefore inaccessible (except, in journalistic jargon, for a "mad collector"). Probable discreet return through the Insurance Company? These mysteries are beyond us, let's not pretend to be the manipulating hands. All I do is sketch the scene. The life of a passerby. The passerby passionate about the past. Everyone seemed surprised that on that night, the movers should have neglected Titian's *The Rape of Europa*. Why that considerate hommage to Venice? But the "Latin-American networks" and those of the "Far East" were mentioned, certain clues, as long as they weren't followed.

The rape of Europa.

"IS YOUR MEMORY good?"

"Excellent."

* * *

LUZ TELLS ME one of her dreams "in two parts," yes, a diptych; for fun, she records on film my interpretation. The idea of stocking the archives came to me gradually, when I became convinced that no one listened to anyone anymore, paid no attention to anyone. What are we? Where are we headed? What will we become? Disappearances, appearances, departures . . . Will there still be transmissions? How will they be transmitted? Through amorous gestures? Ancient animal markings still fresh?

The reproduction of *L'Assemblée dans un parc* was exactly across from my bed, last thing seen before switching off the light. My sight, when awake, began and ended at that place on the wall. There was the bustle of the day, the gossip of the adult extras, and then, in the evening, stretching out under the sheets, the pillow under the head, the real-time assembly calling, the bark cracking open, a yellow-orange couple walking towards the lake, the curtain rises, close your eyes, let go, be trusting. Painting is, before anything else, linked to night. And yet there were numerous paintings, landscapes, Bibles, battles, nudes; all one had to do was open the books. The only one I kept was the little Watteau, glossy paper, bad color reproductions, mediocre text printed in large type, a treasure. Paris's apple appears too dark, and anyway, let's not be in too much of a hurry to choose, each of the three goddesses has her charms, let's carry on with the audition, please undress once again, I must consider carefully . . . Yes, yes, maybe tomorrow we'll go to the island . . . *Charm,* from the Latin *carmen, carminis*: a formula in prose or verse to which one attributed the power of upsetting the order of nature. Yes, by all means, let's upset her since she's so upsetting. "The most charming of riches cannot compare/To the torrents of pleasure that flood our hearts." One learns that in high school, in Racine's *Esther.* After school, the woman at the newsstand sold under the table the first girlie magazines. She was ugly, miserable, brave, perverting the youth at the risk of being denounced to the police, in a wooden shack painted gray, a witch's hut . . . "You have new ones?" Quick, home on the bike, unmolested perusal in one of the attics . . . *Les Charmes de la vie*: where does it take place? The Tuileries? The garden of Luxembourg? He lived over the garden of Luxembourg in Audran's house, Watteau; he was able to observe in the flesh, and from close by, the Rubens of Marie de Medicis, but what a decision to make, what a step taken in broad daylight. *Charm* comes from the Sanskrit *to celebrate,* it's also a tree, and why deprive ourselves of *charmille,* French for "arbor" . . . To fine-tune one's lute just like that, erect, in front of everyone? Lute, from the Arabic *al-ud*. A common French expression: to marry the lute with the voice. Mme. de Sevigne: "Mme. de Marans would marry the lute with the voice, and spiritual matters with vulgarities too horrible to mention."

What's the contrary of charming? Distressing, shocking, unpleasant, unpleasing, bothersome, gloomy, uninviting, invidious, offensive. The charm is a magic medium that is used in conjurations, incantations (the conjuration being the act of chasing away the mysterious evil agent, *or of calling upon him to perform his evil*).

One writer: "We can eternally regret that Adam, in Paradise, should not have known of a charm against the Serpent."

Powerful seduction, great amenity, physical attraction—

but also remedy and relief. Like a charm: in a wonderful way, surprising in its ease. Being under a charm: like being hypnotized. It can be stopped by blowing lightly over the eyes. But once the eyes close, the charmed person, simply by being told so, can suffer hallucinations, paralysis or automatic reflexes. Once awakened, he hardly remembers what has taken place.

Charm: a magic virtue one possesses. Nowadays, it is applied, in physics, to certain particles.

"WATTEAU HAS OFTEN been accused of having succumbed to a typically French brio."

Brio, from the nineteenth century onwards, and now definitively, has become a reproach, the equivalent of inessential, gratuitous, superfluous, vain, misleading, much ado about nothing, useless. *Brio*, coupled with *French*, enhances the reproach.

Brio: the brilliant and resolute character of a musical composition. From the Italian *brio*, vivacity. Provencal, *briu*. Old French, *a-brive* (active, ready). Celtic origin. Gaelic: *brigh*, force. Old Irish: *brig*. General sense: warmth, life, vitality.

Current usage: "Maybe, maybe (disdainful gesture); it certainly doesn't lack *brio*" . . .

NOTHING PREVENTS US from reading the authors of Watteau's time:

"It is usual to see nightingales, when they are in love, gather in the woods to the sound of certain instruments, or of a beautiful singing voice which they will try to answer so forcefully with their chirping, that I have many times seen them fall exhausted at the feet of a person who sang like a nightingale—as it is commonly said to indicate the flexibility of a beautiful voice. Oftentimes, she and I would enjoy this entertainment in the woods near her country house."

"During the month of May, in the Tuileries Gardens, one can very often find people who go there in the morning with their lutes and guitars and other instruments, to enjoy themselves. The nightingales and warblers come and perch almost on the instruments themselves in order to better listen, which proves that birds are more sensitive to the charms of music than to their own freedom."

"Monsieur de—, captain in the Navarra regiment, was sent for six months to the Bastille for having spoken too freely to Monsieur de Louvois; he begged the governor to grant him permission to have his lute with him to make his prison less bitter. He was very surprised to see that after four days, during the time he would play, the mice would come out of their holes, and the spiders descend from their webs, forming a circle around him to listen with rapt attention, which surprised him so much the first time it happened that he became unable to move; so that having stopped playing, all this vermin withdrew quietly to their nests; this assembly made this officer reflect upon what the ancients have told us regarding Orpheus, Arion and Amphion."

PAINTING CANNOT BE separated from music, dance, architecture, sculpture, poetry, novels, drama, opera and, widening the circle of relationships, from bedrooms, offices, outdoor cafes, cellars, streets, bars, brothels, cemeteries, sewers, factories, ministeries, laboratories, observatories, newspaper offices, studies, gardens, mountains, rivers, seas. And vice versa.

Nor does anything prevent us from reading François Couperin:

"At first one should play nothing except a spinet or a single harpsichord keyboard during early childhood. And one or the other should be fingered very gently. This matter is of infinite consequence, since a beautiful execution depends far more on the suppleness and freedom of the fingers, than on force."

Or this: "People beginning late in life or who have been badly taught, must pay attention since the nerves can become hardened or turned the wrong way, and they must either untangle their fingers themselves or have them untangled by someone else before beginning to play, that is to say pull their fingers or have them pulled in all directions. This has the added advantage of unfettering the mind, and allowing a greater freedom."

Or this: "I've already mentioned that the suppleness of the nerves contributes far more to playing well than brute force. My proof lies in the difference between the hands of women and the hands of men. Furthermore, a man's left hand, which he uses far less in the exercises, is ordinarily the most adaptable for the harpsichord."

Unit of time, place, action and diction:

"Along the river, you'll see every day and at all times, a number of those small boats that for two, three or four *sols*, according to where you are, per person, will take you to those neighboring villages most agreeable to visit and best-known for their fine food, such as Chaillot, Passy, Auteuil, Boulogne, Saint-Cloud, Le Moulin de Javelle. At the foot of the Pont-

Royal, you'll find the boat for Versailles: it leaves every morning at eight."

One saw him frequently at Pont-Royal . . .

WHAT IS A meeting? Two rhythms in step with another, spurring one another on: the lute, the voice. This is the miraculous side of meetings, not of those that go up in smoke (but those too are beautiful by definition, they celebrate the instant, that is all), but of those that last *as meetings*. Point Luz. Complex nerves, positive conflict, harmony. A fine contradiction: melody. The chemistry of chance is not measurable: someone is born there, leaves from there, is shaped this way or that, the result, in principle, should be punched into the program and then: a meeting. Everything can be explained after the fact, sure, we all do it, but what for? There should have been the usual boredom, hatred and discord? No, the birds, the mice and the spiders don't come to listen to the music, but *it's just as if they did*. "As if" is the key. Too bad for the never-ceasing preachers of authenticity who require Santa's old-fashioned toy bag, infantile but crafty preachers, keen—out of self-interest—on Father Christmas, on love-fusion-unification, on ballads in which one voice drowns the other, that is to say, their own. Two, always and still two. Is death in all this? Of course, and with good reason, that is what makes it so enjoyable. But, with your permission, let's *respect the proprieties*.

And too bad for abstract generalities: men are this, women are that, he or she was of this social background, they were of different color, different language, different religion, different education, different values, different value, incommunication is the rule . . . If one listened to abstract generalities, one wouldn't ever meet anyone. And that's usually what happens.

Watteau's contemporaries had a fondness (which their successors exaggerated for them) for battle scenes, great deeds, heroic and sublime sentiments, heights, craftsmanship, sacrifices, frozen nudes, expressive landscapes, passion. What? You don't build, you don't complain, you don't sing the lasting pain of a battered life, the shame of the roots, the absurdity of history: you make no suggestions, you don't exaggerate anything, you don't lament, you don't show the way? Watteau indeed dies (it was to be expected): in his agony, the priest places a crucifix in front of his face. And what has he got to say, this charming dying man? "Take that thing away, *it's badly sculpted.*" It's not even a blasphemy, it's an observation. What else is wrong? Ah yes, he doesn't clean his palette properly, he uses oil paints that are too greasy, he's therefore lazy and in a hurry, his canvases will be ruined, what is he going to leave behind, it's impossible to reason with him, one might say that he doesn't give a damn, and in that case, what about the inheritance? The families (friends, art lovers) are already thinking of their lost fortunes, the frittering away of their capitals, expensive restorations. *The Indifferent.* Refusing to place himself in the only true perspective there is: that of those who'll come after him. So much cleaning up to consider! Because everything seems to require cleaning these days: tombs, canvases. We want the Sistine Chapel *just as Michelangelo saw it.* And what about Masaccio? We are at the same time the executors, the parents, the popes, the clergy, the counsellors, and in short, the artist himself. We, Insurance

Company H., chain of department stores W., offer you, united spectators, works of art constantly renovated, finally revealed in their restored authenticity. Here they are, sparkling, barely sprung forth from the mind and joints of the painter. How lovely, just like TV! And who'd dare confess that he'd rather have his canvas dirty, covered in mold, filth, indifference, obvious proofs of the ignorance and incompetence of those who have preceded us? What? You don't like that admirable crudity of Eve bursting with health, stuffed with vitamins and ozone, become here, in front of your very eyes, thanks to our efforts, a fresh hors d'oeuvre, tomatoes, cucumbers, artichokes, carrots, lettuce? You don't feel exalted by that Mary Magdalen finally bleeding, when up to now she'd simply been there, gray, prostrated, slumped under the dust, in the corner of an obscurantist church? You wanted her to carry on, palpitating, penned up, clandestine? Odd perversity, unworthy of this world of scrubbers, overexposed and radiant, about to take over. Clean interiors, sparkling conveniences, gleaming canvases. What's that? You say in a whisper that Adam and Eve, banished from the Earthly Paradise, look, after the restoration, like panic-stricken tourists escaping a forest fire or like refugees demanding a bottle of Pepsi at once? Well, maybe. So be it. And then what? Does the Bible forbid publicity? Have we set up a sign in neon lights inside St. Peter's? No: everything is done tastefully, discreetly, efficiently, for the good of Art as well as for the good of Corporate Enterprise. Who are the woolly-minded thinkers who maintain that the one doesn't follow the same path as the others? Take for example the fascist display or the huge and miserable communist bazaar: well, had they not existed, we would have had to invent them. If necessary, we'll make our new devils. Who's to be our candidate? In the future, the market will develop from a single movement built on the ruins of those errors. Watteau's *L'Enseigne de Gersaint* was chosen in the past to proclaim the merits of American Express? Good choice. A day of shopping in Paris, Faubourg Saint-Honoré, spring and the paradise of shop windows. Speaking of which, what are the forthcoming contracts?

Where was I? Ah, yes: meetings that remain meetings. So what? You want to kill off the novel? Everyone knows that fictional characters must, as in real life, proceed along a fatal curve, from the first shock of initial blinding leading to the drama, the deception, the disillusionment, the disappearance. Law. Gravity. Oh dear, Watteau, your story is certainly not grave enough!

Watteau, in hell, grabs hold of Paris's staff and breaks the chandeliers of the lively merchants' carnival and of the depressive, bloodsucking fake beggars, and says:

"*Non serviam!*"

Stendhal: "All good reasoning offends."

"The bitter pedantry of dejected prigs."

A LATE TWENTIETH-CENTURY dictionary:

"Watteau (Antoine), 1684–1721: After breaking with the academic school of the seventeenth century and borrowing from Rubens and the Venetian painters, he developed, in the midst of a refined society, a talent for comedy scenes and "*fêtes galantes*," a genre of his own creation, culminating with *Le Pèlerinage a l'île de Cythère* (Paris, Louvre; copy in Berlin). Watteau is a first-rate draftsman and colorist: his brush is feverishly original and his inspiration of a penetrating and nostalgic poetry (*Le Jugement de Paris*, Paris, Louvre; *Les Charmes de la vie*, London; *L'Enseigne de Gersaint*, Berlin)."

If one were not *nostalgic*, would one be a poet? And a *penetrating* poet? With a lute, I suppose. Carrying with him "the black sun of melancholia."

PROUST: "LET US not imitate the revolutionaries who, out of 'civil duty' would scorn, if not actually destroy, the work of Watteau and La Tour, painters who do more honor to France than all those of the Revolution."

But who said we were revolutionary? We don't despise, we don't destroy, we buy, we render posthumous, we restore, we exhibit!

INFORMATION AND ADVICE on *Minitel*, the French computerized telephone service:

Have you met famous or very famous people? You want to write your memoirs? Easy: recall the dullest memories possible which anyone might have had, employing a maximum of cliches accessible to everyone. Conclusion: they are like us, we are like them. Success.

Do you want to know what intellectuals are thinking these days? Their latest ambition, after a profitable apology of the Declaration of Human Rights, is a defense of complex thought against oversimplifications, stereotypes and cliches leading to exclusion and intolerance. Question: What should intellectuals do? Answer: Defend complexity. Objection: But if you repeat the same sentence over and over again, including that one, doesn't it become a cliche? Answer: So what?

How many authors still write their own books themselves? Is it the right thing to do? Should one appraise the market before writing?

Answers: 1) Very few. 2) It's the wrong thing to do. 3) Obviously.

You're concerned with the activities of the Mafia? Big problem. Quickly: the economy is at a standstill? Inflation? Unemployment? The film loses credibility? Create a conflict. This stimulates the Stock Exchange which tends to slumber. Arms sales perk up, popular emotions are stirred (don't forget close-ups of the soldiers' families at the foot of the warships—entire families can be recruited for the filming—or of the support demonstrations for whatever party). Each time find a new gadget: helicopters, mines, tanks, missiles, gas masks, etc. Or this: announce a ruthless war against drugs, publicly lending your support to the new Mafia against the old. Amusing example: it's been revealed that more than half of the luxury yachts docked in Palermo don't belong to their declared proprietors. A street flower salesman was supposed to own a superb ship. To be continued.

MEETINGS THAT REMAIN meetings depend *on one point*: physical, mental, social, historical. Sex is a matter of a point within a point: that particular detail, precise, deep-set, which will touch one person at one specific moment. Several people, several points. Never many during one lifetime. Two? That's plenty. Seven or eight? An avalanche. Everything else is line, surface, fold, decor, soap opera, many layers. The point: value through usage, repeated, inexhaustible. In other words: exchange currency. Just like painting: one buys the surface to deny the point. The point one uses is a present infinitive. Now, infinity . . .

". . . is the absolute affirmation of an existence of any given nature."

"Thank you, Spinoza."

"Is the practical value something forbidden?"

"No one must even suspect it's there."

"Says who?"

"No one. It happens automatically."

"The use one makes of one's own body, of oneself?"

"Same thing. Constant loathing of the original."

". . . of its intimacy, of its desires, of its dreams?"

"No respite, complete expropriation. And to top it all, amnesia and robotization. Impossible to stop and to demonstrate, since the phenomenon happens 'in and of itself.' No guilty parties, therefore no victims, or rather, everyone guilty, everyone a victim. Which doesn't mean that the system doesn't pull out from time to time a big bad wolf for the sake of a required massacre. If the slave were in his master's place, he'd act just like the master, it's a well-known refrain. The same thing, but not as well. Less and less well? Maybe, but harder and harder."

"Nevertheless, these carnations exist?"

"For you and me, right this instant."

"Throughout infinity?"

"If you like. As every use becomes more and more strictly forbidden, the conscious use of oneself, gratuitous, takes on vertiginous dimensions. One can reach ecstasy this way, if the word doesn't frighten you."

"It does."

"Then we'll delete it."

Luz eats her fish and drinks her glass of white wine with good appetite. She lights a cigarette.

"Smoking forbidden?"

"For instance."

(And a woman? Utility or exchange? Both, and most of the time she doesn't know on what side she finds herself. The key to hysteria, hatred of the self.)

"MOZART, WHAT IF we had a baby?"

"Oh, sir!"

"Yes, I insist, I'd like that. I've been meaning to suggest it for some time now, it's not all business, you know, we must also think of things creative. Fine then, you can drop into the clinic anytime you like."

"Which clinic, sir?"

"It depends on what city you happen to be in. One of the ones in the Group, of course. Ask for Dr. Stock, there's one in each of the clinics. They'll know what to do. They'll keep me informed."

"Thank you, sir."

"And remind me to take you out to lunch one of these days."

"Too kind, sir."

TRUE . . . FALSE . . . TRUE-FALSE and false-true . . . Tango-waltz . . . Suppose you were to organize a terrorist act against the state. Which one? That's circumstantial. There'd be then a certain spiritual refinement in you that would lead part of you to denounce you, but in such a way that this denunciation would appear as absurd or false. True-false-true as a passing gesture, almost just for the pleasure. What is truth? someone once said to someone else who, it seems, thought it best at the time to remain silent. True-true-false . . . False-true-true . . . The list can be continued into infinity, establishing all by itself the initiatory hierarchy of those able to understand it, tending towards a lovely legal expression: lack of evidence. Nothing will be evident except the evidence of nonevidence. "Ah, dear sir, if you only knew how many authentic fakes there are in the museums, private collections, art galleries, auction sales!" "Oh well, too bad. Only connect."

Richard insists with his project of generalized cloning, and according to him the special German and Japanese reproduction systems are nowadays undetectable to the naked eye. He wants to *give back* the Louvre. Talk, at night, in the great solitary and icy gallery:

Dürer:

"But do you really think that no one would notice the switch? The general public, granted, but a specialist, a curator, a critic . . ."

Andy:

"Come on, they've got other things on their minds. So, Froissart, what will it be? *Le Jugement de Paris*? *L'Indifferent*? *La Finette*? Decide. The time has come."

THE *PLAYER II* and the *Sea Sky* are there, flying an English flag, at the corner of the Rio San Vio. Aboard the *Player*, a couple (true or false) and two blond kids. Aboard the *Sea Sky*, two guys to be dealt with by Richard, who's just arrived from New York (Guillermo had to be replaced at the last minute).

The transfer is scheduled for the day after tomorrow, at night, following the latest secret negotiations (Geena and Nicole).

The woman aboard the *Player* is English, thirty years old, outdoor type, blond (the kids' mother), rather pretty. I immediately conjured up Geena's large fine handwriting in her fax, in New York, when she said: "Froissart? Cézanne."

Welcome, Cézanne (in fact her name is Elodie, and the guy she's with is Walter, code name Roy). Good news from Mozart? From Dürer? Excellent. Yes, Andy's there.

It's like a dream, it is a dream. Who'd believe me if I told them? And who'd believe that the ship of the French Consulate in Venice (passing right now in front of me, coming from the Marco Polo Airport, aboard two employees whose guns can be seen under the dark blue jackets, carrying the diplomatic pouch and important funds) is called *La Nouvelle Héloïse*? And yet, it is so. You can check. And why not, since we've gone this far, *La Chartreuse de Parme* with the following dialogue: "Monsier Stendhal, you're forgetting your weapon." "Ah, yes, sorry."

At this point, a few realistic objections:

1) Is it likely that a brilliant young American woman studying astrophysics would leave just like that, to holiday in Venice with a French gentleman she hardly knows, would live with him, would have no knowledge of his shady activities or would rather not ask any questions, would share his withdrawn existence with his literary and philosophical musings (plus, if we read carefully, cocaine), knowing full well that she'll never see him again two months later?

2) Can one imagine that business transactions as serious and professional as these, linked after all to international

crime, be entrusted to inconsequential amateurs (even if they change their identities twice a year), risking that mountains of money go up in smoke, and tearing a political-financial web as fragile as it is powerful, rigorous and costly?

To which we can answer:

1) The eminent reader or critic, male or female, an employee from the visible part of the iceberg, has no wish to know the world of today, is happy with cliches lifted from vague detective novels produced by the entertainment industry in charge of amusing their ignorance and that of their social, sexual and emotional partners.

2) The new "innocent" delinquents, as they are now known, other than having the advantage of lacking, by and large, a police record, are specialists in playing games, and have often come from the dissolved and dissolute extreme left of the seventies. The thus-employed eminent pseudoreader and critic, male and female, has never met them, only by hearsay, knows nothing of their real life, and judges them with the same severity as their time which has applied itself to ignoring them in every domain, which was exactly what was needed to create excellent agents (also excellent teachers of the following generations).

It's over a century and a half that Stendhal called out, as a last resource, to the "benevolent reader," that is to say, as he knew so well, to practically no one. The preface to *Lucien Leuwen*, "Cityold" (Civitavecchia), 1835: "Farewell, friendly reader, bear in mind not to spend your life in hatred and in fear."

After this burst of lightning in the night, propaganda regarding the novel hasn't stopped: a straightforward life is forbidden, "one must choose between life and the written word," Flaubert's catechism: "Human life is a sorry shop, no doubt about it, something ugly, cumbersome, complicated. For those with a lively mind, art has no other purpose than to dodge the load and its bitterness." (Concerning this, Sartre—himself trapped, it's true, in another cul-de-sac—was right in commenting: "As aristocratic orgies were beyond their means, they replaced the joyful squandering of riches by the systematic denial of reality.") But what if I said that the novel is a passageway between life and life, a footbridge stretched out from one moment to another, from one momentary place to another momentary place? That it's an act of life like any other, and here are the actors, the actresses, formed in our special studio, workshop? They carry on their adventures after the story is told, don't you know? Their misdeeds don't stop here, and they also existed before the story started. Narration: gap, jump, a deep descent in the fall and blooming of these bodies, *clinamen*. Luz in Los Angeles, Geena and Richard in New York, Nicole and I in Paris, many others. Why should they be affected by the curse against life, uttered with such rage and stubbornness, and bend to the morose rule that says that a novel *must* tell of the obligatory failure of life, when every minute, every square or cubic meter won in the name of free space or time, constitutes, for each and every individual, the only true revolutionary war? Tell us about that war, that will be enough.

I am not a child of this century. I've not been conceived by the famous and monstrous comic-strip couple fascism-Stalinism (who's been running after me ever since my birth in order *to adopt me*); neither am I the funereal and frightened spawn of the previous century, narrow-minded clump born from some obscure disaster. If I make use of the eighteenth century (good-bye, nineteenth century, good-bye twentieth century), it's just to be able to breathe, don't you see. The twenty-first century will be the century of renewal and of unexpected deepening in every sense, the Century of Lights, or it will be nothing. Having said that, the instant novel can take place just about anywhere, at any time, and just as well being motionless in a little room in the country, it's up to you to prove it. One doesn't have to become involved with a Watteau sailing through Venice, to lodge in a pink and white palazzo under the sun, to lie on a terrace over the port or sit in a garden with a swimming pool, next to a stone coffin from the beginning of our calendar, in the midst of acacias, oleanders, nightingales, carnations and roses. But if this be the case, should one apologize? Invent an existential angst, in the suburbs or in black and white, as if I were Yugsolav, Hungarian, German, Austrian, Czech? "You don't have the right to put words on paper because you are alive." This has been for a long time now the nihilist dogma. You live? What a monstrosity! And furthermore, *women cross your landscape*? Without tears? Without going mad? Without committing suicide? "One cannot live and write, you can't have everything." But what is this Law? Who decreed it? Is it carved in the heavens? Did it come down from Mount Sinai? From Golgotha? Was it dictated in Mecca? And why should I obey it? *Les Charmes de la vie*: practical value. Is it a question of money? Not really. Sickness and health, virtue and vice: in a word, you want to make a profit *on all paintings*?

All paintings.

* * *

IN 1727, SIX years after Watteau's death, *Le Mercure de France* hesitates with all seriousness: Was Watteau better skilled than Cheron and Santerre? Doubtful. After all, the Regent didn't recognize him, Voltaire was to disdain him, Diderot despises him already. Eventually his chance of survival will consist of having died young, at the same age as Raphael and Mozart. The human species enjoys the scenario of a Christlike transposition. What would he have become, what else had he in store for us, would he have, in the end, developed his tragic qualities? Alas, the tomb snatched away this genius just as he was beginning to perceive the Promised Land, that is to say, maturity. So much the better, when all is said and done, he was a bit of a pain, he was moody, he'd fight with his friends over trifles, he'd have been a terrible husband and an execrable father, he had gone as far as he could, he'd only have deepened the gap between himself and our laborious creations. Would we have ended up by killing him off? Don't tempt us.

After that, who will be fond of Watteau? Reynolds, Ingres, Delacroix, Turner, Monet: lucid technicians. And then Gautier, Baudelaire, Nerval, the Goncourt, Verlaine, Pierre Louÿs, Proust, with usually one condition, the nostalgic overlay, the "endless sorrow." Even now, I read: "Watteau has a place of honor among the artistic pantheon for having introduced that melancholy and sentimental tone in art, appreciated by so many art lovers." Too kind, too kind. Or this: "Watteau's world, static above all." An opinion which coincides with that of Caylus, in 1748: "His compositions have no purpose. They don't express passion, they are therefore lacking one of painting's most entertaining features: I refer to the action."

Your action displeases me, therefore it doesn't exist. Or else: the relaxed activity, effortlessly developed in these joyful and voluptuous canvases, disturbs and shocks me deeply. Such a universe is therefore impossible. So: 1) Nothing is taking place; 2) as the canvases persist, I command them to be sorrowful: they become sorrowful at once.

A variant: why is the *Pèlerinage a l'île de Cythère* such a melancholy painting? Isn't it because instead of the boarding of a ship, it depicts a homecoming? These couples aren't *traveling to* the realm of love, they're *returning from* it. That explains their despair, their moans and groans, their sobbing (the invisible snail jammed in the bush, the tubercular sparrow hidden in the branches): what is more satisfactory than the act of love, the source of so many primitive regrets and nightmares? Of course, Watteau didn't paint this gloomy dejection directly, but evidently it's implicit. And that is why this painting is one of the most sinister of all time.

After all, the male or female critic seems always to fear that his or her partner, male or female, will betray him or her in such-and-such a novel or such-and-such a painting, as if it were particularly difficult to submit *there* to disgusting or guilty frolics. Careful with the words, with the images: careful with their relationships to one another!

So IT'S AFTER a long battle that lasts 170 years (imagine that this book can't actually be read until the year 2160, and why not), a battle fought with grim determination by snipers or amateur terrorists, that it finally becomes impossible to rid ourselves of Watteau. Let's say: after 1890, the year in which van Gogh, suicide of society, begins postmortem his messianic ascension. Of course, Watteau is considered still a *minor* artist (he'll never acquire the grandeur and sublime vehemence of a Rubens, etc.) but, oh well, a major minor. He must be accommodated, he can sleep eternally in peace (I never was, I was, I am not, I don't care). Even Claudel is alerted on December 18, 1939 (the eve of great destructions can obviously be instructive) by *L'Indifferent*, "a mother-of-pearl messenger, a forerunner of Dawn." However, this same Claudel had no qualms to write, in 1925, this revealing enormity in his *Journal*: "A woman is only intelligent to the detriment of her mystery. I've always detested, above all, the type of intelligent eighteenth-century woman, the titillating Frenchwoman. The La Tour collection at the Louvre inspires me with real horror."

There it is! You said it! And all the self-proclaimed poets are with you in this! Let's chop the head of this "titillating Frenchwoman" and lift it on the end of a spear. "A woman is only intelligent to the detriment of her mystery." God preserve us from such a *mystery*! La Tour (Maurice Quentin de), 1704–1788, and not the other, Georges, the nocturnal medievalist with his candlelight, of course.

You say that the titillating Frenchwoman was reincarnated far away, on the Pacific coast, through galaxies, computers, emulsions of cosmic matter, tennis, swimming pools and equations? Through an Italian-Swedish mélange and a Spanish name? And that her *mystery* hasn't suffered, on the contrary? "But what if the 21st century is not as you foresee it? If it's essentially religious and metaphysical, as other prophets have assured us?" "Well, in that case we'll wait for 22d, the 23d, or the 30th, we're in no hurry, the Greek disappeared for a thousand years." "But what about the end of the world? The Apocalypse?" "Oh come on, really."

"All that's very well, but how could that sort of individual exist in the future? Where do you see them growing from?"

"From right here."

"But everything seems to point to the contrary."

"And the contrary of the contrary."

"Is it really foreseeable?"

"Two answers are possible: 1) I hope not. 2) I hope so. I've observed so, therefore I hope so. Time will tell."

"One has the impression that your real characters are Watteau and Stendhal: so we're dealing with the past?"

"I've expressed myself badly. I wanted to show that Watteau and Stendhal are, because of a *very personal* aspect, 'of all time,' and that there'll always be characters 'of all time.' This evident fact seemed to me to have been obscured. Having said that, I agree with the rest."

(Is Froissart satisfied simply with watching Luz asleep? Isn't there anything else going on? What does he feel at night touching her warm skin, her cheeks, her neck, her breasts, her ass, her thighs, her legs, her arms, her hands, her feet, her ears? Does he enjoy kissing her? On the eyes? In the mouth? What does he feel combing her in the dark, intuitively, against this impalpable cave wall, while the city, down below, drapes itself in its luminous black canals?)

"I'M FROM LASCAUX."

"The caves?"

"Montignac, in the Dordogne. I could show you where:

wonderful gray-green-silver landscape, my family still owns a small abandoned piece of land straight down the Vézère, with a big rock, in the grass. A cemetery with names almost worn away. And below, minus seventeen thousand years of cave paintings discovered in September 1940. A crucial year because of that. Everything had to be shut down in 1963, human breath infected the stone, an algae invasion. In 1984, they built a facsimile next door for the benefit of the public. Pretty fable, isn't it? The real deer, bull, horses, ibex, oxen, cows, bison are locked up again. They continue their millenary voyage underground, red, black, white, rounded and mobile, airy ghosts, beautiful as Watteaus."

"Or Courbets?"

"Yes, *La Grotte humide*. It went on sale not so long ago. A hole in the rock and a thin stream of water, two skull-shaped stones linked tightly at the entrance, a great greasy vaginal contraction, ochre and round, a clearly visible signature in red: G. Courbet. Same inspiration as with *Le Torse*. Where is it now?"

Prehistory (it is I, the pebble speaking to you) is entering its third millennium, peacefully. Like a black hole, really. There'll be time enough to go in search of lost time, and to return, with Proust, to Venice. Look: a hundred and thirty of his letters on sale at the Sporting d'Hiver in Monte Carlo. No? Yes. And very interesting ones too, since they escaped the clutches of the family, which means that they're addressed to Reynaldo Hahn. Writing to him, Proust usually signs off: "Your pony, Marcel." Isn't that charming? He also writes to Hahn's dog, called Zadig. Six hundred thousand francs to start off with for these words addressed to Robert de Montesquiou: "Your verses have the mysterious honey of sunbeams possessed with the sweetness of heaven." Absurdly nice. These words on sale at the Sporting d'Hiver? Everything's possible. What we must do is organize pleasant catacombs out in the open.

Silence.

"GOOD MEMORY?"

"Yes."

"Then remember this:

"—The cat alley and its iron grill, the scent of honeysuckle in the evening.

"—The great bronze door of the Church of La Salute at night, and the sound it brings to mind.

"—The *motoscafo* called *Desdemona*, docked at the Grand Canal.

"—The red bench on the pontoon, across from the Societa Canottieri Bucintoro, founded in 1882, across from San Giorgio.

"—The three-mast *Activ*, also from Gibraltar, anchored across from the Dogana.

"—The terrace, bristling with antennae at the very top of the Benedetto Marcello conservatory, a large gray-white palazzo impossible to visit in its entirety and which always looks abandoned, and in which nevertheless *people are living*.

"—Yet another red bench, in the shadows, on the Camp San Agnese, across from the Gesuati.

"—The convex character of the green water that should overflow on stormy days and which simply remains there, balanced, as if to astound the eye and make it feel its relativity.

"—The Ca' Bala Bridge which, as its name makes clear, is the prettiest bridge in Venice.

"—The young girl in a mauve jogging outfit, with her Walkman, running and from time to time dancing on her own, on the quays.

"—The word *giornata* which lasts far longer than a day, which occupies a year within a day; '*una splendida giornata*.'

"—When you said "the moon is inhaled by the fog," on the Zattere Al Spirito Santo.

"—The piano-bar-discotheque *Linea d'Ombra* (*Shadow Line* on the bill), at the foot of the Ponte dell'Umilita, June 30 at 8:45 P.M., Sarah Vaughan's voice, and the dirty thing you said laughing.

"—The bellowing of the transatlantic jets in the mist, sometimes, in the morning, the oleanders in the garden, when the shutters are opened, caught in the mist."

For example.

All this depicts reality itself, alive, and if need be, I'll carry with me the caves, the chapels,the flip side of museums where the souls are kept, *that which cannot be reproduced* in itself. Explain to me why your world exhibitions are so successful, with their scientific catalogues and unique security systems, while reproductions dirty the colors to such a degree: Michelangelo rusted, Titian blackened or a rancid yellow . . . The more paintings are washed and modernized, the more photographs grow doddery, heavy, malevolent, in mourning. All-powerful technology has no answer to this problem? Or is it done *on purpose*? In order not to upset the home buyers? Or maybe you don't even notice it? You've simply taken a snapshot of your own nature, a spontaneous chromo?

ANTOINE DE LA Roque (1721): "The charm in the expression of Watteau's faces, especially in those of women and children, can be felt everywhere . . . The skies of his paintings are tender, light and varied, the trees are full of leaves, set out artfully, the locations of his landscapes are admirable and his terraces have a naive truthfulness, as do the animals and the flowers. The complexion of his figures is animated and soft, the cloth of his draperies is simple rather than rich, but it is downy, with beautiful folds and true and bright colors."

(Bravo! This contemporary is indeed contemporary.)

Jean de Julienne (1726): "He was of medium height and feeble constitution. His mind was quick and piercing, and his sentiments noble. He spoke little but well, and wrote much the same. He was almost always deep in thought, a great admirer of nature and of all the masters who copied her. Assiduous work has made him somewhat melancholic, of cold and embarrassed manners, which rendered him sometimes unpleasant to his friends and to himself; he had no other defects than those of affecting indifference and enjoying change."

(Respectful, but his foul-mouthed character puts in an appearance.)

Gersaint (1744): "Back in Paris, he came to see me and asked if I'd receive him at my home and allow him, in his own words in order to warm up his fingers, to paint a ceiling that I was to exhibit outside . . . The work took eight days . . . An object seen in front of him for longer than a certain time would bore him, all he wanted was to flit from subject to subject."

(The legend of his instability is reinforced.)

Caylus (1748): "Hardly had he settled in a lodging, that he would take a dislike to it. He'd change lodgings a hundred times over, and always with pretexts which, because they shamed him, he studiously made special. There where he stayed the longest was in certain rooms which I had in several Paris neighborhoods which served for little more than keeping the model . . . The purity of his habits hardly allowed him to enjoy the libertine nature of his spirit."

(Unstable, maybe, but don't you believe that he did those things he painted.)

Taillasson (1802): "Perhaps nowadays it's a crime to speak of Watteau . . . No doubt his characters lack the proud and high-minded truth of austere warriors and philosophers; they don't have the good-naturedness of the bourgeois nor the touching simplicity of country folk; they have the only truth that they must have, that of gallant heroes, men of pleasure, actors, musicians, dancers, and of all those who spend their time amusing themselves and amusing others, of all those whose studies are not conducted in secluded corners, in the glow of solitary lamps, but in places lit by a hundred candles, in the midst of numerous people and the tumultuous clapping of hands. Who like him has painted these charming assemblies in which the two sexes attack one another with everything that glitters to the eye, where everything, even thought, even feeling, has a manicured look, when to be ridiculous is the only vice, and the art of pleasing the only virtue . . . After having completed many canvases, drained by his genius and by the pleasures he had depicted, Watteau died young, leaving behind him a great reputation which, since a few years ago, has lost some of the brilliance which had made it shine so brightly, and which will no doubt be restored to him one day by our grateful nephews."

(No doubt Taillasson is being prudent, while representing the official neoclassical tradition in painting: maybe he writes this to annoy David in the midst of Napoleon's coronation.)

Lecarpentier (1821): "Having arrived as a young man in Paris, towards the end of a reign both great and glorious, brusquely succeeded by the empire of folly, at a time when she had spread throughout a realm in which licentiousness was replacing extreme devotion, when she could be seen shaking her bells even at the court . . . it was natural that a painter whose imagination gave birth to nothing except gallant and voluptuous scenes, would be favorably received by his contemporaries."

(These mad contemporaries didn't manage to produce a golden age, and for this, they—Watteau among them—were justly punished.)

Vivant Denon (1829): "He possessed the true harmony of the entire Venetian school . . . Chance made him cross paths with members of the Comedie Italienne which the government had recently invited over from Italy. He became intimate with them, and from then onwards painted nothing except harlequins, columbines, doctors and buffoons, which explains why the greater part of his delightful work has become improper company in the galleries where reigns a certain gravity of style."

(Watteau kept bad Italian company, the notion of the

"carnival" makes its appearance. And yet, the elderly Vivant Denon, who had such a strange career under Robespierre, Napoleon and Louis XVIII, this specialist in Egyptian art who died in 1825, who maybe still remembers having published in his youth *Point de lendemain*, "No Tomorrow," wishes to save, nostalgic, *L'Embarquement pour Cythère*: "Everything here breathes love, the air is thick with it, filling the sails . . .")

1830: Stendhal publishes *Le Rouge et le Noir*.

On June 20, 1832, as we perhaps recall, in Rome, Stendhal himself, "moved like the Pythian Sibyl," writes that his readers are now ten or twelve years old. "The eyes that will read this are barely open to the light." Neptune had not yet been discovered. Finally, he'll postpone the possibility of the reading of his books to the second half of the next century: he could renew his prediction today, and so on and so on.

It's midday, Luz has just come in, the sun is shining on the gray phones, and the novel is also a veiled judgment of History. You doubted it? I never did. I don't like spinach, I love Saint-Simon, the Cardinal de Retz remains a durable passion ("I remained faithful to my point and found marvelous commodities"), I don't like everything Stendhal ever wrote, but most of the time, I do: "Every time I went to piss behind the lime trees at the bottom of the garden, my soul was *refreshed* by the sight of these dear friends. I love them still, even after thirty-six years of separation." Or this: "It seems that I refused to have earth cast on my mother's coffin, saying that it would hurt her." Or finally this (endless affair): "I'm immoral because I wrote women into *L'Amour* and because, in spite of myself, I make fun of the hypocrites."

"So finally, your characters aren't guilty?"

"The more people will become corrupt and patently criminal through conformism, the more those others will become innocent and honest, and end up the only philosophers of an unprecedented abnormal age."

POINT DE LENDEMAIN appears in June 1777, in *Mélange littéraires, ou journal des dames*, signed M.D.O.G.T.K. (the initials of Monsieur Denon, Ordinary Gentleman To the King):

"There are kisses that are like confidences: they attract one another, they speed one another on, they warm one another. Indeed, as soon as the first one is given the second follows; then another: they hasten, they cut into the conversation, they replace it; barely do they allow the sighs the chance to escape. Silence follows, it is heard (because sometimes silence can be heard): it was frightening."

Or this:

"The darkness was too great to make out any object; but through the transparent gauze of a lovely summer's night, our imagination transformed an island across from our pavilion into an enchanted place. The river seemed covered with winged loves that played amongst the waves. Never were the woods of Cnidus so full of lovers like the ones with which we filled the other shore. For us, there was nothing in nature except happy couples, and we were the happiest of them all."

The goddess of Cnidus: Aphrodite. *Le Temple de Cnide* by Monstesquieu, dated 1725.

The large *Gilles* by Watteau, today in the Louvre since 1869, whose meaning is so mysterious, did not reappear until 1804 when Vivan Denon bought it for 150 or 300 francs at the Place du Carrousel, in spite of David's reproaches ("improper company in the galleries where reigns a certain gravity of style"). That man always knew what he was up to.

RICHARD IS ALSO armed, he speaks little, he's always with Elodie-Cézanne (I'd like to know why she chose that name). They mustn't have liked my being there with Luz, even if Geena knows I'm overly prudent. Or maybe business isn't booming, good times are in decline, the dollar hesitates before rising as usual. But my intention was to stick to those facts, never mind. If I write this story, no problem either. Purloined letter, openly displayed never found. In the meantime, everyone will have changed identity, or dispersed. What are you talking about? Nice invention, writing as a hobby. Froissart? But who's ever been called Froissart? And come see the Calle di Mezzo: yes, certainly it exists, but was there ever a palazzo there, even a small one, a garden, a sarcophagus, a swimming pool? Has anyone registered the docking of a *Sea Sky* en route from London to Cyprus, a *Player II* cruising from Gibraltar to Capri? Maybe, but that is pure coincidence. We know what he does and how he lives. A young American woman, Luz? No, never mentioned. The police is so well organized, you can trust it blindly, not the police-police, of course, but that of the airwaves, the one of "it's rumored." What? A never-catalogued Watteau on board ship? *La Fête à Venise*? Venice? Go on, someone's been pulling your leg.

We won't be there then, will we, Luzita? The bustle, the traffic, the wars won't stop, beginning of the century, end of the century, beginnings of centuries, ends of centuries, systolic-diastolic, we will have met in the *enormous* tapestry of bodies, we will have made a hook, a loop, dregs of atoms sent back into the shadows, appearing, disappearing, out of sight, out of mind.

And then what? The sky?

Right now, it's raining, the city lies behind the curtain, it's our luck, we continue to lie in bed in your room, every fifteen minutes I go to the window, I repeat to myself that phrase of one, I don't know which, of Watteau's contemporaries: "He wanted to live according to his fantasies and also remain unknown." I think as well of the never-ending rainy afternoons, children's holidays in Montignac, a boxed-in river green and black, how vast time is, how it offers itself, if one is deserving, how deeply time loves itself.

It was raining like this on Amsterdam Avenue this past winter, broken sidewalks, muddy pools, trucks, taxis, an ambulance; I see the phone booth again, standing in the water, attaché case clenched between my legs, I made a date with Geena at the *Carlyle*. Later, the Haitian taxi driver, his name was Joseph Edison, was listening to a screaming radio belting out Beethoven's *Concert No.* 2 for piano, afterwards, long muddled speech on the city rotten with disease and drugs, the imminent coming of Jesus Christ chasing the merchants from the temple. New York cubes, Venice mirrors . . . "Modern glass contains iron; when thick, it becomes green." First night at a friend's home, on the couch, right under De Kooning's *Park Rosenberg*: one should always sleep under paintings, to sleep in churches or museums, my fantasy. Have you got a one-room apartment for me at the Louvre, Versailles, the Palazzo Ducale? I'll be very discreet, I promise. First contacts: the IBM garden atrium, the Trump Tower: near the bamboo, in front of the tulips.

The sun shines again around four. The slow sailboats depart, the motorboats raised on the water avoid them at full speed, the water prairie has turned blue. Both ships rock quietly one next to the other, under the same flag.

"Will you come have a drink a little later aboard the *Player II*?"

"Won't I be in the way?"

"Not at all, it's just among friends."

Second phone call from Geena, nervous:

"What's the weather like?"

"Getting better."

"At what time?" (She already knows, through Elodie or Richard).

"Three in the morning."

"What do you think of Andy?"

"Ordinary."

"And Cézanne?"

"Charming. Dürer?"

"Perfect. You call me afterwards? I'll be having dinner at the *Pleiades*, I'll be home after midnight." (Six in the morning here.)

"Have a nice evening."

"Have a nice fête."

I kiss Luz leisurely.

She:

"Should we dress formally?"

"Somewhat."

4

. . . .

The painting will not touch the ground. It's there, 56 × 46 cm in the converted safe of the *Player II*. Elodie and Walter allowed us to examine it for a long while, Richard and myself, before the two guys from the *Sea Sky*. Now I'm here, alone, on guard, on the aft deck. Everything went smoothly.

It's two in the morning, Luz is sleeping. I observe the loaded gun, lying next to me on the blue pillow: useless, but it's Richard and Geena's Hollywood side, their likeable touch of madness.

The *Player II* barely moves, the water slaps regularly against the stone quay. High above me, to my left, the Big Dipper; behind me, in perspective, the facade of the church with its two angels surrounding the burning wheel (the projector that illuminates them is switched off at ten); in front of me, above the white wall, a parasol pine tree.

Have I ever before looked at a tree in this manner? So much from the inside? No.

Richard:

"So, excited? A bit of national pride? You've got to admit that it's lively. I checked points J1, O2 and Y3. What about you?"

"A7, D8, N9. The little blond in red, there, to the left."

"Next to the staircase?"

"That's it. Lower the top spot a little, to the right. More. Pass me the magnifying glass."

She'd fit between my two fingers, Luz . . . I'm King Kong. I jump out of the canvas, I put her in my pocket, I leave . . .

"No need for a frottis?"

"Only one."

"Gently. Don't hurt it."

Richard knows what he's doing. Match, damp cotton, point O, analysis. Yes, the brush of Antoine Watteau himself has indeed touched this wall.

"Fine then, delivery."

"The guys next door, what are they like?"

"OK. One Lebanese, one German."

"German?"

"Forget your prejudices. Walter also has German blood."

"Elodie?"

"The English woman? Top class."

"Why 'Cézanne'?"

"Ask her some other time. Lovely, this airy thing, isn't it? Not exactly my taste, but what a talent for staging!"

"What's the stage, in your opinion?"

"You tell me."

IT'S NOT THE painting that overpowers me, there, that very second, but the tree, the branch of the black pine gleaming in the moonlight. The masts, the riggings, the tree. The sound of the water's silence. The masts, the riggings, the water, the branch of the pine tree, the unfolding story of Watteau's trees, the safe, the gun, the night, the tree. And once again, the masts, the riggings, the tree, the Big Dipper, the white wall. It wants to tell me something, that pine tree, or rather, do I want to tell myself something through its presence? No. *Something said but unspoken.* Something said before being said. And after, without anything being said. Start again. Oh yes, start again, since everything starts again, endlessly.

Geena:

"So?"

"No hitches."

"You're going to bed?"

"I don't think so. There's a beautiful pine tree across from the ships. Just like Cézanne's sketch in Zurich."

"Oh?"

"Nothing, nothing at all."

* * *

I'M THINKING OF the steely nerves of the man who went and used an Exacto knife to slice the Renoir at the Louvre. It took him only a few seconds. Very difficult work, high precision, diamond cutting, optical lens polishing, cataract laser operation. I imagine him taking a deep breath, wondering for the hundredth time about the razor's edge. Quickly done, well done, in the bag. All that remains is to exit normally, leaving the guard to snooze away. Did he go and deposit it at Dürer's feet? Had he heard, even once, of Spinoza? "Everything precious is as difficult as it is rare." Spinoza writes in Latin: *praeclara. Omnia praeclara tam difficilia quam rara sunt*. Latin is as beautiful as the pine tree. Two branches to be heard: *tam, quam*. Dry wood, dark red, delicious scent, brought onto the paper by the draftsman's hand, painted, written in a book. The pine forests burn like paper. *Praeclarus*: that which is clear, luminous, dazzling, brilliant, remarkable, transformation of hydrogen into helium, the core of the sun: fourteen million degrees, in four billion years total consumption in flames. *Nihil praeclarius*: nothing more remarkable. *Res praeclarissimae*: the finest acts. *Praeclara*: plural. *Qui habet corpus ad plurima* . . . Translations read: "Having a body fit for the largest number of activities," and that's true but how to explain what that would really be like, *a plural body*?

"He who has a plural body, has a spirit whose largest part is eternal."

What? Beg your pardon? Body? Plural? Spirit? Part? Eternal? Would you go through that once again, step by step?

Omnia praeclara . . .rara. All things (or acts) that are clear are as difficult as they are rare. That which is clearest is also that which is rarest and most precious. That which is well conceived is well articulated, and the words to express it come easily. Tell me something that is *very clear*. Clearer. No, clearer. No clearer, still.

And I making myself clear?

The eye sees only part of the light (which takes eight minutes to reach us from that secondary star, the sun). Our eye doesn't see X rays, gamma rays, infrared rays, ultraviolet rays, radioactive rays. Someone capable of seeing radioactivity would be permanently bathed in a brilliant glow. For him there would be no longer day or night. If you want to study the sun's core and the impalpable neutrinos, you have to dig yourself deep below earth and water, protected from the cosmic rays. Patience, length of time, listen carefully, investigate with care.

Cézanne's *Étude pour un arbre* (1895–1900) measures 27.5 × 43.5 cm. It hangs at the Zurich Kunsthaus. Gray, green, bluish, cloudless, tight, empty, and affirmative, white from having been drawn through a lively black, it is far more explicit, in its absolute relativity, than a thousand treatises on physics, fifty on metaphysics, twenty on ethics or ten thousand on zen virtuosities from Japan. The Japanese show it without being able to know it in detail. We don't. Therein lies the mystery.

What beauty.

The really amusing scene would be to recite to Geena, without any reason, La Fontaine's verses—she in New York at midnight, I in Venice at six in the morning—while the blue-red day and the gulls flood the sky and while I watch, from the terrace, the *Sea Sky* unfurl its sails with its *dainty cargo*.

Hello?

"I enjoy playing games, the art of love, books, music,
City and countryside, in fact all things. Nothing there is
That isn't for my soul an overwhelming bliss,
Even the sombre pleasure of a heart that's melancholic."

Pardon me? What's that? Explain to me how all things can become "an overwhelming bliss"? And above all, how to derive a somber pleasure from a melancholic heart. You'd be somber and *yet* it would give you pleasure? And what about neglect, death, suffering? Those too, an overwhelming bliss?

Incomprehensible.
Branch of pine tree.
Too difficult or rare.
Too clear.

The *Sea Sky* sails away, the two men aboard like perfect nonchalant yachtsmen. Elodie and Walter, on the aft deck of the *Player II*, are breakfasting with their handsome blond kids. Happy family. Richard should be by now on a *motoscafo* on his way to the airport. Luz and Geena are asleep. Nicole is listening to her first batch of news on the radio.

This just in: pseudotourists on a ship were caught as they were attempting to transboard in Venice, together with a considerable cargo of heroin, a series of stolen paintings, among them an important Watteau. An international network has been dismantled, the secret trafficking of works of art has been laid to rest. Police chief Monique Copp will be the guest on our special broadcast.

But no, nothing. The crisis, the threats of war, the draft,

the bushfires in the French Midi, traffic accidents, a few rapes, that's all. Nicole won't hear anything either, and more's the pity:

Who was Watteau? Why are his paintings so valuable? As much as those of van Gogh? Tonight, the moment of truth with the distinguished Mr. Norpois, world-renowned art specialist.

"Mr. Norpois, what can we learn from this new incident?"

"The market's extreme sensitivity and fickleness, its new laws, its worldwide scope."

"And what else?"

"The inventiveness of the new dealers, and the fact that their identity is becoming more and more difficult to unmask, the daring of unknown silent partners, and what we might call a mixing of types."

"Ah yes?"

"The symptom of an entire age, the stability of established values unanimously recognized, the expansion of the yen and the dollar in their reciprocal movements, the prestige of France, the weight of its brand name of which unfortunately our fellow citizens are barely conscious."

"And why?"

"It's not uncommon that civilizations about to be destroyed recognize themselves as mortal. Consider the Mayans when the Spaniards arrived."

"And Watteau, Mr. Norpois? Was he a master?"

"Ah, yes, indeed. A great master."

"The meaning of his art, in a couple of minutes?"

"Immense nostalgia. Consider the magnificent embarking for the burial at Cythera which is, contrary to what is commonly supposed, the Greek island of the dead. As Baudelaire has seen so clearly, that was where the funeral pyres were built. Watteau's characters appear to be having fun but in reality they're wringing they're hands, they moan, they weep, they know they are irredeemably condemned."

A commercial break.

"Mr. Norpois, what is your opinion regarding the writer who was arrested in the Watteau affair, in Venice? Isn't that surprising?"

"Froissart? I vaguely knew him, long ago. Not without talent, but a misguided intelligence. Like most intellectuals, he spent his time being mistaken. The fanatics of self-blinding narcissism end up usually in the whirlwind of the media, or amongst terrorists or delinquents. I'm not in the least pleased about it."

"Do you think that a case like this is a matter for psychiatry?"

"For psychoanalysis, rather."

"Has he written anything of interest?"

"I don't remember. Possibly. First hermetic stuff, then pornography or fashion . . . You know, with ex-leftists, everything is possible."

"Mr. Norpois, coming back to van Gogh . . ."

"Watteau."

"Sorry, Watteau. He died very young. Did he commit suicide?"

"No, but certainly he didn't want to go on living."

"Homosexual?"

"It's been said."

"Drugs?"

"New research might establish that, perhaps."

"Suffering from a neurosis, then?"

"No doubt about it."

"Still rated on the stock market?"

"Immutable."

"Why?"

"I've told you: he depicted like no one else the disenchantment and the *ennui* of love, the dark side of desire which is no other than the hidden side of death."

YES, THE *SEA Sky* sails away peacefully, over there, and the *Player II* will sail away this evening towards Capri and new adventures. An Etruscan tomb? The back of an isolated church? Marble? Bronze? On its way, the merchandise might change its destination. I put my gun away in the drawer, it will stay there for the immediate future. Luz joins me on the terrace, asks if I've slept well, looks out into the distance, with me, Elodie, Walter and their blond kids running on the deck, pushing one another, go back into their cabins, come out again. It's Sunday. In a while, they'll go for a walk, impeccable, crossing their little gangway to come out onto the quay. Careful, hold on to the rope. But the children are nimble. They're not really going to go to mass *on top of everything else?*

Charming Cézanne: she has just lifted the receiver of the portable phone, she speaks and laughs in the sun, maybe it's Geena calling her, or Richard from the airport, or Nicole, or one of the guys from the *Sea Sky*, or someone else again. Not once does she look in our direction.

Luz:

"Can I film them?"

"Why not. Can you zoom down on the pine tree, there, to your left?"

"Yes?"

"Like that, yes. Catch the masts and the pine tree, especially the branch sticking out over the wall. The children, the riggings, the masts, the flags, the pine tree."

(She films.)

"Hubble had transmission problems. But Magellan seems to be working on Venus. Excellent photographs."

"Good."

"Do you want to say anything on camera?"

"No."

"In a bad mood?"

"Not really."

Canvas on the waters, locked safe . . .

"TELL ME, MOZART, how did it go with the transfer of the Watteau?"

"Perfectly, sir. But we changed partners at sea, sir."

"Ah yes? No more Arabs?"

"The area is a little overcrowded at present. Maybe we'll ship the painting to the Caribbean."

"Saint-Martin?"

"Of course. We could leave it there for a time."

"The Japanese don't want it?"

"Yes, but you know that they're still in their impressionist passion."

"Still Monet?"

"Still Monet."

"Don't they get bored?"

"Apparently not. They'd jumped on the Renoir, but our agent wasn't careful enough. He's just been arrested coming back from Venice."

"The Renoir cut out with an Exacto knife in the Louvre, in broad daylight? Whoever had the idea was a genius."

"Thank you, sir."

Luz:

"Won't you leave your Memoirs behind?"

"No. I don't want to be stigmatized with the label of show-off."

"Will someone write your biography?"

"Oh yes, no doubt. But not before 2030 or 2050. Many bodies have to disappear first. The living become dead and coming back to life as if they'd never died. The living, the dead: we used to say that, long ago."

She's lying on the couch in the living room, I'm sitting on the blue Chinese carpet, I'm holding her left ankle in my hands, the drawing of Diana in her bath, Actaeon having been accepted, no dogs, the truth of the foot, two sections, three movements, calm.

" 'Two sections, three movements'?"

"When the time of an instant has been found. Just a phrase."

"For example?"

"This man was a living paradox: he grew soft in his discipline and hard in his pleasures."

"A self-portrait?"

"If you like."

* * *

NIGHT, SKIN: YOU? me? The mouths, the hands, the shoulders, the legs. And in the morning, over there, across from us, the face somewhat puffed up of the auburn young woman at the window; she too must have been caressed for a long time in the dark. With the sun in her eyes, she smiles.

"DARK MATTER? THE MACHOS?"

"Massive Compact Halo Objects. Dark matter is simply the continuation of Copernicus's revolution. Wasn't the Earth the center of the world? Now, if dark matter exists, that means that everything visible is not all that important. Make room for the evanescent, the uncertain, the interval, the echo, the gap, the accent, the minute disturbance, the reflection, the rebound. Make room for the billions of billions of billions of particles that fill this too, too flimsy world. That which glitters doesn't hold. That which can be seen doesn't contain. Everyone holds on to the image right at the time when the image is questioned, made relative, exploded. Advertising against a faint background, galaxies of foam. Death can be looked at indirectly, the sun is a detail, night gives us new energy, hurrah for painting in action, you, I, hello. A moment of silence, it's a neutrino. But you have every right to prefer the neutralinos or the axions. How's your critical density, fine? Are you not yourself a gravitational mirage?"

"Quintessence?"

"Just a figure of speech. Anyway, there's ten times more hidden mass than apparent mass. The psychological consequences? Imagine an unending catastrophe."

"And pleasure?"

"Is that a question?"

"Dark matter?"

"Maybe."

IT'S NOT IMPOSSIBLE that one day it might be said: in those days, enlarged and conglomerated appearances would show themselves in military fashion against a background of illuminated skyscrapers and moving screens. Their names were Lou Dobbs, host of *Moneyline* on CNN, or Terry Keenan (who'd look a bit like you if you'd been taken and frozen by the incessant apology of merchandise immediately converted into figures, including the human body), the impeccable and quick host of New York's *Business News*. God's name was Dow Jones, the international specialist in his religion William Sterling (you can't invent a name like that). The T-shirt correspondent in Saudi Arabia, as much at ease in the desert as next to a swimming pool, was called Carl Rochelle. Kodak's stocks were high, while the others were suffering from a noticeable and temporary decline. The oil barrels burned high, then low, up again, down again. The silent market of drugs, white matter for black results, was booming as usual, and was coming more and more under the beneficial wing of the official state. No one kept count of the stolen paintings. A disabused magistrate about to be murdered realized twenty years too late that the whole of Italy was in the hands of the Mafia. The pope warned timidly against the ravages of TV, while there were celebrations for the 450th anniversary of the creation of the Jesuits (plenary indulgence for those going on pilgrimage to Loyola). Real-fake books were being published everywhere and sold as if by magic without anyone reading them. The *Sea Sky* crossed paths, as it left Venice, with the

Ocean Free, coming from Capri. A French writer in exile was reading a moralist, also French, who wrote, "The world becoming fake is also the fake becoming worldly," asking himself how many people would understand this sentence. He recalled that an idealist philosopher had noted that, in our time, "the notion of unscathed is disappearing." That word, *unscathed*, made him think of Watteau's *L'Indifferent*. The philosopher's words were: "Only Being lends the unscathed their serenity, and the wrathful their feverish race towards the abyss." Yes. Cézanne's pine tree branch. "Such a thought bears no result. It produces no effect. It satisfies its essence, since it exists. But, in its expression it is also that which it wishes to express. At each moment in history, there is only one expression of that which thought wants to express, which is of the same nature as that which it wishes to express." There you are.

He would have wished that in Venice mass would begin like this: "In the name of Titian, Tintoretto, Tiepolo; in the name of Watteau, Rubens, Manet, Monet, Cézanne and Picasso; in the name of all their brushes; in the name of what was once called Italy, France, Spain, China; in the name of the defeated South and Secession itself abolishing slavery within itself; in the name of the Spanish Republicans, the last insurgents before the great defeat against the North (United States, Germany, Russia, Japan): memory and art, bread and wine, for ever and ever, amen."

CLAUDE MONET AND his wife, Alice, arrive in Venice for the first time and last time, on October 1, 1908. First they stay at the Palazzo Barbaro, with Mary Hunter, then at the Hotel

Britannia, today Hotel Europa, which was Turner's, across from La Salute. On December 7, the day before their return to France, Monet writes to Gustave Geffroy: "My enthusiasm keeps growing . . . How unfortunate that I didn't come here when I was younger, when I was daring! Ah well . . . I've spent some delightful moments here, almost forgetting that I wasn't the old man that I am."

Astounding sentence. Ordinarily, he should have written "almost forgetting that I was the old man that I am." He's 68 years old then. He'll die aged 86, in 1926.

The explanation lies in the series of paintings he exhibits in 1912 at Bernheim's. A curious mind might investigate the one called *La Maison rouge*.

The letters of Alice Monet to her daughter, Germaine Salerou, describe their stay almost hour by hour. "I live as in a dream, that arrival in Venice, so marvelous, the calm sweeping over you, Mary Hunter's numerous attentions, the admirable palazzo, a real fairy tale . . . Here, as I expected, everything is luxurious, but calm and easy . . . Too beautiful to be painted, Monet says, I hope he'll change his mind . . . Monet says it's 'inexpressible' and that no one has ever rendered an idea of Venice . . . Monet wants to leave so early that I can only scrawl you this one page . . . Days pass, pass, always in this state of dream and delight . . . Here, it is always the same wonder, and Monet working well, our life is absolutely well-ordered . . . He wants to come back next year . . . Every day, he begins new canvases, as long as the fine weather lasts he won't think of leaving . . . Today not the shadow of a fog, a radiant sun, so he's hard at work. At 8, every morning, we're set up in front of the first subject until 10; so we have to get up at 6. Then another subject from 10 to midday. From 2 to 4, in the canal, from 4 to 6, through our window—as you can see, the hours are full, and, truly, I don't know how at his age he does all this without getting tired . . . Monet has now twelve paintings under way and he's more and more enthusiastic . . . While I think of it, in the morning, in his tea, Monet now takes English orange marmalade . . . Truly we've spent a terrible time with this torrential rain, Monet not wanting to leave the room and not being able even to work through the window . . . Yesterday we had wonderful weather, so warm in fact that I put on a cotton dress, and I was as hot as in midsummer. This morning, it's foggy . . . At this moment, while I write you these lines and Monet, grumbling, has set himself up to paint, I'm watching a parade of fishing boats with those amazing red and white sails with images of saints or horses, or even the moon. Here comes a large three-masted ship, then several real ships, one that stops here on its way to Egypt to pick up passengers, what a spectacle, and the reflection of it all in the pearly water . . . You know how it pains you when you see him doubting himself . . . We've been delighted with the news from Renoir and hope to see him in full form, Monet is quite looking forward to seeing him again . . . You ask me, dear Germaine, what I do with myself during Monet's working hours. You'll be surprised, because other than write letters, which takes me all morning, during the periods of work at San Giorgio where I can sit next to him on firm ground, I spend the rest of my time next to him in the gondola, allowing ourselves to be rocked by the passing ships, oil-powered boats, etc. and can do nothing, not even move, while Monet paints. Hours pass in contemplation, after lunch, that is to say from 2 to 6:30; then we take a walk to the paint shop or the tobacco stand or the postcard shop . . . Yesterday evening, we had another marvelous sunset, how I'd have loved to have you admire it: the sky all red and blue, but so soft, the waves of fire and pearl, the moon's crescent appearing on the silent lagoons and us two rocked in the gondola . . . Our life follows lines as straight as those of a sheet of music . . . I require, I assure you, a great deal of courage to bear such moments of enthusiasms or despair, never seeming to end . . . Good Lord, with Monet one never knows what one will be doing. How often has he told me to pack up our bags, that he won't touch another brush, and an hour later he's working and sometimes even beginning a new canvas . . . I agree with you not to say anything to Mme. Renoir, who's such a gossip . . . I'm happy here to see Monet so full of passion, and doing such beautiful things and, between us, something other than those eternal water lilies, and I think it will be a great triumph for him . . . Last evening we went to a puppet show, what a curious thing! There were ballets where these string puppets stood on tiptoe like real dancers. Monet found it wonderful . . . November 28, two months since our departure from Giverny: we are truly living it up, I think it also means we're ready to leave . . . Yesterday, we had a little celebration . . . Monet's works, he was still working on 8 canvases yesterday. It's too much, he's been working from 8 in the morning to 5 in the afternoon, with just one hour for lunch. Last night he was so tired, it worried me, but if it makes him happy . . ."

* * *

MONET, IN VENICE, painted thirty-seven canvases. Contrary to his expectations and wishes, he never returned. Alice died three years later, and there he was, locked up in Giverny with his "eternal water lilies." Alice Monet, we have only just realized it, was an extraordinary woman. Very beautiful, not in the least a slave, strong handwriting, bursting with life in a photo by Nadar in 1900. The usual SAP commentary (SAP: Sentimental Anguished Puritan) on this fabulous Venetian series is this: "The painting born, or reborn, under the brush of the old Monet, signals the death of Venice."

There you have it.

So we can now publish the dictionary of premodern, modern and postmodern cliches, the dogma of the new negative religion, as obsessed as it is stubborn.

Venice: recto, tourist banalities, spectacular views. Verso: evident death, slow sinking into the waters, never-ending end, castration (Sartre).

Debauchery: always morose.

Enchantment, delight, ecstasy: depression, viral hepatitis, nervous breakdown.

Casanova: constantly sick.

The flesh: unsatisfying, alas, which is why we won't read any more books.

Feast: always ends in sadness.

Ek-sistence: incomprehensible word whose definition isn't given by any of the sociological police. It was concocted by an abject philosopher ("Ek-sistence: ecstasy experienced in the truth of Being") and cannot but lead to criminal fantasies. If an individual were to ek-sist, we would no longer exist and we would lack an essence. Therefore, it's absurd. Anyone might then, after a SAP alert, insolently declare: "I don't exist, I ek-sist." And where would we be then?

Of course, just like Proust at the same time, Monet wanted on the contrary to celebrate the unexpected resurrection of Venice through his irrepressible and intimate feeling and his technical evolution. Obviously! With his Alice in Wonderland. At the house of the Queen of Time. No, no! I'll grant you as a gesture Delacroix or Matisse's Morocco or Algeria, but not Monet's Venice! But why not? The churches bother you? You sense burnings at the stake? The Inquisition is after you? You tremble at the thought of being subjected to the question ordinary and extraordinary? No nymphs in Venice (Luz, go hide!)? At a pinch, you'd rather have odalisques, women in pantaloons and pointy slippers? You definitely don't like this frenzy of Monet's? No?

Off to Japan!

Luz brought it to my attention: not a single French flag on the water. All the yachts are English, or almost all.

She:

"Will you end your days in Tokyo?"

"Why not? I'll give a permanent course on impressionism to rich budding young girls. I'll come here three times a year with ten of the best students. I'll wait for the young Chinese girls: they'll arrive in the end as well.

La Maison rouge (65 × 81 cm): it's the house next door. To have a sense of where we are: no photo or film angle will do, but the little patch of pink wall, to the right, in the *Rio de la Salute* (the canal of health)—100 × 65 cm—signed very legibly in black, lower left-hand corner: Claude Monet 1908.

Cézanne: "The sky is blue, isn't it? Well, it's Monet who found that out!"

TITIAN, 93 YEARS OLD, heard this summer lecture:

IN PRAISE OF VENICE
BY LUIGI GROTTO CIECO D'HADRIA,
PRONOUNCED FOR THE CONSECRATION
OF HIS SERENE HIGHNESS
THE DOGE OF VENICE LUIGI MOCENIGO
AUGUST 23, 1570

This is a city that astounds all who see her. And I would add that all the dispersed virtues of Italy, fleeing the barbarians' fury, assembled here and having received from heaven the privilege of halcyons, made on these waters, in this city, their nest. And I would conclude thus: who praises her not is unworthy of his tongue, who observes her not is unworthy of the light, who admires her not is unworthy of his mind, who honors her not is unworthy of honor. Who has not seen her believes not what is said about her, and he who sees her hardly believes what he sees. Who hears of her glory is moved to see her, and he who sees her is moved to see her again. Who sees her once falls in love for life and never leaves her again, or if he does, it is only soon to come back to her, and if he doesn't come back to her he becomes heartbroken for not seeing her again. From that desire to return which weighs upon all those who leave her, she took the name of *venetia*, as if to say to all those who leave her, in a soft prayer:

veni etiam, come back again.

It's been so hot, after the departure of the *Player II*, that we've started bathing in the pool even at midnight. The pool is lit from underneath, we dive from the darkness into the very clear blue. I bought a large transparent ball, a globe with the continents drawn in green, pink, yellow, and red. It floats there, in front of us. A little push and it races to the other end.

Luz seems happy. She spends long hours in the library with her incomprehensible books. She writes, verifying certain equations. Every so often, I join her in her room, unless we stay in the living room, on the carpet, till two or three in the morning. Music. Gestures. Precise.

> *"Tutto gioisco e si di gioia abbondo*
> *Che de la gioia mia gioisce il mondo."*

Gesualdo, end of the Sixth Book. A classical commentary: "With a note of joyful bliss, with a composition full of light and overwhelming rhythmical vitality, Gesualdo's madrigal work comes to an end. The last message of this violent and unbridled music, dictated in one of his darker and unhappiest moments of his tormented life is, curiously, a hymn to love and joy."

Why *curiously*?

I go back to my room, I lie on my bed, my eyes open. One shouldn't sleep at a time like this, the time of *objective* love, always surprising beyond oneself, dazzling, deep, without images, quenching beyond all thirst. She has entered my madness, and I hers, very reasonable, the world enjoys my own joy, curtain.

From time to time, I go down into the garden and sit on the

sarcophagus to smoke a cigarette. One always has a hard time imagining how the bodies lay themselves down, how they slept. Stendhal undressing in Old City; Watteau flopping in the corner of a room in Paris; Proust seeking his breath, waiting for daybreak; Monet dreaming a hundred feet away, dazzled by the ten hours of color, curious brain turned to spots on the fresh pillowcase. The sleep of Titian: magnificent vanished canvas, painted by himself. Spinoza up against the wall: nothing has changed in the demonstration of principles. Joyce in Triest? Céline in Meudon? Nabokov in Lausanne? Ditto. Cézanne realizing more clearly how to introduce his skulls among the fruit. Picasso posing gallantly for a photograph, his split head in his hand. Vanity? No: defiance. My image is my corpse, and it's got fuck all to do with me. One could dedicate to all of them these lines by Jalaluddin Rumi:

Strange night, when you heard the voice of your companion,
Escaping the serpent's bite, saved from the horror of ants,
The intoxication of love bringing to your tomb like a gift
The wine, the woman, the light, the food, the sweets, the perfume.
In those days when the lamp of intelligence was lit,
What a clamor rose from the buried dead!
The earth of the graveyard is upheaved by their cries,
By the drum of resurrection and the spark of the homecoming."

All right, fine, sh! A breeze in the red oleanders. Froissart, go to bed.

* * *

MONET'S VENICES ARE to be found nowadays in London, Cardiff, Chicago, San Francisco, Boston, Washington, New York, Indianapolis, Berne, Tokyo, Nantes—or in private collections. The one in Nantes is the farewell painting, December 3, 1908, a gondola tied to the posts, black and mauve, mourning and faith, Chinese strength. Water lilies or not, he becomes attached and remains there. The two Crepuscules, blue, yellow and red over San Giorgio Maggiore, are vivid and mad. The second one (now in Japan) is the most successful of the two, I find.

One senses that, in that spread of open air, Monet tried to go through his entire life at full speed: poplars, banks of the Seine, haystacks, verticals, horizontals, cathedrals, changes in ponds, reflections of reflections of reflections, inverted ascents, armfuls of flowers, children, dresses, parasols, hats, poppies, lunches, days of warm and days of cool weather, diffusion, steam, explosions, bushes of atoms. "The Venetians": the expression comes back again and again, towards the end, in Cézanne's remarks. Both of them, Monet and Cézanne, had the certainty of feverishly returning to the truth obscured by a deluge of conformism and untruths. Glory to the place for the sake of the place itself. Here.

Céline: "The impressionists were hard workers."

The Palazzo Ducale, as seen by Monet, contains, like a paint box in music, Giorgione, Titian, Tintoretto, Veronese, Tiepolo. One carries on, one boxes in, one surrounds, with the tips of one's fingers, within the interior eye. It's endless. Neither Canaletto nor Guardi: trembling with an open certitude.

Question to Cézanne: "What do you hope for?" Answer: "Certitude."

Mount Saint-Victoire is in Venice. And Venice is not in Venice, but in a celestial double called Venice.

Cézanne: "Art is a harmony parallel to nature; what can one say of the idiots who tell you that an artist is always inferior to nature?"

To be parallel: *that's it.*

"The prices of Cézanne's paintings are going up slowly . . . In 1899, a landscape is pushed up to 6,750 francs. The announcement of this price causes an uproar in the sales room and the public shouts: 'It's rigged! It's rigged! Where's the buyer?' Someone stands up: 'It's me, Claude Monet.' The sale can then proceed quietly."

Brushstroke after brushstroke, surface after surface . . . No arguments, silence, work, despondency, astonishment, infinitesimal progress; wordless learning speaking to himself, lightheartedness, levitation, certitude. That which was given immediately to Watteau can no longer be obtained, two centuries later, except through strict discipline. And in one more century? Oblivion.

Picasso, in his old age, would get up at night to perform, in the dark, to do toning-up exercises. Artaud, shortly before his death, not knowing what to write anymore, would draw straight lines in his school notebooks with color crayons.

"The unscathed" has disappeared, but also the notion of *little by little* which leads even the feeblest to salvation. Cram now that imagined flesh. Combustible. Where are now the skulls of Monet, of Cézanne? I want to look at them on oriental carpets.

"Why were there that many Frenchmen of genius at the time?"

"Indeed, sir. But after 93, Napoleon, the Commune, the bloodletting of 1914 reduced the gap."

"Are they convinced, in Paris, that they were provincial in regard to the Vienna of the early twentieth century?"

"We are constantly saying it, sir."

"Do they adore the Bauhaus, Klimt, Schiele?"

"Increasingly."

"Do they resist?"

"Less and less."

"Do they know that, since 1945, they've been crossed off the map?"

"They're resigned."

"Do they revolt against it?"

"A little, in the past, in a haphazard manner. Not anymore. Anyway, for quite some time now the slightest nationalist vindication is immediately labeled as fascist. May I remind you that we subscribe largely to this movement in charge of so outrageously representing this current of opinion."

"To the point of caricature?"

"To an abject point of caricature, sir."

"Fine. Go raid those Monets for me."

WHAT WAS IT that pushed this Monet, this Cézanne, out-of-doors, or apparently out-of-doors? Did they experience before and better than others the great closure promised to the entire world? The enormous roundup? The general confiscation? The plumping up of flat images? Probably. Certainly. The obsession of the subject, the terror of being grabbed by the collar (the famous "*noli me tangere*" of Cézanne, forbidden to touch, even delicately), the endless sessions in a corner of the woods, on the water, at the window, next to a significant bend in the river, in front of a lake, a kitchen table, a plaster cast, a skull, apples; the walk under the sun as if seeking a stroke; the senseless comings and goings, exhausting for the near and dear; distrust seen as positive fanaticism; controlled paranoia, always justified; the sudden quarrels; the "instability" trick, a particular manner of being stable; fussiness in every sense, palette, timetable, use of studios, gardens, flowers, fruit, women—everything indicating a passion not to fall into the hands of a society mounting guard over everything before the act, not to allow oneself to be pushed to suicide by it. How can one make use of the enemy who comes to you as a friend? At what point does the friend become the necessary enemy who will work for you back to front, with all his fixed animosity? How to wear down the dealers who wear you down? How to foresee the increase in value of your own death with regard to the sum total of your paintings? What should be kept? What destroyed? With what false projects should one pretend to be busy? What betrayals? What alliances? What coded messages quoting the past in order to be decoded in the future? Only one evident fact: no one ever sees what is *there*, so no one is really *there*. "Art addresses itself to an excessively restrained number of individuals" (Cézanne). Above all, do not divulge this fact! Keep quiet, you fool! The new gospel is that any one person is capable of being an artist! "Taste is the best judge. It is extremely rare." Quiet, you wicked old man!

I've offered myself as candidate for the post of permanent

correspondent in Venice. Geena (tight-lipped): "Really? You want nothing else? And what about your wife? Your daughter? Bella? Fleur?" Richard: "From my point of view, no problem. But *all year round?*" Nicole (on her guard): "Ah yes?"

It seems, however, that *my request is proceeding*.

Jokingly, I tell Luz at lunch: "If I lived here, rather than in Tokyo, would you come see me from time to time?" And she, suddenly serious: "Possibly."

I'd like to be able to paint her, here, right now: her profile against the water, eyes in the shimmering blue water, gulls, bunch of white and yellow carnations . . . Maybe I'll have all winter to watch on the TV screen the videocassettes filmed during the summer . . . The series of canvases would be called: *Venice with Model*. There'd be two kinds: *A Little Beforehand, Just Afterwards*. But no one paints models anymore! Exactly: *Almost* no one. And also, you're not a painter! So? Who knows?

Cézanne: "To paint from nature is not to copy what is objective; it is to realize one's sensations."

"The strongest will be he who has seen deepest and achieves the fullest, like the great Venetians."

Cézanne still, speaking of Monet: "Monet's cliffs will remain as a prodigious series, and a hundred more canvases of his. When I recall that they rejected his *Été* at the Salon! All juries are pigs. He'll be in the Louvre, you'll see, next to Constable, Turner. Shit, he's even greater than they are . . . His is the only eye, the only hand capable of following a sunset in all its transparencies, and of shading a canvas without having to go back. And also, he's a lordly gentlemen who gets any haystacks he wants. He likes a certain field, he buys it. With a hefty servant and guard dogs so that he won't be bothered. That's what I'd need."

And at the Louvre with Joachim Gasquet, speaking of Veronese: "That man, he was a happy man. And all those who understand him are made happy by him. It's a remarkable thing. He painted just as we see, without any greater effort. Dancing. Torrents of shades ran through his brain. He spoke in colors. I have the sense of always having known him. I see him walk, come, go, love, in Venice, in front of his canvases, with his friends . . . Everything entered his soul with the sun, nothing separated him from the light. No drafting, no abstraction, everything in full color . . . We've lost that fluid light that comes from undercoats . . . Look at that dress, that woman against that cloth, there where the shadow begins at her smile, where the light caresses, or drinks, soaks in that shadow, we don't know. The tones all invade one another, the forms turn as they fit into one another. There's continuity here . . . Magnificent: to have bathed an entire and infinite composition with the same warm and subdued clarity and to give the eye the vivid impression that all these breasts are indeed breathing right there, like you or I, the golden air that floods them. Ultimately, I am certain that it is the undercoatings, the secret soul of the undercoatings which, holding everything together, give such strength and lightness to the whole . . . The daring of all that foliage, the cloths echoing one another, the linking arabesques, the continuing gestures . . . You can look at the details: the rest of the painting will always follow you, will always be present, you'll hear its buzzing around your ears, around the detail you are studying. You cannot tear anything away from the entire composition."

* * *

I SEE THAT a New York paper has published a tight-lipped article on a retrospective, in Boston, of Monet's "series." How curious, says the writer, that a painting that seems so harmless today might have seemed once so revolutionary. You said it, porky. You are, without knowing it, the worthy descendant of the confined nineteenth-century bourgeois. You lord high above Monet, you are far superior to him in everything (*Moneyline!*), your *interior clock* is set like an ad, a projector, "we have ways of making you blind!" All these stories about nymphs, nymphettes or water lilies are amateurish, simpleminded. Can one imagine, nowadays, a painter setting up his easel on the top of the World Trade Center in order to study the nuances of the setting sun on Wall Street? Warhol was right: to paint in a series the dollar sign is enough. The *sensation*? What sensation? "We must become classic again through nature, that is to say, through sensation." What nature? What are you talking about? "It's ten in morning," Cézanne complains, a guerrillero on all fours in the midst of the bushes, "daylight's fading." Or this: "Have you noticed how the light grabs the apricots from all sides and how it's surly with the peaches?" Or this: "Advice to a young painter? To paint well the pipe of his stove." Salvation is to him who listens well. Hide away that cylinder I don't want to see. The cone frightens me. A cube or a sphere, I'll accept. But a cylinder! "It must both turn and interpose itself at the same time. Only the volumes are important. It must bulge. The contrasts must become apparent in the exact opposition of tones." Ah, these Latins! Obsessed with sex! "From the reindeer on the walls of the caves, to Monet on the walls of a pork butcher, mankind's path can be followed" (still Cézanne). So we're pork butchers, are we? Certainly not. Rockets, cannons, OK, if you insist on cylinders. "False painters don't see that tree, your face, that dog, but the tree, the face, the dog. They see nothing. Nothing is ever the same. All they see is a sort of fixed type, foggy, which they pass from one to the other, floating constantly between their eyes—do they have eyes?—and their model." Incomprehensible. Why would we waste time, i.e., money on *that* tree, *that* face, *that* dog? All that has a single name: *how much? How* leads us directly to *how much*. Why? No whys. For whom? For Mr. and Mrs. How-Much. Who are they? The representatives of How-Much Inc. Ltd. "When the tones are harmoniously juxtaposed and they are all in place, the painting models itself." Moving, charming, but a bit stupid, Gramps. "Great tints are analyzed through their modulations." Explain to this Cézanne person that he's got to be more flexible, otherwise he's not going to go far in the advertising world. Anyway: what's his lifestyle? A hermit? A maniac? Badly dressed? Never stopping for lunch? He can survive without selling? He never phones Mrs. How-Much? "Nature is not on the surface, but in the depth. These colors are the expression of that surface, of that depth." But this man is a savage! Let him go smoke his peace pipe on the reservation, and get him off our backs!

THE OBSERVATIONS GATHERED by Joachim Gasquet, Cézanne's young friend (the son of one of the painter's ex-fellow students), are generally thought dubious, especially by the Anglo-Saxon art historians. They find him edgy, emphatic, lyrical, preaching a confused Provençal renaissance, leading head-on to a reactionary nationalist revolution, or in other words to Vichy-Pétain (even though he died in 1921). According to them, he reconstructed a Cézanne the way he wanted him, traditionalist, vehement, mystico-Catholic, refusing to paint Clemenceau's portrait because the man didn't believe in God, etc. Monet would have been "leftist" and Cézanne, therefore, "rightist." To efface that nasty reality (since Cézanne represents for Picasso and Matisse the God of painting, and he's certainly very pricey), they decide not to take Gasquet's opinions seriously, but call them exaggerated, oh yes, full of personal intrusions, but whose authentic tones and sincere enthusiasm cannot be doubted. I myself believe in that fanatical Cézanne visiting the Louvre and endlessly praising those Venetians and Spaniards." "When you are ignorant, you think that those who stop you are those who know. On the contrary, if you see them often, instead of being cumbersome they take you by the hand and gently have you mumble your story." Yes, it's him. Did he really say that David killed painting off by trying to be goody-goody and overpolished? Did he really call him "bloody Jacobin" and "bloody classicist"? Sartre did indeed call Titian "a traitor," accusing him of having gone onto the side of those in power. Tintoretto left-wing, Veronese and Titian right? Too bad . . . Poor intellectuals still arguing, while the steamroller *Moneyline* passes through . . . Proust center-right, Stendhal more and more to the right, Joyce left-right, Nabokov back-right, Céline extreme left-right, all favorite readings, as everyone knows, of Hitler, Pétain, Franco, Mussolini. While Stalin was an enlightened fan of Kafka and Walter Benjamin, common knowledge. Hitler, failed watercolorist, crazy about Cézanne's

Baigneuses? No? De Gaulle didn't understand Monet? Churchill, who often had his picture taken while he was painting, had never heard of Picasso? Carry on with the list: PAINTING IS TRUTH. You can pretend to have read (up to a point) but never to have *seen*. "This David, he even managed, in his art, to cut the balls of that dirty-minded Ingres who, nevertheless, loved the female." Did Cézanne use the word "female," carried away by his young companion? "What I deplore, is that those young people in which you believe are rarely seen in Italy, don't spend their days here (in the Louvre), ready to throw themselves into nature afterwards. Everything, especially in art, is nothing but a theory developed and applied in touch with nature." And then: "Sensation is at the root of everything, I'll repeat it again and again." Yes, it's him.

"Tell me, that Tintoretto, that *Temptation of Christ*, at San Rocco, I think, that busty angel with bracelets, that pederastic demon who offers stones to Jesus with lesbian lust, he never painted anything so perverted . . . Chaste and sensual, brutal and cerebral, willful and yet inspired, anything except sentimental: I think he experienced everything, this Tintoretto . . . Listen, I can't talk about it without trembling. He would have his daughter put him to sleep, he would have his daughter play the cello to him, for hours on end . . . Alone with her, with all those red sparkles . . . His gods go round and round, their paradise is not at peace. That resting place is a tempest . . ." Yes, yes, it is indeed Cézanne, and that's also the reason why everyone tries so hard to hide the account of this unbelievable visit to the Louvre. Not enough "modern art," no doubt, not at all new *tabula rasa* painting, futuristic, dadaist, constructivist, suprematist, cubist, surrealist, impossible to teach at the university these days, especially in the United States, you wouldn't think of it, such a disturbance in the words . . . Wasn't Cézanne an iconoclastic puritan? An ascetic? Well-crafted painting leads to its own demise? "There are only two modern artists here: Delacroix and Courbet. Everyone else is trash . . . And one is missing: Manet. He'll come, just like Monet and Renoir." Cézanne, furious advocate of sensuality? Is Picasso already imminent? "Look at those *Femmes d'Alger*, those pale pink tones, those stuffed cushions, those slippers, all that limpid quality enters your eyes like a glass of wine down your throat, you're immediately drunk . . . If I had done something bad, I think I'd come stand in front of it to seek my composure. It's full to the brim. The tones enter one another like silk. Everything is in opposition, crafted within the whole, and that is why the whole thing clicks. This is the first time anyone has painted a volume, ever since the greats . . . For a painter, nothing counts except the real colors, you're not going to transpose a Racine tragedy into prose . . ." Courbet? "He's profound, serene, velvety. Some of his nudes are golden as a harvest. His palette reeks of hay. His *Vanneuse* at the Nantes Museum, so thickly blond, with her big reddish sheet, the hay dust, the crooked bun on the neck like in the loveliest Veronese, and the arm, that milky arm in the sun, that stretched-out peasant's arm, polished like a washing stone . . . His sister posed for it . . . You could stick it next to Velázquez, she'll hold her place, I give you my word . . . Isn't she fleshy, dense, grainy? Isn't she alive? Of course she is. And snow! He painted snow like no one else . . . And those lakes in Savoy, with their lapping water, the fog climbing from the banks and wrapping itself around the mountains . . . And the great *Vagues,* the one in Berlin, prodigious, one of the findings of our century, with its disheveled foam, its tide coming from the depth of time . . . One gets it right in the middle of the chest. One draws back. The entire room smells of sea spray . . . And the *Demoiselles* . . . It's a crime that this painting isn't here . . . You might say it was Titian . . . No, no, it's Courbet. Those *Demoiselles*! An ardor, a languor, a happy exhaustion, a sprawling . . . The gloves, the lace, the silk of the dresses, the russet . . . The bulges of the necks, the roundness of the flesh . . . Nature becomes a slut in their company. And the low sky, cut off, the landscape sweating, the inclined perspective forcing us to search . . . The dampness, the hot pearls . . . There's no one but Courbet to lay on black without making a hole in the canvas . . ."

Must we believe Gasquet when he shows us Cézanne, in order to better see a badly hung Courbet, take a ladder, climb up on it, hop onto the landing, while the guards come running, calling out to him? Cézanne suddenly a '68 leftist, turning red, delivering an actual harangue, something like: "It's disgraceful, good Lord! . . . No, but what the hell? . . . We're always letting you get away with everything . . . It's a crime . . . We are the State . . . Painting, *c'est moi!* . . . Who understands Courbet? You throw him into prison, in this dungeon . . . I protest! I'll go to the papers, to Valles! . . ." He shouts louder and louder . . . Finally he gets off the ladder and says to the guards: "I'm Cézanne." Gasquet ends with these words: "He turns even redder . . . He searches in his pockets.

He stuffs money into the hands of the guards . . . He runs away dragging me with him . . . He's in tears."

Yes, I believe it.

Valles? Just this, about Michelet: "France, alive on the page—with her laughter and sadness, her feline grace and wild beast's vigor, crowned with her fresh lilies and her somber grapes."

Come on, come on, no displays of emotion, please, the Louvre is closing, Monsieur Cézanne. Come back tomorrow, we'll transmit your suggestions to the minister. No, it's useless to bring the archbishop into this, he's got nothing to do with us. Because you think maybe that the cardinal-archbishop has a thing for the *Demoiselles* or for the *Olympia*? What? What's that you say? That no one likes painting? Oh well, it's possible . . . What? We live in the midst of the sensational and hate sensations? Maybe. But you forget that you're a *dear departed*, Monsieur Cézanne! You didn't know! Didn't you realize you were dead, as one used to say, long dead? Come on, come, good-night, go back into your Mountain, your *Montagne* . . .

AFTER WHICH COME, most logically, Picasso and his communist wanderings, and Matisse and his chapel. After them, remove the ladder, painting becomes the cleaning lady of the destroyed environment, the writer, the flunkey of the bla-bla market. So much the flunkey, in fact, that he affects noble airs, speaks of times long past or vanished civilizations, is as well behaved as a picture (his wife can vouch for that), embroiders nicely on past subjects, above all avoids thinking, stammers, clouds over, keeps silent. Painting? He's not going to get his feet wet for so little. And then the sensation might be unexpected, bothersome, too vivid, disturbing, too much. Samuel Beckett, in a letter from 1948: "I dreamt of Matisse, in Dublin brogue he was saying, *I'm bet*. My father, in a semicomatose state, answered: Fight, fight, fight." Quite something. Fuck, fuck, fuck. André Breton would call Cézanne "a greengrocer." We're only quoting the most important ones here, since the comments and tastes of others are generally sheer desolation. Beckett's name used to be Becquet, from Huguenot French ancestors who sought refuge in Ireland. That's where that lip, all those parrot stories come from (what does the parrot say, since the days of Flaubert? "Shit asshole motherfucker fuck," and has every reason to.) "I want a theater without painting and without music, without embellishments. That's Protestantism, if you like, we are what we are." And Thomas Bernhard: Bach, that fat fool; St. Peter in Rome, that piece of crap, etc. "Oh, to end it all."

OK.

No more painting, music, literature; no more words, gestures, notes, colors, sensations or bodies. No more nothing. Well done and thanks, kids, go and commit suicide, disappear, clear the stage, and now: advertising screen.

No, no, that's not what we had in mind!

But yes, of course, a trick of the Devil!

Cézanne in the Louvre, already (the ecstatic subjective cylinder, having been laminated): "We're nothing, we're not even capable of understanding . . . To think that a long time ago I wanted to shatter it all. Because of an urge to be original, to invent . . ."

What does Picasso do towards the end? Grecos, Velázquezes, Delacroixs, Courbets, Manets . . . I, "modern art"? Certainly not! He takes his paintings with him, into his Ark, he locks them up, he X-rays them, he duplicates them, he duplicates them again, he leaves carrying them with him, skidding in the downpour, farewell. A final kiss! The deadly faun! The narrow spasm of the bacchanal!

He doesn't lay a finger on Cézanne, Picasso. Cézanne is sacred. From New York, they'll have to offer him a small Cézanne for him to be willing to give up one of his first guitars. Give and take. Cézanne can't be imitated, can't be waylaid, can't be parodied. One barters Cézanne, one doesn't sell him.

Something like that has no value.

Utility.

Demoiselles, Baigneuses, Demoiselles: who can understand?

And there's Monet again, painting ten canvases at once like a chess master playing ten games simultaneously, fast. There they are, on the quay, in the sun, the chess players, across from Luz and me, wooden chairs and table, concentrated, right hand against the cheek, indifferent to everything except the constant calculation of the pieces, the landscape has disappeared, the passersby have vanished, noises and movements have gone up in smoke while the possible decision is taking place. And yet, it's evident that *they are the ones who see.*

Just like the characters in *Joueurs de cartes* see the painting in the painting in the painting.

While the big Palladio, orange and khaki, bringing the weekend visitors, glides in front of my eyes, right behind the two young bluish players who never lift their heads from the board.

Luz is reading a treatise on theoretical physics, taking notes in a small apple-green Pignastyl booklet. Hundreds of researchers must be doing more or less the same, around the world, at this very moment. So what about those *Machos*? Are we getting anywhere near them?

Gray jacket, rings under the eyes. Not much sleep.

Claude and Alice Monet didn't miss having their picture taken at the Piazza San Marco, like every tourist. She's wearing a coat with a fur collar, a funny feathered hat, a peaceful-looking pigeon on her left arm, another, wings open, on her right hand. Monet, bearded and stocky, in a light gray suit has one on his right hand and another calmly sitting on his cap. "You think we really should have this picture taken?" Yes, of course, yes. "Don't move!" A morning in October 1908. The weather's fine.

I have the same photo, or almost the same, of my parents here, after the War (1948). Pose for the camera, obligatory picture. Mamma looks splendid. Pappa not so good.

Ah, Venice.

Two young Japanese women are taking one another's pictures. The player on the right moves his rook forward.

When he paints *Impression, soleil levant*—morning seen through the window, in Le Havre—forty brushstrokes to give the reflection of the red disk of the sun—Monet signs his name to the left and adds the year: 72. He's thirty-two years old. All the Venice canvases, on the other hand, are dated 1908. It's impossible to write 08. That's what is meant by bridging a century. Sixty-eight years old, blasé, unimpressed, identical technique, but younger. Cézanne too, growing older, realizes that he's heading towards greater and greater freshness.

Titian "traitor," Watteau "superficial and unstable," Monet "harmless," Cézanne "greengrocer"—I read an Italian note on Ceźanne: "Should one reproach him for his indifference towards social issues, for not having broached the great problems of his time, the Franco-Prussian War, the Commune?" On Picasso: "Did he plunge, towards the end, into a senile obsession?" General conclusion: "Should we accept the elitist notion that artists or writers are in the best position to judge what they themselves do?"

Oh Lord, start everything again, endlessly.

Again, again. And again.

"One must begin neutral." "Gray is of a frightening difficulty to grasp" (Cézanne).

The gray of trousers of one of the two men in the *Déjeuner sur l'herbe.*

Let's go back home, my lovely.

IN ORDER FOR the modern slaves to accept or even vindicate their condition, they must be drugged with permanent images and tall tales, and they must lack the smallest distance, the slightest perspective on their own situation. Except to be aghast by their degree of servility and lack of remuneration, which leads them to a renewed submission, reinforced by distress. Does it work? Yes. We've succeeded. They'd never dream of looking at anything by their own means, and if ever the confused notion were to form itself, the alarm would sound: danger. Are they going to ask for permission to experience a perception which they feel must be imminent? Not even that. Best to give it all up in one fell swoop. That's what I was saying: the lines outside the museums are like those in the past outside the embassies to get a visa. They come *to punch in their cards* or to be sanctioned in front of the hidden cameras. We've been to see the paintings, the Master keeps telling us that they're very precious, he'll be pleased. Some of us even made the effort of buying a book which, of course, we'll never read, no time. Ah, dinner, to the table. TV.

And in life? Same thing. Not see too much, avoid touching, not hear more than necessary, not listen if a comment oversteps the threshold of prefixed banality. The machine is self-regulated, warm, hormonal, fetal, past passions are past.

Let's be technical: images, in themselves, are depressing. The less they impact, the more they depress. That's easily understood: they block the sex in puberty, titillating without satisfying. To reach orgasm, however, implies a "black hole" (the collapse of the realized fantasy), a spasm and a sonogram, trembling but palpable. All women know this instinctively. "What are you thinking about?" "Oh, nothing."

No orgasms, then, as little pleasure as possible: too dangerous for the irradiated installation. Endlessly excited, endlessly depressed, this is how the spectator of the spectacle will be. He, or she, is a reproduction. He, or she, will be used as the reproducer of reproductions.

The terrace here faces south. The water is to the right, in front, to the left. The sun crosses from left to right, slowly, before returning to the night.

Now let's take a map of France: Monet firmly holds his position in Le Havre and environs. Impossible to move him from Giverny. Renoir has reinforcements, Courbet has taken the woods as well as women in their sleep. Cézanne reigns over the Midi. If Monet is at sea, Cézanne is in the mountains, the blocks, geology, hot solid shadows, artillery constructions in Vauban, aerial fortifications. Matisse is in charge of the interiors: bedrooms, palaces, royal chapels, swimming pools, musical background. But we need a general in Paris to succeed Manet and Delacroix. An energetic Spaniard? Picasso? Agreed.

They'll be defeated, of course, but as so often occurs, the defeated will be the winners. For the time being, send them a few exotic dancers, to relax with. Not to Cézanne, he's unsociable. He'll tell you to go stuff it.

You make Watteau supreme commanding officer to concentrate on the final objective? Yes. Stendhal wishes to enlist? Has he definitively renounced Napoleon and David? And his sentimental crystallizations? Let him come.

No doubt the situation is desperate. We wouldn't have wanted it otherwise. Froissart, you'll hold this terrace to the bitter end. No prisoners. If you manage to escape at the very last minute, good for you. I was told you're terrific at stealing away. This time, you'll need all the luck you can get. But that you have. And don't forget you're responsible for all papers, letters, documents, numbers. You're the free-shooter in the film, you delay the adversary, you cause him individual losses with your long-range silent rifle, aim straight for the head each time, eh? No flesh wounds.

Code name of the operation: Cythera. General purpose: the rape of Europa. Commanding site: high sea. War cry: cylinder! Your enemies are two-dimensional, they have no knowledge of the third. You possess the third in the second thanks to the fourth. The fifth, diffuse all over, supports you. Anarchist? Black flag? An old formula. You wear all colors. Dark matter has no flag. In the name of black holes, singularities and colored sensations, you reconquer France. Why France? We'll tell you later. Instructions for the next stage are in envelopes sealed on June 18. Let every man do his duty.

GEENA:

"I'm coming to Paris. I need to see you."

"When?"

"Saturday. Nicole would like to see you too."

They'll see me. We'll go have lunch at Bagatelle, on the grass. My *dossier*? Maybe. For the time being, terrace and shifting immobile blue. Luz lying down there by the pool, reading the "modern art" supplement of the *Corriere* which shows *Les Demoiselles d'Avignon* on the cover. She leafs through the pages, she lights a cigarette, she leafs through the pages again, she looks carefully at—what? *La Montagne Sainte-Victoire*, 1904–1908, 60 × 73, in Zurich? Renoir's *La Première Sortie*? Will I film her, from a distance, blond profile, naked breasts, while dreaming quickly about *Le Moulin de la galette*? Daddy (the cardiologist) must be the one who loves these things, while Mummy (the chemist) is probably more reserved, Protestant-style, but not hostile, curious. But to hell with the parents, shadows quickly blotted out, snapshots. To have been conceived by photos, by film or TV images—or by paintings (and which ones): the moment comes when one must choose. But science? Ah, science, ladies and gentlemen, science is something else . . . My advice is rather that you make arrangements with partners who move among equations, the sense of relativity, the arbitrary nature of measurements, if A then B, beginning and end are hypotheses, God, Mummy and Daddy are not every instant retired, compressed in humanity's future, truth exists as the development of itself. "In my home all I wish for/Is a woman with all her faculties" (Apollinaire). It's touching to think that the name of Apollinaire was the last name spoken by Picasso just before his death (Paris, belle epoque, heroic charge of the artistic forms). Note this, sergeant: Apollinaire, back from the German front, enlists in the Confederate Army. Not too many erotic books in his luggage? Sade should suffice him to get his bearings on the bridge.

The sun is playing with the clouds. Chimneys, cracks, gray blots, rays. Blue plunging necklines make a strong comeback . . . Quick, Monet, five seconds for that light yellow . . . Hold on, Cézanne: the areas, the distance, the cone. We'll fly over it all in a couple of hours. Lovely Cézanne, those Alps, in the window of the plane. Lovely Monet at takeoff, the lagoon. "A body isn't limited by a thought, nor a thought by a body." And then: "A body in movement or at rest must have been determined in movement or at rest by another body, and that other in turn by another, and so on into infinity." And then this: "Falsity consists of a deprivation of knowledge surrounding inadequate ideas, that is to say, ones that are mutilated and confused."

Matisse: "I give a fragment, and I lead the spectator in through the rhythm, I tempt him to pursue the movement of the fraction he sees, so as to give him the sense of whole. The point—as in painting in general—certainly lies in giving, through a very limited surface, the idea of immensity."

A 1948 example? *Intérieur à la fougère noire.*

"A tiny detail might reveal to us a huge mechanism."

"The linear, graphic equivalent of the sensation of flying."

"These successive flights of doves, their circles, their curves, glide within me as if in a vast interior space."

"My instant draftsmanship is not my number one performance. It is nothing but the film of a series of visions that I'm constantly following during a session of serious work."

"The eyes less than a meter away from the model, knee capable of touching the knee."

"A sort of flirting with myself which ends up in rape. Whose rape? My own."

To rape oneself through a tiny detail, during the fraction of a second, like a flight of doves in a vast interior space.

You manage? Great.

One is either gifted for this sort of thing in the cradle, or never. It's impossible to learn, to transmit. It can be perfected if one survives the repression which always follows. Lots of mistakes and illusions, but a compass: flowers, knees, circles, curves, hand, eye, breathing, knees.

IT'S ONLY at the age of thirty-three that Goethe reveals a certain love for himself, in Italy. On his return, he'll marry his faithful worker. Spring of 1790: the *Roman Idylls* and the *Venetian Epigrams* appear. Stendhal: "Goethe the flat." And in 1808, concerning two visitors: "They are nothing, sweetness, virtue, but of a terrifying slowness. As German as possible."

Freud instead goes on his first journey in 1876, at the age

of twenty. He's received a scholarship to travel to Trieste and study the male organs of eels. A male eel of Homeric grandeur will soon make his appearance in Trieste: Joyce. Freud in 1895, with his mother and his wife: "Venice makes us deeply drunk." He's again in Venice in 1900 (this time it's Proust who's in a corner of the picture). And again in 1913 with his daughter Anna, then in Rome, a place for him intensely neurotic, with his sister-in-law, Minna. Problem: who was Michelangelo's Moses? Each one has his own questions. Signorelli, Leonardo da Vinci, Michelangelo . . . Not the slightest mention of Titian or the Venetians. And yet, Doctor, that *Venus with a Mirror* . . . 1895, a letter to his wife: "Deeply drunk by Venice, we feel wonderfully well and all day long we do nothing but walk, ride in boats, look around, eat, drink."

Standard but a bit on the short side. Later drift towards antiquity and Pompeii: fatal move.

Let's bypass Nietszche, pastor's son ("Luther, that grievous monk") who ends up, immediately afterwards, taking himself for the Antichrist in the name of Dionysius. Come now, come now, my dear philologist, let me show you *at the same level* the *Pentecost* of Titian and *Marsyas Punished by Apollo*. Or *Venus Binding the Eyes of Eros* and *St. John Begging for Alms*. A contradiction? Not in the least. It's irritating? No doubt. Bothersome, genial, genital Italy. "Are you making an apology of the Counter-Reformation against the nihilism that has been reigning for the past two centuries?" "Exactly." "You monster!"

In Paris, on my way home, I pass by No. 34 Rue de l'Observatoire. Someone has come to lay a bunch of red carnations in memory of Cavaillès. Till when will this commemorative ritual continue? Everything is forgotten, but the plaque will remain as long as the building remains, in the shadows. I see, right next to it, the statue of Theophile Roussel (1816–1903), senator, member of the Institut and the Academy of Medicine. It seems that he fought against alcoholism and for the protection of children. He's represented accordingly, towering over a woman who is leaning over two infants. And no doubt Tissier was correct, when on his jubilee, celebrated in his honor on October 20, 1896, he wrote these words: "To protect children is to love men twice over."

We won't deny that.

Everything seemed normal with Geena and Nicole. Of course, there'll be sometimes *visits* to the palazzo. Another transfer by boat? Next month. "Cézanne" again? Always accompanied by her lovely blond children, but this time with another husband? Nothing has been decided.

Geena:

"You really don't want to come to New York?"

"The ball is in Europe's court."

"So they say. But what about winter there? And the floods?"

"Merely a question of comfort."

"Your American stays with you?"

"She's got her studies in California."

"Richard thought she was pretty."

"She is."

Nicole:

"And the Titian exhibition?"

"Terrific."

"Many paintings missing?"

"Thankfully: it's exhausting enough as it is."

"I'm coming back in three weeks. Can we go together?"

It will last however long it lasts.

Froissart, hold the terrace.

Luz returns from a congress in Rome. How was it? Fine. A bit hot. We have one last drink at *Linea d'Ombra*. I find my city again, made of water and night, quickly sketched and blindly painted. My hand is on her naked arm, I shut my eyes.

WE ENTER ONCE again through the small door to the left, the exhibition closes at 11:00 P.M.; they stop selling tickets at ten, the best time is between eleven and midnight. The palazzo empties slowly; it seems as if the paintings, impassive but offended, breathe once more. They seemed monumental, now they become enormous, threatening, overpowering, wicked, they possess an aggressive force which they never possessed before. "You're not obligated to come." "I'm coming." For the third time, I amused her by going down on all fours like a dog, in the first room. We're all dogs. Guided by smell. I asked for a ladder in order to better smell—or pretend I'd smell—the surfaces. Seven times at night, it's only the beginning, dozens of times would be necessary, to sleep there, on the spot, to live there, painting demands it, it's the very least we can do, to live simultaneously with it. What's required is the casual glance, the look that doesn't expect to see but sees nonetheless. Well, we can always pretend. Here we go, we come down from the upper chambers after dinner, we walk once again through the big room full of paintings, nothing special, out of habit, distracted. It will arrange itself all on its own. I need this armor to go in, portrait of Francesco Maria della Rovere, unexpected in the dark and the roundness of its glitter, with its tubes, its sticks, its cylindrical treatment of spheres. Is there a man inside all that, a look that can cut through all that, the iron, the bronze, the erected stone, the wood, the drapery? Turn my back to the painting. The man with a glove (the finger), the man with blue-green eyes . . . And the self-portrait, still black, the grim old man with eyes more distant than time, brush directed towards himself pointing to the absent sex (the sex is the entire collection of paintings). OK, now the women: all the Venetian blonds, mirror, bed and music, virgins if you like, rather Venuses, that one binding the eyes of her love child, a yellow-orange knotted ribbon, two assistants ready for the hunt. We have the secret nude, we have the source of power. Money? Three revelations. First, simony, the bribing of Christ (absolutely not, who do you take me for?). Then alms: coin thrown towards the supplicant bottom of the painting, by a St. John in white surplice, balanced book, blue sky, head turned for an instant, thanks. Finally, the shower of gold: Danae, naked, on her bed, fills up with a stream of golden change. Prostitution is the rule, here it is, generously evaporated as it should be, we all prefer Mary Magdalen. Death? Oh yes, but with no pathos, no crucifixion or resurrection, a simple entombment in stormy weather. All this is taken seriously, that is to say, as close as possible to volume and shadows, he buries himself in his chiaroscuro, this Titian, but what is a corpse if not a technical equation to be treated, like the rest, in the light of a flame, of a torch, as a torso? A St. Sebastian is preferable to a Crucifixion because the arrows, stuck at different angles, shape the composition. He ties, he unties, he makes it turn, he puffs it out, he excavates, he echoes all over the place, on low or high flame, the look upon the organ player's face never reaches the place between the blond woman's thighs, nor do our eyes either, as it was foreseen. In the end, Titian is no longer convinced by the eye, he trusts the fingers, the brain branching out from head to foot, color comes, hot and deep, like blood on the paintable skin. He arrives at straightforward tattoos, pink child and rust-colored dog, the fleshy muzzle sniffing the meat, yes: the trace of blood, the animals on the wall. He sniffs, he laps, he whines in silence. Tip of the fingers, tip of the tongue: he licks, he mops himself up, he snorts, he breathes in watching his lungs, his bronchial tubes, suggesting leaves and branches, the shadowing of the entire undergrowth. He sees better by touching, oh well, he punches holes in your vision, cruel sadistic, joyfully excited. Did Marsyas, hanging by his hindquarters, dare defy Apollo? Good, learn a lesson: he is to be flayed alive to the sound of violins, slowly, delicately, so that his eye, down below, gradually widens with horror. He's being cut with a knife, a little dog tasting the dripping blood, a satyr bringing along a bucket—that *bucket*!—all done with curiosity and a smile. It's awful, it's magnificent. Don't go defying Apollo in a singing contest! You'd find yourself hanging in this forest burchery being poked with a knife all over the place for the greater glory of our mingling on the palette. Young lady, new Lucretia, don't you go resisting that crazy Tarquin either! Immediate rape in response: perfid albino Albion raped at knifepoint by a Spaniard from the Inquisition. This is the great painting of the Counter-Reformation. Madame Reformation hurled into the righthand corner, the movement of her arm lifted against the assailant is a tour de force, the left arm seems to spring from her belly, she uncovers three blank intimations of a breast by lifting her right arm held by the assailant with the straight knife. No exit, their knees touch, he'll throw her down, cut her throat, take advantage of her. What's that? Don't you want to fuck? You're reticent? You contest the primacy of Rome? The virginity of Mary? The cult of the saints? The desires of Venus? The brush of Venice? You want to limit the depth of these images, after all the time it's taken, since prehistory, sculpted antiquity, flat Middle Ages, to represent finally, correctly, in flesh and full color a naked woman? You are already thinking of banning them, you little pest, the Demoiselles on the banks of the Seine, the Olympia, the Baigneuses, the Odalisques, the Demoiselles d'Avignon? You are thinking of doing business with this filthy sex, in the wings? Get the bastards! Into bed!

Admiral Titian sends this to Phillip II, who hasn't thought long enough about the plan before sending his invincible armada northwards, against the Puritan heresy. Too bad, said the admiral. Painting is a form of rape, one must keep a close eye on it, it has always been that, it will always be that. It is necessary therefore to anesthesize it. Give a bromide to that Titian, he's going to paint us scenes of torture as if they were Gardens of Eden, sacred love, profane love . . . What a fingering Magdalen-freak! Maybe he's eaten some prehistoric oxen? Bisons? And such a refined man, too, and yet so reflective, and at the same time that fury, that science . . . Is such a convergence of gifts humanly possible? Let's hope not.

But alas, it is.

I'd almost forgotten Luz sitting in front of that *Tarquin and Lucretia*.

I walk around the painting, I go, I come, the Palazzo Ducale has become a grotto, we're in Lascaux, I look at the painting by trembling candlelight, inspecting it by the carbon 14 method, by the dome of the skull. And now everything becomes entangled, the sarcophagus, the cavern, the well, the deer swimming in the mist, the sexually aroused shaman with a bird's head, Actaeon pursued by Diana and her hounds, Paris and his erection in Watteau's painting in the Louvre, *La Fête à Venise* in its safe on the waters, the walls, the lute, the hands, all these tombless tombs . . .

"Hello."

The last of the conniving guards turns off the lights. We must leave.

EXHAUSTING TITIAN . . . REALLY good painting kills you and lightens your heart at the same time. Your body shouldn't ever be there with its fat physical baggage . . . An avalanche of paintings annihilates you, a single one is enough to call you into question. What were all these painters after? To be right where you are wrong, there, dumped in the fake time, the pseudospace. With them, we're in century C, year Y, month M, day D, hour H. Whether this takes place in 1560, 1720, 1863, 1908 or 1970, the stakes are the same. Fifteen thousand years ago, ditto.

Strange night. Apollo pursues Marsyas, and Tarquin, Lucretia, bathers turn into trees and Actaeon into a Lascaux deer, Monet's easle falls into the water, Cézanne has an apoplexy in the midday sun, Watteau's dancers discover a pearly clearing, a Moroccan prostitute flows into deep red, a *demoiselle* from the banks of the Seine goes off with Olympia . . . Luz sleeps quietly next to me. I get up, drink three glasses of water, I go out into the dark garden, I crawl on all fours through the grass . . . Under the moon . . . Funny . . . Painting isn't made to be seen, I tell myself, but to be taken to bed and put to sleep. Better still: *deathened*. The wrong side of dreams. He certainly *deathened* them well, Titian, his emperors, his queens, his page boys, his generals, his princes. Traitor? You bet. Rather a stylish assassin. At the very heart of power. Through the deathening-glass. Like Velàzquez, but freer (he's got all of Venice boosting him). Power must be treated through the cone, the cylinder, the sphere, and the annulment of color. That drapery, there . . . Dark red . . . Marsyas flayed . . . Oneself . . .

Daylight is here, now, a stain of color on the page. Where am I? I haven't slept, I've slept, I don't sleep anymore, no worries. Red sun, mist, blue water. It's six in the morning. The gulls are squawking.

At 7:30, I go and prepare Luz's breakfast. I like watching her, pink, propped up against the white pillow. "Why are you looking at me like that?" "Painting." "I won't be able to move my arm." "Yes, you will." Portraits of Geena. Soon, portraits of Nicole. All the portraits, long ago, of Bella and Fleur.

Cézanne: "So you see, this little, little shade, this minuscule shade darkening the spot under her eyelid, has moved . . . Well, I'll correct it. But now my light green, next to it, I see it, it stands out too much. I tone it down . . . I'm in one of my good days, today. I tighten my muscles. I master my will. I continue all around with imperceptible brushstrokes. The eye sees better now . . . But the other eye! I think he's cross-eyed. The eye sees, it sees me. But the other one sees its own life, its past, sees you, I don't know what, something that's not me, that's not us."

It should be noticed that in this anecdote, retold by Joachim Gasquet, Cézanne is painting the portrait of the father (Henri Gasquet) in the presence of the son, in his studio at Jas de Bouffan, one later winter afternoon.

The two Gasquets are now, one in Prague (the son) and the other (the father) in San Antonio, Texas.

Cézanne: "Regarding one's art, one must be incorruptible, and to be so in one's art, one must practice being incorruptible in one's life."

"In the end, there's the know-how and the how-know. When you know how, you don't need to know *how* to know. You always know."

Joachim Gasquet on Cézanne: "He looks at his fist. He follows there the passage of shadows to light . . . He carries on painting. The portrait is well advanced, on the cheek and forehead are two white squares. The eyes are alive. Two fine blue lines prolong the outline of the hat up to the edges of the canvas. He's started to cover and diffuse one of these lines by thinning down the background. A bird flies against the windows . . ."

Cezanne: "To hell with them if they don't understand how, joining a shaded green to a red, you can make a mouth sadder or a cheek smile."

Gasquet: "He goes up to a stack of canvases, searches . . . He takes out three still lifes, places them against the wall, on the floor. They burst out, warm, deep, alive, like an uncanny patch of wall and all rooted however in everyday reality. In one of them, on a tablecloth, a bowl with four apples, grapes, a long-stemmed glass, flared like a chalice, half full of wine, a knife. The apples stand out against a flowered tapestry. To the left, in the corner, the painting carries half a signature."

Cézanne: "Objects penetrate one another . . . They don't stop living, you see? . . . They spread insensibly around them through intimate reflections, as we do through our looks and through our words."

To hell with them if they don't understand how you, bringing together from far away four adjectives or repeating a verb, change your vision of the world or your philosophy, in any way you like.

"SO, YOU PLUNDER backwards, so to speak?"

"If you like."

"These gatherings, these quotes, these collages: the novel seen as an encyclopedia, a Noah's Ark? *Après vous le déluge?*

"That's it. In the open. The scattered members of Osiris. Including the phallus. Transmitting to the improbable future. If someone existed, then someone might exist."

"Let's go back: your idea is that of a tyranny and a barbarian slave society on the rise."

"Exactly."

"A new illiteracy instituted on the basis of technology and domesticated science? Based on memory loss, obligatory morbidity, the omnipotence of the image live the pointless excess of information, the destruction or manipulation of sources, the theft or biased and uninspired interpretation of documents and works of art?"

"Plunder of the South."

"Ah yes, your thing about the South. You're a committed writer, an *engagé*, I take it?"

"Most certainly. In the invisible, ghostly and yet still gray and yellow divisions of generals Beauregard and Lee."

"Political, then."

"To the hilt."

"You'll accept the consequences?"

"It seems so."

"You don't hesitate to place yourself beyond the law?"

"Useful phrase."

"Is your goal different from that of your predecessors?"

"Isn't it?"

"Isn't it too ambitious? Laughable?"

"From the enemy's point of view, no doubt."

"Your obsession is this then: to save, to conserve, to stock up, in hope of better days to come? And to pretend, on top of that, that your action is subversive?"

"You got it."

"No doubt you find the literature of your time of no value whatsoever."

"More or less."

"Painting also?"

"Its ugliness and vulgarity jumps out at you."

"The Maoist sympathies of your youth and your subsequent papist tendencies were also inspired by the South?"

"Evidently."

"Explain."

"I have already."

"Why Venice? The struggle against the Turks?"

"Among other things."

"Are you for love?"

"Totally."

"No regrets?"

"None."

"An understanding between man and woman is impossible. And yet, you say that it can be conceived. How so?"

"Distanced thought. Irony."

"More precisely?"

"In verse:

On Simcoe Lake we sailed about.
I hated her, she hated me.
We came together with a shout:
You fuck great with your contrary."

"Clever."

"Rather."

LUZ IS EATING a croissant. I watch her eating that croissant. It's amazing to watch a young beautiful woman eat a croissant.

I like linen, cotton, canvas.

Yesterday, entering the Benedetto Marcello Conservatory at ten in the evening, through a door that had been left open, we discovered, in one of the back rooms, three musicians in rehearsal: a violinist, a cellist and a young auburn-haired woman at the piano. Seeing us, they stopped all of a sudden.

At midnight, a rock band was playing on the quays: a girl at the mike, guys with electric guitars. They were very loud. Two girls started dancing together, drunk.

Luz lying down on the library couch, warm sunset, white

T-shirt, bare legs. She reads a book on theoretical physics: "Shit, something's wrong, but I don't know what."

A red-brown butterfly on my table: there are very few butterflies here.

Gray sky, very still, typewriter, letters in relief: strange to say one is going *to compose French*.

DNA: 6 million "words." Each word is made up of 5000 syllables for the shortest words and over 2 million for the longest. Components: adenine, thymine, cytosine, guanine. Combination: the result is you, you alone.

The old stationery (there since 1890), near the Accademia: "Monsieur, they want to relocate us, it's an act of murder." Drawing paper, crayons, brushes, tubes of color, palettes. Monet must have bought supplies here.

The priest, once again, after the Elevation: "*Mistero della fede.*" It doesn't seem to bore him. Twice a day.

A cardinal has just stated that the risorgimento was certainly at the basis of the following accelerated spread of fascism and communism. A civil and socialist clamor: To slander such a great age! National! Worldwide! Moral! The return of darkest clericalism!

Three young Franciscan monks observe Titian's *Venus with a Mirror*, overflowing with golden sensuality. I say: "You look at that? Aren't you afraid it might be a sin?" Hardly disturbed, they laugh. One of them looks at the title of the small book showing in my left pocket: Stendhal, *Vie du Henry Brulard*.

Luz is being cruised by a tall auburn-haired man, thirtyish: "Are you on your own?" "My husband is expecting me."

A Japanese man in the restaurant takes a picture of his lobster dish before touching it.

Monet's red house is boarded up. Construction work. "How long?" "A month." I'm one of the last people to have seen it.

The president of the Italian Republic regularly consoles, under compunction, the families of the judges who have been victims of Mafia murders. He looks like an old exhausted vampire. Full-time job.

Evidently, new sacrifices are required from all. Tax increase. The Communist Party, like everywhere else, is looking for another name.

Once again, the *Odysseus*, blue and white, passes by.

In a trattoria, one evening, the waitress, forty years old, auburn hair, hefty, very cheerful, pinches Luz's cheek as she goes by.

Sometimes, when it's very warm, the gulls come down onto the grass, next to the pool.

The Russians try to murder the pope: they're lumbered with the return of their priests. They had been warned. To no avail.

In order to extend the realm of democracy, will it be necessary now to kill many Arabs at once? The matter is under discussion.

Taiwan is celebrating with pomp and circumstance the memory of Confucious: at least according to the news agency photos.

This morning, an emotional moment for Luz. Brief tears. "We shouldn't have to die."

The presidents meet. Summit meetings follow one after the other. The true figures are not known. On earth, from time to time, dissatisfaction is timidly expressed. It is severely reprimanded.

All the art historians are astonished: the successive and cruel bereavements in Titian's life don't seem to have slowed down his creative process. Only the plague will kill him. For that reason, after the epidemic, the Church of Health is erected.

With Luz, in a blue coat, in front of San Michele cemetery, the pink island of the dead. I've bought beautiful pearl binoculars.

She phones San Francisco. "Everything fine?" "Yes."

A journalist friend asks me: "What to do?" "The same thing." "Why?" "No reason." "I'd like to see you try." "No." "Well, of course, you're a writer." "A writer is no longer anything." "That's what they say."

And yet, that's how it is: everything can be written, but there's no one left to read.

A woman—in her thirties, blond, bourgeoise, jewelry, refined—cruises Luz in the restaurant. Laughter, seduction, openings. While I'm in the toilet: "Won't you come to my place?" Luz: "Sorry, I've a plane to catch tomorrow morning." "*Peccato*" (Too bad).

A look at women: evaluation, refusal or roundabout acceptance: some other time, maybe. How much paper must have been filled!

Couperin, publication of the *Concerts royaux*, 1722 (a year after Watteau's death): "The following pieces are of another kind from that which I have published to this date. They are not only excellent for the Harpsichord, but also for the Violin, the Flute, the Oboe, the Viola and the Bassoon. I composed them for the small Chamber Concerts which Louis XIV had me attend almost every Sunday in the year. These pieces were played by Messieurs Duval, Philidor, Alarius and Dubois.

I played the Harpsichord. If they were to please the Public as much as they pleased the late King, I have enough of them to publish several complete volumes more. I've arranged them by Tone, and have kept the Titles by which they were known at the Court in 1714 and 1715."

Are they irreducible? So are you. Pass on.

Have I said nothing about the magnolia tree? Deeper silence regarding the acacia. The tree catches the night upside down, deepens it, varnishes it, absorbs it. Acacia: early and clear afternoon. The oleanders, on the other hand, occupy the fresh shadowy width of space.

Long red evenings, light wind, light wrinkles, thumbing one's nose for a laugh in the early gray-blue of the night.

The scent of cut branches. Feline ears. The endless bundles of twilight in Monteverdi: the choir singing a round, each male and each female voice delaying as much as possible the disappearance of sound, amen, amen, and once more, the contrary of the collective Lutheran mobilization, farewell, adieu, good-bye, for ever and ever, amen.

BUT NO, THE cock's crow, here we are, sitting up: Forever Watteau! Unflappable *Gilles*! Drugged *Mezetin*! Holding the terrace!

As time goes by, or seems to go by, these paintings become even more incredible. I project them again on the white wall: *Gilles, Mezetin, L'Indifferent, La Finette, Le Donneur de serenade, La Toilette intime, Le Jugement de Paris, L'Embarquement pour Cythère, La Fête à Venise, Les Charmes de la vie, Les Plaisirs du bal*. They end by flowing into one another, white innocent sun of the big *Gilles*, with its explicit fauna to the right, and the not less declaratory eye of the donkey below; clarinet player and water fountain in the Plaisirs, a painting copied by Turner and which Constable says seems to have been "painted with honey, so melting, so tender, so soft, so delicious"; insensitive canes of the characters of Cythera, masts and loves, lend me your arm, come here; the broken folds, the silk, the leaves, the columns, the trunks of trees and the benches of stone; the hands playing, pushing away, inviting, articulating; the guitars, the fans, the conversations, the salutations during the dance; the rusty colors, the bluish tones, the greens, the penetrating reds . . . No one is less indifferent than *L'Indifferent* deploying in front of you, from left to right—right to left for him—the magnetic line, not represented, impossible to cross, of the stuff in which he floats. Arms falsely open (he is closing in) responding to the flowering left foot, vegetable body made of sky, illusory velvet cape on his shoulders, he is looking at the absent world from which we think we are observing him. Everything is empty. Everything is one and different for him who knows how to dance the pleasures of emptiness, to play, to enjoy and to disappear in an instant. Sex does not deserve death, no, but we must surely inflict sex upon death. There's no other sense to be found in it. These dreamy paintings are so violent, so sure of themselves, so solemn in their diffuse joy, that they will never stop preceding us in time. *L'Indifferent, La Finette*: what a couple. The only couple, I think, that was ever thought of in equal terms, without reducing them in any way. Play, guitarist, on your stone bench, for these only two real inhabitants of the drama. Rise, Gilles-sun, light their definitive absence of guilt. As for you, people of Cythera, of the *Bal*, of the *Fête à Venise*, you are not required even a thought of thanks, you are free to forget all. Speaking of which, who are you giving that apple to? To the lovely libertine of *La Toilette intime*? Obviously.

I switch off the projector. I think of the safes on the *Player II*, on the *Sea Sky*. Good-night at sea my children.

A fax from Geena: "OK for the watch."

I wonder what face someone, he or she, would make finding this message in my place: "OK for the watch, *Mozart*."

A bottle of champagne. Six P.M., it's midday there, bells, fog.

I switch the slides on again, lingering over *Les Charmes de la vie* in order to see, once again, the little blond and green Luz playing the guitar, to the left, in her red chair. The detail I'm projecting is life-size. So many things taking place on such a limited surface? Indeed.

The painting is in London. It's after Watteau's trip to England, whose climate does not agree with him at all, that his cough intensifies, and he begins to drift towards his end: July 18, 1721, in Nogent-sur-Marne. Death in midsummer: what joy.

Now . . . What? No . . . Hallucination? No, not at all . . . Something in *L'Indifferent* . . . That left-right bulge between the jacket and the trousers . . . That signaled peaking roughness, that cylindered slant, that hump . . . You're not going to tell me that . . . Well, yes . . . Mount St. Victoire . . . Slanting, canonical, in the trousers . . . Oh, but an erection isn't thought of *like that*, you see . . . All the elements and all the natural materials must take part . . . It's exactly what I was saying: the elegant pearly messenger, sweet, casual, charming, with his thread cutting through space, in his whitewashed forest clearing, silvery, isn't indifferent at all, on the contrary . . . *Il bande,* he has a hard-on, there's no doubt about it . . . Yes, in French, that's how one says it. I can't help it if it's the same word for "blind-folding," "*bander les yeux,*" for instance. So, according to you, Cézanne is delivering the same message? But of course . . . Don't tell the critics, curators, university professors or officials . . . Gratuitous imaginings . . . Any old nonsense . . . Obsessed . . . Because painters aren't obsessed, are they? In its time, *Olympia* caused a scandal? What one always forgets is that she was painted by a thirty-one-year-old Manet . . . Oh really? As young as that? How old was he when he died, remind me? Fifty-one? Born in 1832 . . . Two years after *Le Rouge et le noir* . . . Generations, passing the flame, secretly . . . "The eyes that will read this are barely opening now to the light" . . . That's one way to retell the whole story . . . The point of view of the fibers, down South . . . If you prefer: Joyce is born a year before Manet's death . . . Céline was four when Mallarmé kicked the bucket . . . Proust is twenty-three the day Céline was born . . . Joyce is seven when the Eiffel Tower is built . . . When Sade dies, Stendhal is thirty-three . . . And so on . . . Complete the list . . . The wind bloweth where it listeth, a secret history, to the detriment of the global police . . . Each one does what he can, according to the repression of his own age . . . The author of these lines makes his appearance at the same time as *Guernica,* he's nursed by solid Basque peasant-women refugees . . . He hears their voices . . . Their prehistoric language . . . He's pressed against their breasts . . . He smells their hair, their necks, their scents; he wakes among their laughter . . . In his room, later on, a reproduction of the *Assemblée dans un parc*, by Watteau . . . The deed is done, nothing more is needed . . . An image, a skin, an accent, a curve . . .

Yes, one really has to make the decision not to see that hump . . . Underlined by the opening-closing of the arms . . . And the tip of Cézanne's mountain of ten different blues, topped by its little cloud smudged with green . . . The sense of the white islands left on the canvas. A lightening, a breath of air, plane after plane . . . You don't really believe that Monet, Cézanne or the others were interested in the landscape itself, rising sun, setting sun, reflections in the water, water lilies, haystacks, poplars, pine trees, mountains? It's all right. Never was a block so carefully understood, so morally, with so much localized precision, brushstroke after brushstroke, a freshly colored animal . . . And the indifferent messenger, 22.5 × 19, like *La Finette*? So small? So big?

Wandering thoughts . . . "A curious mind, a bit crazy," Nicole would say . . . "Amusing" (Geena) . . . "Too classic" (Richard) . . . Do I tell Luz? After three glasses of champagne? One mustn't speak of painting in action. For example: "Can you tell me by what miracle that red cloth, to the right, in Titian's *Profane and Sacred Love* holds itself in the air as if that woman had two left arms? "It's for the effect." "Effective."

I'm keeping nothing but *L'Indifferent* on the wall. Hallucination. Allusion? Illusion? Inadmissible collision-collusion? I'm not the one writing the text for the catalogue, nor do I take the schoolchildren and the tourists to the museum. Let's carry on with discussing the exaggerated charms of an age gone by, or the hard Flaubertian Northern labor of the out-of-doors painters. Can you see anything *there*? Can you? What?

* * *

I MUST CHANGE dollars, I go to the bank. Everyone's annoyed, long lines, the computers are down. Another bank, then? No, sir, *it's the entire network.* No financial operation can take place, the whole system works electronically. One of the employees nervously fingers his keyboard, white screen, black screen, immediate rectangles cut out, memory display not working. "And my check?" asks a fat German woman, "my check?" "It's inside, madame, it will come out, don't worry." "I want my check."

The network? But which one? The neighborhood? The city? The country? The planet? Black hole or virus in the circuits? Interruption of the sale at Sotheby's or Christie's? Of the arms delivery? Airport activity? Ports? Interruption of the gunpowder dispensers? Generalized hostage taking? Oh no, in the end it was a false alarm. All eyes are fixed on the screens. But one must wait for the machinery to recover, that it may retrace its data from the very beginning.

I ACCOMPANY LUZ to Paris to catch her plane, I come back . . . Winter preparations, now. Is the heating working? Are the windows well sealed? The swimming pool covered, books and records bought, three warm jackets, boots . . . October, still a few days of high atmospheric pressure, beautiful days. The *Player II* is on its way. Will Luz be here for Christmas and the New Year? Next spring and next summer? She said so, we'll decipher her fluctuations over the phone. Froissart, you asked for it. You're now in your meditation cell. Long empty hours ahead. So now, those Memoirs? Why not? While the wind blows, the rain pours down, everything closed, black, opaque? And from time to time, tunnels of cold light? In the secluded library? Between *visits*? Beginning by writing on the upper left hand corner VE and the date, in numbers, like the license plates of the boats out here?

Quick or slow beginning?

"I arrive, the small palazzo is in order, the sun is shining on the gray telephones."

Or this:

"As always, here, towards the tenth of June, there is no drawing back, the sky turns, the horizon displays its unchanging warm mist, one enters the true arena of the evenings."

The day drifts on, the white moon replaces the red sun of the morning; the sounds of the quay, in the green and black night, break loose and rise.

I wink at the sarcophagus in the garden.

About the Author

Philippe Sollers is editor of the French avant-garde journal *L'infini*. He has won numerous international literary awards, including the Medici Prize. He and his wife, Julia Kristeva, have been described by the *Village Voice* as our generation's Jean-Paul Sartre and Simone de Beauvoir. They live in Paris.